Kody Keplinger

SHUT OUT

Hodder
Children's
Books

A division of Hachette Children's Books

For the nomadic novelists:
Michelle, Kirsten, Leila, Kate, Lee, Kaitlin,
Amanda, Emilia, Kristin Jr and Kristin Sr.

So many words I could put here, but the Beatles
said it best. 'I get by with a little help from my friends.'
Thanks for keeping me sane.

1

There is nothing more humiliating than being topless in the backseat of your boyfriend's car when someone decides to throw an egg at the windshield.

Wait. Scratch that.

Having your boyfriend jump off you, climb out of the car and chase after the guy, completely forgetting that you're still half-naked – that trumps it.

And there is one thing even worse than that.

Having it happen repeatedly.

I rolled on to my stomach and reached an arm down to the floor, searching for my tank top and praying the windows of Randy's new Buick Skylark were as tinted as the ones on his old Cougar, the one he'd wrapped around a telephone pole last month. The Buick was older and used, but Randy considered the bigger back seat an improvement over his other car.

Not that it was being used at the moment.

I pulled on my top and climbed into the front seat. This was the third time the car had been vandalized – with us inside – since Randy and I had started dating sixteen months ago. The other two times had happened last fall, when the rivalry was in full swing, and both times I'd been left in the car, humiliated, while Randy chased after the culprit. Not exactly my definition of a good time.

It had been almost a year since then, though, and I'd hoped to avoid the embarrassment this time around, but apparently I was too optimistic. Here I was again – forgotten, alone and fighting back tears.

Part of me knew I should be mad, but I was mostly just hurt. After more than a year together, I hoped I came first to Randy. But the fact that he forgot me so easily because of a stupid egg on his car? It stung.

I shut off the sexy R&B CD Randy had been playing and flipped through the presets on his stereo, stopping at a crackling oldies station to hear the last few seconds of 'Night Moves' by Bob Seger while I pulled my messy make-out hair into the elastic band I wore around my wrist.

Thirteen and a half minutes later, Randy returned.

'Soccer fags! I'm gonna kill those assholes.'

2

I shot him a look. He knew I hated it when he talked like that.

'Sorry,' he muttered, falling into the driver's seat with a thud. He stared at the egg-splattered windshield, grinding his teeth. 'I just can't believe they did that.'

'You can't?'

'Well, OK, I can, but I'm pissed off.'

'Uh-huh.'

'That's going to be a pain in the ass to clean off.'

'Probably.'

He turned to face me. 'I hate those assholes. God, I can't believe I didn't catch the guy. Shane and I are going to have to get them back good for this.'

I didn't say anything. I'd tried to explain the whole 'cycle of violence' concept to Randy before, but it just didn't stick. He didn't seem to understand that retaliating against the soccer players would lead to them attacking him again. He was giving them what they wanted. Feeding into this stupid rivalry. It would never end if he kept fighting back.

Logic wasn't Randy's strong suit, though. He was the spontaneous 'act now, think later' type. That was part of the reason I loved him. The whole 'opposites attract' thing was way true in our case. But sometimes Randy's impulsiveness was more stressful than sexy.

3

He sighed dramatically before turning to me.

'So,' he said, a suggestive grin sliding across his face. He tilted his head forward, letting his sandy blond hair fall into his eyes. 'Now that that's over with . . . where were we?'

'We,' I said, pushing him away as he leaned in to kiss me, 'were at the part where you take me home.'

'What?' Randy sat back, looking wounded. 'Lissa, it's only ten thirty.'

'I'm aware.'

'Look, I know that guy ruined the moment, but we can start over. Please don't be pissed off with me. If anything, be pissed off with the guy who threw the egg.'

'I'm not pissed off, I'm just . . . frustrated.'

'It's not my fault,' he said.

'It's both of your faults.'

'Come on, Lissa. What was I supposed to do?' he asked. 'He egged my car. He ruined our moment. He could have been spying on us – on you. A good boyfriend wouldn't let some jerk get away with that.'

'He did get away with it,' I reminded him. 'They always get away with it. Whether you go chasing them or not, they get away. So what's the point?'

I wanted to be honest with Randy. To open up and tell him how much it hurt when he left me alone like

4

that. How worthless and cheap it made me feel. We'd been together for so long; we loved each other; it should have been easy to tell him the truth. To let it all out.

But all I could make myself say was, 'I'm not cool with coming second to this stupid rivalry all season.'

'You aren't second, babe.'

'Prove it,' I retorted.

Randy stared at me. The corners of his mouth twitched a little, like he was going to spit out a cute answer and then thought better of it. His eyes perked up once before going blank again. He had nothing.

I turned away from him, messing with the dials on his radio again. 'Just take me home, OK?'

'Lissa,' he murmured. His hand closed around mine, gently pulling it away from the radio and lifting it to his lips. He kissed my knuckle, whispering, 'I'm sorry. I'm sorry that jerk ruined our night.'

That wasn't what I wanted him to apologize for.

'I know you are.'

His hand slid down my wrist and danced its way back up my forearm and shoulder, stopping when it reached my neck. His fingers cupped my cheek and turned me to face him. 'I love you,' he said.

'You too.'

He moved forward, and I let him kiss me this time. Just a quick, light kiss, not the kind I knew he was hoping for.

'You still want me to take you home, don't you?'

'Yes.'

Randy shook his head, half laughing as he reached into the back seat and blindly attempted to locate his own shirt. 'You amaze me, Lissa Daniels. Most girls would cave as soon as I gave them the puppy-dog look with these amazing eyes.'

'Sorry. I like boys. Not dogs. You should've dated a different girl if you wanted someone to bend to your will.'

'That's all right,' he said, pulling the shirt over his head and turning to fiddle with the keys, still dangling from the ignition. 'I like having a girl who can keep me in line. You're tough and smart and sexy and—'

'And you're still taking me home,' I said, giving him a sweet smile.

'Yeah, I figured. But, hey, doesn't make it any less true.'

I shook my head, unable to hold back a little bit of laughter now. 'Oh, just drive me home, you brown-noser.'

And, just like that, the night's drama was almost forgotten.

Almost, but not entirely.

2

'Dad!' I called out as I walked down the stairs the next night. 'Where is Logan? He should be home already.' I paused in the doorway, staring at my father. Or, more accurately, at the big bowl of ice cream in his lap.

'Hey, honey,' he said, trying to conceal the bowl from my line of sight and failing oh so miserably. 'I'm sure Logan is—'

'Dad, what are you eating?'

'Um . . .'

I walked over to him and jerked the bowl out of his hands. 'I can't believe you,' I said, taking it into the kitchen. I could hear the wheels of Dad's chair squeaking across the carpet, rounding the corner after me as I dumped the remaining chocolate-swirl ice cream into the garbage disposal.

'Oh, come on, Lissa.'

'You heard what Dr Collins said. You're supposed to be watching your diet.' I ran the water to rinse out the bowl. 'You need to lose some of the weight you've put on since the accident or you're going to have more health problems. Eating this isn't going to help you with that, Dad.'

'One bowl of ice cream isn't going to kill me,' he argued.

'You don't know that.' I reached for a paper towel and turned to face Dad as I dried the bowl. The look on his face tore at me a little. The one that said he knew I was right but didn't want to hear it.

This wouldn't have been an issue five years ago, before the accident; his construction job and love of sports kept him in great shape. But it all changed on the January night his car slid on a patch of ice and sent him and my mother careening into the opposite lane. Even after Mom's funeral, with all the food no one could touch; after he started his new job as a counsellor at the elementary school; after he began smiling again – he was still in the wheelchair.

No more biking. No more football. For some paraplegics these things were possible, but we couldn't afford any sort of special chair or bike that would keep Dad active.

So it was my job to watch out for them. For him and Logan. Without Mom around, they needed someone to take care of them. That was my responsibility now, even if it meant being a little harsh sometimes.

'So why isn't Logan back?' I asked again, glancing at the clock on the microwave. 'He usually gets in right at five thirty-two. He's almost ten minutes late.'

Dad laughed. My muscles relaxed a little at the sound, even if it was my neurosis he found amusing.

'Lissa, are you really stressing over him being less than ten minutes late?' Dad asked.

'Maybe,' I admitted.

'Well, don't,' he said, rolling his chair up to the kitchen table. 'I'm sure he'll be home before Randy gets here. Randy is coming over to watch the game, right?'

'Yeah,' I said, turning around to put the bowl back into one of the cabinets above the sink. 'He'll be here at six.'

Randy came to my house every Saturday night. First he'd watch whatever game was on ESPN with Dad, then we'd hang out for a couple of hours before he went back home. In the year and a third we'd been together, he'd never missed a date. Even when I was mad at him.

Behind me, I heard the front door open and shut. I turned around and walked past Dad into the living room. 'Where have you been?' I demanded as my brother untied his sneakers and tossed them into the pile of shoes next to the door.

'Um, work?' Logan said. 'Where else would I be?'

'You're late,' I told him.

'No, I'm not.'

'Yes, you are.' I pointed at his wristwatch. 'Look. You're eleven minutes later getting here than usual. I was getting wor—'

'Lissa,' my brother said, reaching out and putting his hands on my shoulders in a way that was so belittling I wanted to scream. 'Chill. I was talking to my boss after work.'

'About what?' I asked.

'Don't worry about it,' he said, patting my cheek and stepping around me to walk into the kitchen. 'Anyone feel like ordering a pizza? If Randy's coming over we should probably make it a large, right?'

I scowled and bent down to straighten up the pile of shoes on the rug. Why couldn't Logan just answer my question? I hated that he had to make me feel like a child. I was ten years younger than him, but I wasn't a baby – and eleven minutes may be nothing to him, but that's enough time for anything to happen. I had a right to worry.

Mom was killed in less than thirty seconds.

'Lissa!' he yelled from the kitchen. 'What kind of pizza do you want? I'm ordering now.'

I stood, having aligned the shoes and feeling happy that at least some part of this house was in order. 'Sausage and ham. But Dad has to have a salad.'

'Oh, come on!' I heard Dad whine as Logan laughed and began reciting his order into the cordless phone.

Through the living-room window, I saw Randy's Buick pull into the driveway. Right on time. That was one of the things I loved most about Randy – he was always punctual, unlike my brother.

I opened the door for him as he made his way up the front steps. 'Hey, babe,' he said, leaning in to kiss me.

I let his lips brush mine for just a moment before pulling back.

'Still mad?' he asked.

'Not mad. Frustrated, remember?'

Randy ran his fingers down my arm, lowering his voice so Dad and Logan wouldn't hear. 'I can un-frustrate you if you want.'

I swatted him away, my whole body stiffening. 'You sure you won't be too busy cleaning your windshield?'

'I'm never too busy for you, baby.'

'You were last night.'

11

He tilted his head to the side, batting his long, perfect eyelashes at me. 'You'll forgive me. I know you will.'

'We'll see.' I meant it to be teasing, but it came out sounding cold.

'You always do!' he called over his shoulder as he strolled into the kitchen.

I shook my head, knowing he was right. I always forgave him, and I was sure I always would. I knew as soon as he walked into the kitchen. As soon as Dad smiled at him. As soon as Logan clapped him on the shoulder. I would always forgive Randy because he was part of my family. He had been since the moment I first brought him home.

Watching them now, as I stood in the kitchen doorway, I knew I'd fallen in love with Randy that first night, when he walked right up to my father as if he didn't even notice the wheelchair and shook his hand. He made my family happy, and after all we'd been through over the past few years, seeing them smile like that . . . well, it made me happy too.

I forced myself to relax, to loosen up a little, as I walked into the kitchen and sat down at the table next to Randy. There was no need to be on edge right now. Not with my family. Not with Randy.

'So how's the season starting up?' Logan asked as he took a seat across from Randy. 'The soccer assholes giving you hell yet?'

'Yeah.' Randy sighed, leaning his chair back on two legs and folding his arms behind his head. 'But whatever. We're giving them hell right back.'

I bit my lip. 'Randy, can you put your chair on four legs, please?' I asked. 'You'll fall that way . . . and hurt the chair.'

'Yes, Miss Daniels,' Randy said, rolling his eyes as he let his chair fall back into its proper position. 'But is it me or the chair you're worried about?'

'I plead the Fifth Amendment.'

Randy gave me a look of mock heartbreak.

'My senior year,' Logan said, ignoring my deliberate change in conversation, 'we gave all the freshmen soccer players swirlies in the boys' bathroom.'

'Dude, that's so lame.' Randy leaned forward, grinning. 'There's actually a plan for tomorrow night that—'

'That you're not going to be a part of,' I snapped before I could stop myself. Randy, Dad and Logan all turned to stare. 'I don't think you should be involved in all that, Randy. It's stupid. What kind of school has a rivalry between two of its own teams? Plus, what if someone gets hurt?'

13

'Oh, come on, Lissa,' Logan scoffed. 'It's harmless. No big deal.'

'Maybe when you were in high school, but the fighting has got worse since then. This time last year, Randy and the football team busted all the windows out of the soccer goalie's car. They could have got into some serious trouble,' I informed him, then turned back to Randy. 'You won't participate, will you? Leave it to Shane and the others if they want to be idiots, but you don't have to do it.'

Randy hesitated for a second, looking between me and Logan.

I gave him a nice hard glare. A wordless warning of what might happen if he didn't side with me here.

'Fine,' he said. 'I won't be a part of it.'

'Promise.'

'I promise.'

'You're so uptight, Lissa,' Logan grumbled.

'Leave her alone,' Dad said. 'She's looking out for people. It's sweet.'

Sweet, I thought bitterly as the doorbell rang behind me. God, it was so condescending. Like I was an overly sensitive little kid. Couldn't they see how ridiculous the rivalry was? How continuing to retaliate would just make it go on forever? Soccer, football –

they were just games. Neither sport was worth this much drama.

I went into the living room to get the door. The delivery boy handed me the large pizza and Dad's salad. From the kitchen I could hear laughter and cheers as the boys discussed the game they'd be watching that night. Betting on who would win and lose, the topic of torturing freshmen dropped and forgotten.

The rivalry wasn't brought up again until later that evening, when Randy and I sat out on the front porch steps, the game having ended and my dad and Logan already off to bed.

'I'm sorry about the other night,' Randy said quietly, his arm sliding around my shoulders, pulling me against him. 'Sorry those assholes had to show up and ruin everything.'

I had to bite back a sigh of frustration. He still didn't get it.

Didn't get that running off and leaving me was the part I was upset about, not the fact that someone had egged his car. But at least he was trying, I guess.

'Shane's got a plan to get back at them,' he continued. 'A good one.'

'You're not going to help, though,' I pressed. 'I know I probably shouldn't have called you out in front of Dad and Logan, but I'm serious. I don't want you involved in all that.'

Randy gave me a hopeless look. 'Shane and the guys are going to give me hell for backing out.'

'Aw. Will they pick on you, sweetie?' I asked. 'Should I call their parents?'

'I'm serious,' he said. 'They'll call me a pussy.'

'And if you help them, I'll call you a dick. So no matter what you do, you're going to be some form of genitalia.' I grinned up at him. Finally, I was feeling relaxed enough to joke around. It had taken all night. 'Shane and the boys may rag you a bit, but will that be any worse than what I could do to you?'

Randy stared down at me for a second. 'What would you do to me?'

'I obviously can't tell you. That'd ruin the surprise.' I poked him in the chest. 'But I can tell you that it wouldn't be this.' I glanced around to make sure there were no cars coming, no neighbours staring out of windows, no one to see. Then slowly, tantalizingly, I leaned up and pressed my lips against his. The kiss was long and hot, but before it got too deep, I pulled back, leaving Randy with an awed, hungry look on his face.

And leaving my cheeks on fire.

'I bet Shane can't do that,' I said.

'Maybe he can. You don't know.'

'How do you know I don't know?'

Randy blinked at me, and I laughed. 'Kidding. I'd never hook up with Shane. You're the only Neanderthal I can deal with.'

'Thanks. I'm flattered.'

I kissed him on the cheek and rested my head on his shoulder. 'Seriously, though. Please don't mess with the soccer players. Just let it go. For me?'

Randy let out a long sigh. 'Yeah . . . I guess.'

'Thank you.'

His fingers wrapped around mine and I snuggled against him. Now that he seemed to be listening to my entreaties, I was sure we would get through this autumn; we'd survive the rivalry. I was sure it would all work out. We fell into a comfortable silence, staring up at one of the last starry nights of the summer.

3

I know that most schools have rivalries with other schools, but that's not how it worked at Hamilton High. Nope. Our biggest battles were fought on the home front.

It all started back when Logan was a junior in high school. That's when the school board decided to start an official school-sponsored soccer team. I don't know all the details — I was in second grade, and anything that didn't involve ponies just wasn't worth my time — but in a small town like ours, taking away half of the football team's funding to create another fall sport was pretty scandalous.

Apparently the football players got pissed off at having to share time in the workout room, and the crowds that usually filled the stands at games began to dwindle as more and more people started going to watch the soccer team play. Hostility rose between them

– and between the teams' coaches – and eventually a full-on war broke out.

Now, you'd think the drama would fade over time, right? Like, after the teams graduated and new players came in, it would die.

So not the case.

A decade later, the rivalry was still going strong. Every fall, when sports season started up, the battle would rage again. And the dumbest part was, I don't think the boys even knew why it had started to begin with. I'd asked Randy once and he'd just shrugged.

'Does it really matter?' he'd asked.

To me, a girl who had to share her boyfriend with the war every autumn, it did. But not to the players. They just knew that they hated one another. That was enough.

'Dickhead!' Randy yelled across the cafeteria as Kyle Forrester, the soccer team's goalie, gave him the middle finger.

I cringed at the volume of the obscenity in my ear, and I tapped Randy on the shoulder. 'Hey, would you mind lowering the volume a little? I'd like my hearing to last a few more years.' He flashed a quick smile at me and hooked an arm around my waist as he turned his attention back to the soccer team's table.

I was glad he didn't notice the way I tensed.

I sat at the lunch table, sandwiched between Randy and my best friend, Chloe. Though Chloe was too busy flirting with Michael Conrad to notice the stares we were getting from the rest of the student body. This was so not what I needed on a Monday.

I already had a headache from staying up too late the night before. That was the fatal flaw in my weekend schedule – with Randy over on Saturday nights, I didn't get to do any homework until Sunday. With three AP classes on my plate, that meant lots of homework and late-night studying. Having people yell insults over my head the next day, while I was still exhausted? Not fun.

And also completely embarrassing. I rapped my knuckles against the table in a fast, anxious rhythm.

'Hey, could you keep it down? Seriously,' I said to Randy just as one of Kyle's buddies yelled, 'Fuck you!' back at us.

Randy shot him a glare before giving me an apologetic nod. 'You OK?' he asked.

'Fine. I just have a headache.'

He put a hand on the side of my head and smoothed back my hair, pushing some of the straight black strands from my eyes. 'Anything I can do to help?'

'Well, you can—'

And that's when the glob of mashed potatoes landed

in a disgusting mound on the table, right in front of me. They'd been flung, undoubtedly, by one of the soccer players at Kyle's table.

'Gross,' I said, scooting my chair away from the table. 'Randy, can you please put an end to this?'

But he wasn't listening. He was too busy glaring at the soccer team's table, a look of deep concentration on his reddening face. For some reason, it reminded me of a caveman contemplating how to make fire. Only Randy didn't want fire. He wanted a way to get revenge without getting detention – or, worse, suspended – in the process.

I stood up just as his best friend, Shane, picked up an orange and pulled back his arm, aiming for one of the soccer players' heads.

'Where you going, babe?' Randy asked, turning away from his enemies and reaching for my hand.

'Library,' I muttered, wrenching my hand from his grasp without even meaning to. I let out a breath and rolled my shoulders, willing myself to relax. It was just Randy, after all.

He wrinkled his nose in disgust at my words. 'Library? Why?'

'I need to finish some homework.' I gave his shoulder a quick, reassuring squeeze to let him know I wasn't

21

pissed off – this embarrassment wasn't entirely his fault; Kyle had been the one to start it, really – before scooping up my tray and edging around the table, heading to the front of the cafeteria so I could dump my barely touched food and hurry away from the madness.

At least, that was the plan.

Running into Cash Sterling kind of ruined it.

One minute I was clearing off my tray and returning it to the rack, thinking of how quiet the library would be, and the next I'd spun around – without checking behind me, of course – and slammed into something hard. For a second I was totally dazed, the top of my head pounding from the impact with something very solid. When my senses came back, I realized that the thing my head had hit was Cash's chin, and the only reason I was still standing was because one of his arms had wrapped quickly around my waist, keeping me from falling backwards into the trash cans.

I knew it was him without even looking up. I blushed, embarrassed by the way I knew his scent. Hating that I remembered.

'You OK?' he asked in his bass voice.

I pulled away from him, hurriedly putting a few feet of space between us. 'I'm fine.'

Cash was still rubbing his chin where we'd collided. 'Sorry. I didn't even see you.'

'It's no big deal,' I told him, pretending I didn't care if he noticed me or not. 'But you shouldn't stand so close behind people. Maybe remember personal bubbles next time or . . . or something.'

He shook his head, half laughing, and ran a hand over his buzzed brown hair. 'Personal bubbles, huh?'

I almost laughed, too. That really had sounded lame. But I forced myself to keep a straight face, to stay cool and aloof. Cash Sterling would not make me smile. I wouldn't let him.

'Yes,' I said stiffly. 'It's, like, a three-foot radius for most people.'

He smiled, his green eyes crinkling at the corners. 'Would it surprise you if I mentioned that I barely passed geometry?'

'Oh,' I said. 'Well, a radius is the distance from any part of a circle's perimeter to the direct centre of the circle. It's half the diameter. So if a circle is six feet across the middle, the radius is three feet and . . .' And I was rambling. I shifted my feet and took a breath. 'And I got an A in geometry.'

'I'm not surprised,' he said. 'Seems like I should have hired you as a tutor, huh?'

'I doubt even I could have saved you if radii are beyond your comprehension.' The joke slipped out before I realized it.

'True,' he said, stepping a little closer to me. 'But if I'd been smart enough to hire you, maybe I would have been smart enough to learn the material.'

I was fighting off a smile when I saw Randy coming up behind Cash. That killed the smile. And in a weird way, I was grateful. It made me uncomfortable to be so comfortable around Cash.

Though I also didn't want to be present for the drama that was about to unfold.

'Hey, loser,' Randy snapped. 'Leave my girl alone.'

Heat flooded my cheeks as Cash's face darkened and he turned to face Randy. 'Sorry. I didn't realize Lissa was your property.'

'Don't get an attitude with me,' Randy said. 'I'll kick your ass right here and—'

'Randy, stop,' I hissed, sliding around Cash to stand between them. 'Don't do something you'll regret. There are teachers around.'

Randy glared up at Cash, who was at least two inches taller. 'If he's messing with you, I'll beat the shit out of him.'

But I knew it wasn't about me. Had Cash been any

other guy – played any other sport – Randy wouldn't have left his seat. He really wasn't a jealous or possessive boyfriend most of the time. This was one hundred per cent about the rivalry and the fact that Cash played soccer. I was just serving as a good excuse for a fight to break out.

And I certainly wasn't OK with that.

'I wasn't messing with anyone,' Cash said. 'I was coming up here to get a fork' – he pointed at the silverware container by the tray rack – 'when I accidentally bumped into her.' He used the same hand to gesture to me. 'I was just making sure she was OK. Didn't realize that was crossing the line. Next time, I'll just let her fall into the trash cans, if that'll make you feel better.'

'You being a smartass?' Randy growled.

'Randy, come on,' I demanded, tugging at his arm. 'You're embarrassing me. Just let it go.'

Randy resisted for a second before finally relenting and letting me pull him away. 'Prick,' he muttered after we'd taken about three steps.

'Yeah, he is,' I said, though I was sure we had very different reasons for thinking so.

'Randy, hold up.'

Despite my efforts to keep dragging him forward,

Randy turned around to face Cash again. 'What?'

I glanced over my shoulder and watched as Cash took a step forward. 'I don't know if you heard, but Pete went to the hospital last night. Tore his knee ligament after that stunt you and your buddies pulled yesterday. He won't be able to play all season. Hope you're proud of yourself.'

I froze. What?

Randy shrugged, and Cash turned and walked away.

'Come on,' Randy said to me. 'The library can wait, right? Let's go sit down and—'

'What stunt?'

'Huh?'

'What "stunt" did you and your buddies pull?' I asked. 'What is Cash talking about? How did Pete tear his knee ligament?'

Randy looked away from me, his eyes darting around for a second before finally coming to rest on the floor. 'Nothing,' he said. 'I mean, we didn't do anything to the kid. It's his own fault. He should have known not to run through the woods when it was so dark, and—'

'We?' I repeated. My hands balled into fists at my sides. 'Randy, two days ago you promised me you weren't going to get involved with that stuff.'

'Lissa, lighten up. It's no big deal,' he assured me.

26

'You promised me,' I whispered. I wanted to yell – I was angry enough – but my voice just wouldn't rise. 'You promised me you wouldn't get involved. Now that kid won't be able to play all season because of you.'

'I swear it isn't a big deal. Besides, it's his own fault. He got hurt when he tried to run away from us.'

'What were you going to do to him if he didn't get away?' Randy started to open his mouth, but I quickly shook my head. 'Never mind. I don't want to know. It doesn't matter any more. What matters is that a poor freshman is in the hospital now, and no matter how you try to excuse it, you lied to me.'

'He'll be fine,' Randy said, shrugging. 'I don't see why you're freaking out so much.'

I just stared at him. After more than a year, I thought we were past this. Past the lying and promise-breaking. After more than a year, I thought he understood me better than anyone. Maybe I was wrong.

An injury kept my father from ever playing sports again. Rationally, I knew that Pete's situation was nothing like Dad's, but to me, it didn't matter. The fact that Randy's actions – the entire football team's actions – had hurt someone, ruined someone's season, made me sick. This was bigger than just an egging or a few shouts across the lunchroom. This was dangerous.

And Randy, the one person I trusted to understand my feelings on this, thought I was 'freaking out'. That was the worst part of all. Worse, even, than having him break his word to me.

'I'm going to the library,' I murmured, scooting past him and heading towards the cafeteria doors. The whole place suddenly felt too loud, too chaotic.

I could feel the familiar panic setting in as I fought to restrain myself. I needed to get out of there.

'Come on, Lissa,' I heard him calling after me. 'Don't be mad. I'm sorry, OK?'

But I just kept walking.

4

'You really expected otherwise?' Chloe asked over the phone that night when I told her about Randy and Pete. 'Come on, Lissa. That rivalry has been going on for, like, ever. Promises or not, there's no way any of those boys are going to miss out on a chance to torture the soccer team.'

'Someone got hurt, Chloe,' I said bitterly. 'Bad this time. And for no reason. There will never be a winner, so what's the point? There is none. The fighting is stupid.'

'Maybe. But there's no use complaining about it. It's not like it'll ever end.'

When I first became friends with Chloe Nelson last year, after Randy and I started dating, I wasn't sure what to think of her. I heard she'd slept with two-thirds of the boys on the football team. I'd thought she was kind of a slut at first – that's what everyone called her – but we

29

became friends fast. Faster than I did with any of the other football girlfriends.

Don't get me wrong – the other girls seemed OK, but I hadn't entirely trusted any of them. Not with my secrets and not with my boyfriend.

But in a weird way, I'd known I could trust Chloe.

I also knew that she was right.

This stupid little war would never end on its own. But I had to do something. I just had to.

'I'm sorry for bitching,' I told her. 'It's just . . . It's getting out of hand, you know? It's too chaotic. Too out of control. And even before that kid got hurt, it was getting in the way of my relationship. I mean, he just forgets about me any time the feud comes up. I hate it.'

'Have you tried telling him that?' Chloe asked.

'Sort of . . .'

Chloe sighed. 'Lissa.'

'I know. You don't have to lecture me.'

'Too bad. I'm going to anyway.' She took a deep breath. 'You need to tell Randy how shitty this whole thing makes you feel. I know you like to be Little Miss Ice Queen and stay cool and aloof and whatever, but he's your boyfriend. You need to relax for once in your life and just let him know that this hurts your feelings.'

'I know, I know. It's just . . . It's hard. I want to, but I always seize up. I mean, we just got back together a few weeks ago.'

'Maybe you two broke up because you weren't open enough with him.'

That so wasn't why we broke up. But I would never tell anyone, not even Chloe, the real reason.

'God damn it, Lissa. You know, you are the only person who can make me sound like a fucking Hallmark card. Just talk to him, all right?'

'Fine.'

'Good. He'll probably be nicer to you than I am, anyway.'

'I like it when you're mean.'

'Meow,' Chloe said. 'Oh, baby.'

I laughed. She was really the only person who could get me this loosened up. If anyone else made the jokes she did, I would get so uncomfortable. Not with Chloe, though.

'I hate this, Chloe. Instead of it being just me and Randy, lately it's been me and Randy and the entire soccer team.'

'Bow-chika-wow-wow. That sounds like a good thing to me.'

'God, Chloe.'

'Sorry. I couldn't resist.' She giggled.

'You know what I mean, though, right? It's—'

Plink.

I frowned and stood up from my desk chair, carrying my phone with me to the window.

'Lissa, you there?'

'Yeah. Just a second, Chloe.' I covered the receiver and leaned against the cool glass of the window, staring into the semi-darkness below.

Plink, plink!

The pebbles hit the other side of the glass, right where my nose was pressed. I squinted, trying to make out the figure standing in the bushes by the edge of my house. The orange glow of the streetlamp fell across sandy hair and a blue T-shirt. Both were unmistakable. Randy had about a million Hamilton Panthers shirts in his drawers. Football pride and all that.

I put the phone back to my ear. 'Chloe, I have to go. Randy's outside. I'll call you tomorrow.'

'Have fun,' Chloe teased. 'Don't do anything I wouldn't do.'

'There isn't anything you wouldn't do.'

'That's the point.'

'Good night, Chloe.'

After tossing the phone on to my bed, I flipped the latch and pushed the window open, careful to move the screen aside before leaning into the warm late-August air.

'You are such a cliché,' I hissed down at Randy.

'Clichés work, though, don't they?'

'What do you want?' I asked.

'I'm proving it.'

'Proving what?'

'Friday night,' Randy reminded me. 'You told me to prove that you meant more to me than the rivalry. I'm here to prove it.' He whipped out a small bouquet of flowers from behind his back and looked up at me with a hopeful gaze, the light from the lamp post glinting off his brown irises. 'I'm sorry about today. I want to make it up to you. See?' He waved the bouquet a little, making sure I didn't miss it.

I couldn't help laughing at him. God, he could be so cute sometimes. A little pathetic, but mostly cute.

It was also cute how he shimmied up the drainpipe, trying desperately not to squish the flowers, and tumbled clumsily through my bedroom window.

He gave me a lopsided grin as I took the flowers from him and put them in a vase on my desk. When I looked again, Randy was lying on my bed. His eyes were on me, and his arms were folded beneath his head, showing off his toned biceps. I blushed and hoped he didn't notice me checking him out. His ego was big enough.

'Carnations,' he said, raising both eyebrows and jerking his chin at them, all cocky. 'You like pink carnations, so that's what I got. Proud?'

'Very,' I admitted. 'I didn't think you'd remember.'

'I remember everything you tell me.' He tapped a finger to his temple. 'It's all right here.'

'There ought to be plenty of room for it there. I mean,you don't have much else in that cavern you call a skull.'

'Ha, ha, very funny.' He rolled his eyes at me. 'Maybe I choose not to study just so I have more room in my brain for Lissa Facts. Ever thought of that? I mean, knowing your favourite colour and your lucky number is going to be way more useful to me than the periodic table or, you know, basic multiplication.'

It surprised me he could actually think that it wasn't useful. 'Actually, basic multiplication is really important for daily life. It—'

He groaned. 'That was a joke, babe.'

'Oh.' I shifted nervously and played with my hair a little, feeling embarrassed. It was sweet of him to come over, but having him drop in on me like this had thrown me off. I took a deep breath and told myself to chill out a bit, to loosen up. 'Well, thank you. For the flowers.'

'You're welcome.'

I could tell by his grin and the sparkle in his eyes that he wanted me to come over to the bed with him, but I didn't budge.

With a sigh, he stood up and walked over to me. One of his hands moved to my hip while the other stroked black locks of hair away from my face. I forced myself to be still, not to shrug away like I did sometimes. There was no reason to be so uptight around him. I closed my eyes, trying to enjoy his touch.

'I'm sorry,' he murmured. 'I shouldn't have lied, but Shane and the others really rode my ass when I told them I wasn't going to do it. I couldn't get out of it without being humiliated. I really didn't mean for that kid to hurt his knee, though. Seriously.'

'I know.'

For a minute I wondered if he'd been bullied by soccer players as a freshman. Randy was too proud to tell me if he had, but it was possible. In that case, I couldn't really blame him for wanting some revenge of his own.

'So we're cool?' he asked, rubbing a thumb across my cheek.

'Hmm.' I opened my eyes. 'Maybe.'

He smirked and leaned forward to kiss my lips, then my jaw, then my neck. I let out a little moan as his mouth travelled down my collarbone. My shoulders relaxed and my arms wrapped around him, my hands resting on his back.

'Are your dad and Logan still awake?' Randy whispered after his lips had travelled back up to my ear. 'Will you get in trouble for having me up here?'

'No,' I said. 'It's Logan's birthday. They went on a gambling boat for the night.'

Randy pulled back, a frown spreading across his full lips. 'Why didn't you tell me? I could have walked through the front door instead of climbing up to your window.'

I ducked my head. 'Well, you're the one who wanted to prove you were sorry. I think climbing the drainpipe was the least you could do.'

He looked a little pissed off for a minute, but he got over it fast. 'OK, you're probably right,' he said with a shrug and a tiny little smile. He leaned down and kissed me again.

We stood there in front of my desk, kissing for a while. Both of his hands were on my waist, and my fingers were twisted into his hair. After a few minutes, he pulled away so we could catch our breath.

'I love you,' he said, touching the tip of his nose to mine.

'You too.'

He pressed his lips to mine again, kissing me for a long moment before easing back just slightly. 'Babe,' he whispered against my mouth, 'do you want to . . . ?'

My eyes opened, travelling momentarily to the bed before moving back to meet his gaze. He was waiting for me. Pleading with me. I kissed him again, relaxing against him, and pressed my hips a little closer to his.

The quiet moments were the best. When our heartbeats had just started to slow down and the only sound was our breathing. It was the most intimate feeling in the world, letting someone hold me like that. Those were the moments when I was reminded just how much we loved each other, when I could finally let myself fully relax, when I thought that maybe Chloe was right and I could really open up to Randy about how I felt. Those were my favourite moments spent with him.

'OK. I'd better get going.'

Well, those moments were great when they lasted more than five seconds.

'What?'

Randy disentangled himself from me and kicked off the comforter that was spread over us. I watched as he climbed off my bed and moved to button his jeans.

'Where are you going?' I sat up and searched for

my shirt in the sheets. Suddenly, I felt too exposed, too vulnerable.

'Shane wants me to meet up with him in the old Fifth Street parking lot. Some soccer idiots wanna start shit with us because of that freshman who hurt himself. I think it'll be a good fight.'

'You're ditching me to go fight with soccer players?' I asked. I yanked my T-shirt over my head and turned to stare at him. 'I thought you were trying to prove that I came first.'

'I did,' he said. 'I came here first, didn't I? I could've gone straight to the fight, but I came to see my girl.' He walked over to me and leaned down, kissing me on the cheek. 'And we had a good time, right?'

'No, *you* had a good—'

'I'll call you later,' he said. 'I was here longer than I expected to be – not that I'm complaining, but Shane's waiting for me. I'll see you tomorrow. I love you.'

He tried to kiss me again, but I jerked away.

Randy sighed and shook his head. 'Don't be like this, Lissa,' he said, and then he turned and walked out of my bedroom.

I started to go after him. I jumped out of bed, momentarily determined to give him a piece of my mind, but stopped in the doorway. I took a deep breath and forced it all back, forced myself to stay in control.

But a minute later – as the front door slammed downstairs and the sound of Randy walking towards his car on the street corner wafted up through my window – I knew this was the last time I would be left behind for this war. I had to do something about it. Put a stop to the stupidity. Get Randy out of this trap he was in. For him. For both of us.

And I knew just how to do it.

5

The next morning, eleven of Hamilton High's female students received an email instructing them to meet in the library during their lunch period. Nine of the girls were dating football players. One had slept with most of the team. And the eleventh girl, a junior named Ellen Brennan, was the longtime girlfriend of the captain of the soccer team . . . and also my ex–best friend.

The email directed each of the girls to take a seat at the round table in the back corner of the library, where they would be given details on a plan to end the fall sports rivalry that had plagued Hamilton High for far too long.

And you know who sent that email?

Me.

'I don't see why you had to send me an email,' Chloe said, leaning her seat back and propping her feet up on the table. She had on really cute white sandals, and her toenails were painted bright red. 'You could have just called me.'

I put a hand on the back of her chair and pushed it forward. Her feet slid off the table as she let the chair's front legs hit the floor again. 'I thought a group email seemed more official,' I said. 'And it's so much more orderly.'

'You're so freaking neurotic.' Chloe ran her fingers through her brown corkscrew curls. I knew she hated them; they were apparently a pain in the ass to manage. But they just looked so adorable on her. 'And I don't get why you won't tell me about this plan of yours.'

'You'll find out soon,' I told her, tapping my fingers on the table in front of me and checking the clock. 'Where is everyone? Lunch started two minutes ago. It can't just be us.'

'Did you really expect everyone to show?'

'Yes.'

'Why?'

'Because everyone else has to hate this just as much as I do,' I said, crossing my arms. 'I can't be the only one sick of this stupid fight.'

'I'm sure you're not,' Chloe said. 'But you're the only one crazy and controlling enough to think you can do shit about it.'

41

Just then, the library doors opened and a group of three girls walked in, all carrying packed lunches. It took them only a second to locate the table I'd specified in the email, and they took their seats across from Chloe and me.

'Hey, Lissa,' they each said in turn.

I nodded in welcome.

They ignored Chloe completely.

She ignored them right back.

'So what's this about again?' Kelsey Foagler asked, twirling a strand of her blond hair around a long manicured finger.

'I have a plan to end the rivalry,' I told her.

'Oh, right. That's adorable.' It was her MO to sound incredibly insincere.

'Um, thanks?'

The doors opened again and a few more girls trickled in with their lunches, taking the remaining places around the table. I smiled at Chloe, realizing that my plan might actually work. Only four more girls had to show up before I'd have everyone from the email list. She just rolled her eyes at me.

One by one, the last batch of girls came through the library doors.

Ellen was the last to walk in, and I admit, I was

shocked she'd decided to come. I'd added her to the email list more on a hopeful whim than with actual faith that she'd show. We hadn't spoken in a year, yet here she was, taking the seat beside me and giving me a smile like nothing had changed. But Ellen had always been a better, more forgiving person than I was.

'Hey,' I said nervously. 'Um, it's nice to see you.'

'You too.'

Across the table, Kelsey was giving her a less-than-welcoming stare, reserved especially for girlfriends of soccer players. I couldn't help cringing. Tensions from the feud had seeped into the lives of the girls, too. That had been what pulled Ellen and me apart last year.

The table was full of chatter. I cleared my throat a couple of times, trying to get their attention, but no one seemed to hear me.

'Hey, bitches, shut up and let Lissa talk!' Chloe shouted, and everyone fell silent. Man, sometimes I wished I had her nerve. At least, I did until I noticed Mrs Hillman, the librarian, shooting us a disapproving glare. Oops.

I cleared my throat again. 'Hi, everyone,' I began. 'So I just wanted to talk to you all about the boys' sports feud. I think it's got way out of hand. People are getting hurt, and it's been causing problems in my relationship. I'm sure you are all in similar situations.'

'Yep,' Susan Port huffed. 'After Luther's tyres were slashed last week, he completely skipped our date on my birthday so he could go have his 'baby' fixed.'

'At least your boyfriend didn't have a busted lip and black eye in your Homecoming photos last year,' Kelsey grumbled.

A general murmur of agreement bubbled around the table.

'Exactly,' I said. 'We're all neglected during the autumn because of the rivalry. So, naturally, we should try to put a stop to it, right? Isn't that what all of you want?'

Another murmur of agreement.

'That would be nice,' Kelsey said, 'in theory. But in reality, what can we really do to end it? Nothing. Those oafs won't stop clubbing one another on the heads until they graduate or go so brain-dead they forget who to hit.'

'Shut up, Kelsey, and just give Lissa a chance,' Chloe snapped.

Kelsey feigned surprise. 'Oh my God, Chloe can speak? I thought her mouth only worked for sucking dicks. It's a miracle.'

'I'll show you a miracle, you little—'

I grabbed Chloe by her T-shirt and yanked her back down into her seat. 'Both of you, please be civil,' I advised.

Kelsey sat back down, growling to herself.

'Anyway,' I said, 'I have to disagree with Kelsey. I think I've finally figured out what we can do to end this once and for all.'

'Nuke the locker room?'

'Seriously?'

'Can we just get the soccer program cancelled?'

'How would we do that?'

'Give her a chance to explain,' Chloe said loudly just as a wave of anxiety washed over me. Too many voices talking over one another. She winked and nodded for me to continue. She knew me too well.

'So you all want to stop the fighting,' I said. 'That's good. I'm glad we're on the same page. The fact is that we've all tried everything we could think of on our own. We've begged, pleaded and fought, and it hasn't done a thing. We can't control them. So the important thing here is to get control of the situation – we need power. And clearly, we haven't been able to get that on our own. That's why I called this meeting. Because together, I believe we can get power over at least one of the sides. And with that power, we can manipulate this war however we want.'

'How many times did you rehearse this speech?' Kelsey asked.

I ignored her, picking up my pen and twisting the cap

back and forth under the table. No way was I telling her that I'd practised this in front of the mirror . . . twice.

'OK, so the thing is to get control of our boys, and to do it all together, as a unified force,' I continued. 'Because when it was just football versus soccer, it was a stalemate and a never-ending cycle. But add in an extra party – the girls – and it's possible to totally upend the balance. Finding our leverage is the hard part, and like you, I didn't think it was possible. I thought we were all just screwed. But last night, I figured it out. I know exactly how we can get control of the boys and end this war for good.'

'Out with it already,' Chloe urged.

I grinned. 'It's the one thing they could never say no to. The one thing they beg and plead and cajole for. Up until now, I didn't realize we could use it to our advantage. But last night, I realized that it's our best shot.' I paused, took a breath. 'We go on . . . a sex strike!'

And . . . silence.

Dead silence.

For at least forty-three seconds.

As I might have predicted, Chloe was the first one to share her opinion, and in typical Chloe fashion, she shared loudly.

'Are you out of your fucking mind?'

The table rumbled with uneasy disapproval, triggered by Chloe's protest. I took a deep breath, twisting the pen cap faster and faster. I had to pull them in. I had to get them back in my court – to show them that this was the best option.

'Think about it,' I pressed, my voice raised. 'Boys only want one thing. They're all horn dogs. If there's anything we can use to get power, it's sex. Specifically, denying it.'

'You might be right,' Chloe said. 'But you're forgetting one key factor here. Won't we be denying ourselves, too?'

Kelsey rolled her eyes. 'Jesus, Chloe. You're such a whore.'

'Fuck you,' Chloe snapped. 'I know for a fact that you screwed Terry on your first date. Don't act so high and mighty.'

'Guys,' I said, a little panicked. 'Fighting among ourselves won't solve anything. We're here to create peace, remember?'

Kelsey shot Chloe one more evil glare before leaning back in her seat and folding her arms over her chest, her bottom lip poked out like a pouting five-year-old.

'Look,' I said. 'You all agreed you wanted to end this stupid war, right? And this is the way to do it. We make them want us, then refuse to give them what they want.

Once they realize we're not giving in, they'll be like putty in our hands. And that's when we spring this on them. They have to call off the rivalry before we'll touch them. I bet they'll cave within two weeks.'

Somehow, I could feel Ellen's eyes on me. I smiled, trying not to look uncomfortable.

'Is that, you know, ethical?' Susan asked. 'I want the rivalry to end and all, but sex as a weapon feels a little sketchy. I think there have been whole Dr Phil episodes about it.'

'Oh, come on,' Chloe said. 'Every girl has a prerogative to say no. There's no reason not to exercise that right . . . even in large groups. Besides, Dr Phil's a quack.'

'Susan, you pay a freshman girl to do your English papers,' Kelsey said. 'Are you really the one to question ethics?'

'Hey, I'm busy. I have basketball practice. No time to read *The Great Gatsby* or whatever. Plus, I pay her. That makes it ethical.'

'This is ethical,' I said, hoping to get them back on track. 'We're not really using sex as a weapon – we're just choosing not to partake until the rivalry ends. We're not manipulating them or anything. We're . . . boycotting.'

'Well, it is a good plan,' Susan said. 'I mean, it will probably work.'

'I don't know.' Mary Grisham's voice was barely loud enough for me to hear over the flutter of whispers at the table. She was a tiny junior with huge blue eyes and dark chocolate-coloured hair. I looked at her, smiling, urging her to continue. She shifted nervously in her seat and said a little louder, 'I, um . . . I can't really do anything,' she said. 'Finn and I aren't sleeping together, so I don't—'

'Seriously?' Chloe said, gawking. 'You and Finn have been together for, like, nine months, right? And you haven't even got it on once?'

Mary shook her head.

'Is he, like, gay?' Chloe asked.

'Just because they haven't slept together yet doesn't make either of them gay.' It came out sounding harsher than I meant it. I glanced at Mary again, then addressed the rest of the table. 'I'm sure some of the rest of you are in the same boat, right?'

More silence.

I had to stop counting after ten seconds. I just didn't get it. These were the same girls who called Chloe a whore for having too much sex. I could see their eyes on Mary. See the mocking or disapproving expressions. Like her virginity was a bad thing.

'Well, thank you for being honest,' I told Mary as her cheeks turned redder and redder. 'It's cool that you're waiting. I know a lot of girls lie about it, so I respect your honesty.'

'You're welcome,' Mary mumbled.

'Oh, honey.' Chloe sighed. 'That's cute, but you don't know what you're missing.'

I elbowed Chloe in the ribs and said loudly to Mary, "But you can still participate. Just don't do other stuff. Don't, um . . . Don't go down on him or touch his . . .' I felt like my face was on fire. I took a deep breath and forced myself to keep going. 'No hand jobs. Or anything he might enjoy too much. If kissing is all you do, don't make out with him. You'll find a way. You don't have to be having sex to make it work. Trust me.'

'But won't they get mad?' one of the girls asked.

'Yeah, they will. And then won't they cheat on us?'

'I don't want that.'

'I do. Then maybe I'll finally be off the hook for kissing that kid from Oak Hill.'

'Stop, stop, stop,' Chloe said over the growing wave of panicked voices. 'Look, maybe I'm not an expert, since I'm not in a relationship or whatever, but is this really something you're worried about? If so, that is seriously fucked up.'

'Girls like you are the reason we have to worry,' Kelsey muttered.

Chloe turned an icy glare on her. 'Despite what you think of me, I've never slept with another girl's boyfriend. And I would never sleep with Terry – whiny ass-kissers aren't my type.' She looked at the rest of the girls again. 'Seriously, if the bastards cheat on you, then they don't deserve you anyway. If that's a legit fear, then you probably shouldn't be with them to begin with.'

'Lissa,' Susan said, "what about you? Aren't you afraid Randy will cheat if you do this?'

'No,' I said. Though I think I sounded a little more certain than I felt. 'I'm not. He loves me. Something like this won't change that. Besides, this will help the boys in the long run, too. They're victims here. But unless we do something, something to force them out of the war, they'll never end it. This is our best option, and a good boyfriend won't hold the no-sex thing against you.'

'Seriously,' Chloe said. 'I mean, I like sex probably about as much as any boy does, and even I know a little bit of abstinence isn't something to end a relationship over. That'd be pretty fucked up.'

'Easy for you to say,' Kelsey snapped. 'Have you ever even been in a relationship, Chloe? A real one. One that continues even after you put your clothes back on.'

'You know what? Screw you, Kelsey. I don't have to be in a relationship to know that a guy is a dick if he dumps you because you won't put out. And no matter what you think of me, I won't be the one the boys run to when they want to get some. Because . . . because I'm going to do it. What Lissa said. I'm going to play along. No sex.'

I gaped at Chloe, amazed. 'Seriously?'

'Yep. I'm in.'

'Me too.'

I turned to my right and saw Ellen watching me with her hazel eyes. Something in them seemed sceptical, and I wondered if I'd misunderstood her. Then she shook her head and the flicker of disbelief was gone.

'I'm sick of this fighting. It's definitely crossed a line.' She gave me a meaningful look before adding, 'I think a sex strike is a great idea, and I can try to get some of the other soccer players' girlfriends in on it. I bet they'll help. We're all fed up.'

'R-really?' I beamed at her, half in shock. 'Ellen, thank you so much.'

After that, a lot of people seemed to hop on the bandwagon.

'I'll do it,' Susan said. 'Damn, Lissa, you've got some brains. I never would have thought of this.'

'I'm in. It'll make this season more entertaining at least.'

'I guess I'll do it. Maybe end-of-rivalry sex will be even better than make-up sex.'

I ducked my head to hide the blush creeping up my face. How could these girls be so open about their sex lives? I barely even talked about mine with Chloe. Hell, I couldn't even say the words for the things I was doing with Randy without cringing.

'We need to make a pact or something,' Chloe said. 'Like, an oath. We need to swear to abstain from all sexual activities.'

'What do we swear on?' Susan asked. 'The Bible?'

'That's kind of inappropriate,' I managed to joke. 'Considering what we're swearing about and all.'

'Here.' Ellen placed her backpack on the table and unzipped it. After a few seconds of digging, she pulled out a new issue of *Cosmo* and tossed it on to the table. 'It's the sex-tips issue. Includes a nice list of all the things we can't do. We can swear on it.'

Chloe picked up the magazine. 'Sweet,' she said, flipping through the pages. She paused and visibly cringed. 'Ugh. No, don't try that. Trust me, not as great as it sounds.'

I grabbed the magazine from Chloe, half wondering and half afraid to see what she was talking about. I held it up for everyone to see. 'OK,' I said. 'So we'll all take a vow. I'll lay out the rules, and if you agree, you put your hand on the magazine and say, "I do". Got it?'

Most of the girls nodded.

I placed the magazine on the table, putting my hand over the model's face on the cover. 'I hereby swear to abstain from all forms of sexual activity. This includes but is not limited to anything involving body parts below the belt. That's either party's belt. Oh, and second base is outlawed, too. Nothing, um, under the shirt.' I forced myself to continue, despite the way this speech made my face heat up. 'I'll stand my ground, even in the toughest of times, and will resist temptation until the rivalry is put to an end.'

I slid the magazine to Ellen, still feeling a little anxious when our eyes met. But I couldn't let my composure falter right now. Not with all these girls watching.

I cleared my throat for, like, the millionth time that afternoon. 'Do you agree?' I asked.

'I do,' Ellen said solemnly.

She passed it on to Susan. 'I do.'

Susan passed it to the girl to her right. 'I do.'

'I do.'

'I do.'

When it came to Mary, I saw her hesitate for a minute.

She looked at me, took a breath and placed her hand on the magazine. 'I do.'

Then she passed it to Kelsey.

'Just pass it on if you're too chicken,' Chloe taunted. 'You call me a whore, but you're more hesitant about giving up sex than I am.'

'Shut up,' Kelsey hissed. 'Give me that.' She yanked the magazine towards her and put her hand in the dead centre of the cover. Her eyes locked with Chloe's as she said, 'I. Do.'

Chloe grinned.

To my amazement, after so much disagreement, all eleven girls at the table – plus me – wound up making the oath. Chloe was the last, and she grinned at me as she swore to be celibate. I knew it would be a challenge for her more than anyone.

But looking at the others, I knew Chloe couldn't have been the only girl who liked sex. So many others had been hesitant to agree right away. Surely some of the girls had the same reason as Chloe, even if the others were reluctant out of fear of losing their boyfriends. I wondered what the ratio was – how many of the girls just didn't want to give up sex versus the ones who were afraid of being cheated on.

And I wondered why Chloe was the only girl willing

to come out and say she liked sex. Maybe because the others knew she was called a slut or a whore for liking it so much? But I didn't understand that, either. Like Chloe said, it wasn't like she slept with other girls' boyfriends.

I also wanted to know why Mary had been the only one willing to confess the opposite – her virginity. Because I didn't think for a second that she was the only one at the table who hadn't yet made that leap.

When everyone had sworn on the magazine, I handed it back to Ellen. 'You can make the soccer girls take the same oath,' I said.

'Sure thing.' She tucked the magazine into her backpack again.

'All right,' I said. 'So here we go. I'm thinking we should all keep in touch via email. We'll need a support group to get through this, and it'll keep us organized. But I definitely think we are on to something here. We can win this way.'

'For your sake,' Kelsey said, getting to her feet just as the bell for third block rang, 'I hope so. This better work, Lissa.'

'It will,' I assured her. 'I know it will.'

The girls began to move in a herd towards the door. I started to turn to Chloe, who was still sitting at the table with me, then noticed Ellen, lingering uncertainly near the library door.

'Hey,' I said, walking over to her. I'd picked up my pen again and was already spinning the cap. 'Thanks for coming. I know this is all really weird. The football girlfriends and being around me and . . . whatever.'

'I'll always come if you want me to, Liss.' She gave another small smile and put a hand on my shoulder, squeezing it briefly. Then she turned and left the library.

I thought I'd lost Ellen for good because of this feud. Because our boyfriends hated each other. But maybe, I realized, I could end the war and get a friend back at the same time. The thought made me smile.

Chloe eased up beside me. 'You ready for AP Bio?'

'Sure,' I said, turning to face her. 'Thanks, by the way. For agreeing to this.'

'Yeah. You owe me.'

'Well, at least the stupid fight will be over soon,' I said. 'Won't that make up for it?'

Chloe rolled her eyes. 'Lissa, I couldn't care less about the problems between the teams. I know it's stupid, and I know it affects you, but it doesn't really have an impact on me, since I'm not really committed to any of the boys.' She shrugged. 'I didn't do this to end the fighting.

I did it because I know it's important to you. And you're important to me.'

I smiled. 'Thank you, Chloe.'

'Yeah, yeah,' she said, picking up her messenger bag. 'I also did it just to spite Kelsey, so it wasn't totally selfless. I hate that bitch.'

I laughed.

'Come on,' she said. 'Mr Hall will flip his shit if we're late.'

6

That afternoon, as Chloe and I walked out to the student parking lot after last block, Randy jogged up behind us. 'Hey, Lissa, hold up a sec.'

We stopped, and I turned to face him. 'Yes?'

He came to a halt a few feet from me, looking momentarily confused. 'Something wrong?' he asked. 'You look upset.'

'It's noth— ow!' Chloe had just elbowed me hard in the side, and now she gave me a stern look. I sighed. 'OK, fine. Yes, I'm a little upset, Randy.'

'Shit. What did I do?'

'OK, my work here is done. I'll give you two some privacy.' Chloe brushed past me and walked over to her convertible. I saw her climb on to the hood and pull her long legs up to her chest.

'So what's wrong?' Randy asked. He was already

dressed in his workout clothes for football practice.

I kicked at a small chunk of loose pavement, a little harder than I'd intended, and it skittered across the parking lot, colliding with a Dumpster a few feet away with a loud thud.

'Didn't your mother teach you to use your words?' Randy joked.

I looked at him sharply.

'I— sorry,' he said. 'I know you don't like to talk about . . . sorry.' He sighed and ran a hand through his hair. 'Let's rewind. What's wrong? What did I do? Tell me.'

'Look,' I said, forcing the word out of my mouth. Chloe was right. I needed to open up and tell Randy how I felt. 'It's just . . . I'm not cool with being your . . .' My eyes stayed trained on my hands, where they wound and unwound in a steady rhythm near my waist. 'Your booty call.'

'Booty call?'

'Last night,' I reminded him. 'My room. You bribed me with flowers before ditching me. You were there; I'm sure you remember.'

Suddenly, the light bulb clicked on over his head. 'What? That? That wasn't a booty call, babe. It's only a booty call if you're not with the girl. But we're in love, so it's cool.'

'Not to me,' I muttered. 'It hurt. I felt used. I'm tired of you ditching me for this stupid fight, Randy. It really bothered me last night. It's been bothering me for a while, actually.' I stared at my feet and shoved my hands in my pockets so I'd stop wringing them.

'Lissa . . .'

I looked up at him.

Randy shuffled his feet and rubbed the back of his neck with one hand. 'OK, I'm sorry. I didn't mean for you to feel that way. Can I make it up to you?'

'How?'

'Let me take you out Friday. Like, on a nice date.'

'Randy—'

'Seriously, Lissa. I mean it. Let me try again. Please?'

I sighed and shifted my weight from one foot to the other. 'Well . . . OK.'

'Cool,' he said, leaning forward and kissing me on the cheek. 'I'll pick you up at seven, OK? Dress up. We'll go somewhere nice. Mom is going to some work retreat this weekend, so we'll have the house to ourselves if you want to come back to my place after.'

'Sounds good.'

'Great. Well, I have to get to practice. I'll see you around.'

I let him give me a quick kiss on the lips before

he ran back towards the double doors that led into the gym.

When he was gone, I turned and walked over to Chloe's car. 'Let's go,' I said, smacking the hood of the black convertible. 'I can't be late for work.'

Chloe slid off the hood as I got into the passenger seat. 'Now, Lissa, was that so hard?' she asked.

'Yes . . . but I'm glad I did it. You were right; it is better for me to just be honest with him.'

'When am I ever wrong?'

'Well, there was that time last year when you attempted to convince me that Harrison Carlyle was straight by going up to him at the Nest and trying to—'

'Hey, hey!' Chloe raised a hand to silence me. 'We do not talk about that night.' She sighed. 'I should have known when he told me what kind of shampoo would help with my frizz.'

'So you can be wrong.'

'Rarely,' she said. 'And I wasn't wrong in this situation – so there.' She winked at me and laughed. 'It's good to know that my dreaded Hallmark moments do pay off.'

I rolled my eyes at her.

She started the engine and pulled out of the parking lot, heading towards the Hamilton Public Library, where

I shelved books every Tuesday and Thursday. Since I couldn't afford a car and Randy had football practice, Chloe usually gave me a ride.

That's how Chloe and I had started hanging out, actually. She heard me talking about needing a ride at the lunch table last year and volunteered to drive me. At first I was kind of nervous. I knew the rumours about Chloe, and I was sure being alone with her would be totally awkward. Like, her car would be full of condom wrappers or freaky sex toys or something. Not exactly the kind of girl I'd usually hang out with.

But I'd misjudged her. Chloe was shockingly normal. She listened to Top 40 radio, wanted to see the same movies I did, and, aside from a few empty bottles of Diet Coke on the floor, kept her car fairly clean. Nothing really set her apart from any of the other girls whose cars I'd ridden in. And, honestly, after talking to her during that first car ride, I'd realized how much I liked her. Chloe started driving me home or to work every afternoon, and within a few weeks, she was my new best friend.

'So Friday, huh?' she said as we sped past the Fifth Street movie rental with the top down and the radio blasting an old Backstreet Boys song.

It was ninety degrees outside, normal for late August,

and I was already dreading the cooler days of autumn that would be coming all too soon.

'Were you eavesdropping?' I asked, unconsciously popping open the glove box the way I always did when I got in Chloe's car.

'Of course I was . . . and will you get out of there?'

'I'm just looking for a CD.'

'No, you're not. You're alphabetizing them.' She reached over and swatted at my hand and, with a sigh, I shut the compartment. 'So if the strike starts ASAP, it looks like your date will be interesting. Poor Randy. He's got that empty house and everything.'

'We'll still go to his house,' I said. 'Maybe we'll watch a movie or something.'

'Yeah, I'm sure that's an alternative he'll be thrilled with.' She laughed and grabbed a cigarette from a pack on the dash. 'Shane wants me to come over to his place Friday night, too,' she said, lighting up and taking a drag. 'I told him I'd love to, but the idiot isn't going to know what hit him when I don't give it up.'

'You could have just said no,' I told her. 'You didn't have to say you'd do it.'

'What's the fun in that?' She took another drag on her cigarette and blew the smoke out between her pink-glossed lips.

'It's not about teasing, remember?'

'I won't tease him . . . Well, not much.' She took another puff on her cigarette. 'What about you? Are you sure you can handle this, Lissa? Being alone with Randy and not jumping his bones? I mean, he is pretty fine. Will you really be able to say no?'

'Trust me, I'll be all right,' I said. 'Randy's hot, but it isn't like he's Adonis.'

She looked sceptical. 'Whatever you say. He may not be a sex god, but I know you like it.'

I blushed. 'God, Chloe. Can we not talk about this?'

'What?' she asked. 'Come on. If you're mature enough to have sex, you should be mature enough to joke about it with your super-fabulous best friend.'

I didn't say anything to that.

We pulled into the library parking lot and I quickly undid my seat belt.

'Have fun at work,' Chloe said.

I watched as she put out her cigarette and left the butt in her ashtray. 'Doesn't your mother see those and get pissed off?' I had to ask.

'Psh. Nah. She bought me the pack.' Chloe shrugged and gestured to the glove compartment. 'She swore she'd quit for real last time. But after the divorce, she asked me to go out and buy her a pack. I told her she could only have one if she bought me one too. I figured she'd be like, "No way in hell," or something, but she just tossed me a twenty and said it was OK.'

'My dad would kill me,' I said.

'Eh. I'm eighteen now. Even if she didn't like it, there isn't much she can do.' Chloe started messing with the radio dial, and I climbed out of the convertible.

'Thanks for the lift.'

'You know it's not a problem. See you tomorrow.'

I slammed the car door and waved over my shoulder as I made my way up the steps to the front entrance.

'About time,' Jenna snapped when I walked over to the front desk.

'I'm five minutes early,' I told her.

She chose to ignore this, of course, and jabbed a finger at the cart of children's books beside her. 'All of those need to be shelved right away,' she informed me, tossing her curtain of cherry-red hair over her shoulder. 'Hurry. There are some kids up there now. What if someone is looking for one of those books and can't find it on the shelf? Chop, chop.'

Jenna was insanely anal-retentive. She was my co-worker, a student at Oak Hill Community College, and a royal pain in my ass. She'd seemed cool for, like, the first week I worked at the library, but I quickly learned that she had serious issues. Working with Jenna was the only part of this job that I hated.

I grabbed a few of the adult fiction books that had accidentally been placed on the children's cart (Ha! Jenna could make mistakes too!) and put them on the correct shelves before walking back to the front desk to grab the cart, which I needed to lug up the stairs. Judging by her attitude, Jenna wasn't going to help me drag the beast to the second floor – great.

'Oh, by the way,' Jenna said, turning away from her computer and meeting my eyes, "you have a new co-worker.'

'Who?' I asked.

'Some high-school kid.' Jenna sighed. She wasn't bothering to hide her agitation. I'm sure she saw it as one more idiot to deal with. Funny, really. As much as she loved to boss people around, you'd think she'd be thrilled to have someone new under her command.

'Name?' I pressed.

'Can't remember. But he's hot. Don't let that distract you from working, though. I don't want it to become a problem.'

I rolled my eyes when she wasn't looking.

'He's late,' Jenna said. 'By two and a half minutes. Not a great way to start a new job, is it?'

I was about to respond when the library doors opened behind me.

'Sorry I'm late. I had to talk to my soccer coach about making up practice.'

My whole body went rigid. I knew that voice.

'There you are,' Jenna said, flicking her red hair over her shoulder in the sassiest way possible. 'OK. I'll excuse your lack of punctuality today, but don't make a habit of it, please.'

She'd excuse it? Jenna was not our boss. She couldn't punish us or anything just because she worked a few more days a week. She might have called herself an "assistant librarian", but she was just another shelver. You needed a degree to be a librarian (I'd Googled it out of curiosity once), and she was still a student. Really, Mrs Coles, the head librarian, was the only one with the power to hire, fire, or punish.

'Sorry,' Jenna said. 'Can't remember your name. What was it again?'

'Cash.'

'Right. Good. Cash, this is Lissa. You'll be working together to keep this place in top order.'

I had to keep myself from blushing as I turned to face him for the first time since he'd walked into the library. I was annoyed to find him smiling at me. Not a sly smile or a knowing smile, just a casual smile. Like he was vaguely happy to see me.

'Hey,' he said.

'Hello.'

'You two stop having a staring contest and get to work. Take those books and shelve them in the children's section,' Jenna ordered, pointing at the cart again. 'Upstairs.'

'I know where the children's section is,' I told her.

'Cash doesn't, though. Now hurry up. What if some poor little kid is looking for *The Velveteen Rabbit* and can't find it because you guys took so long putting these books on the shelves?'

I sighed and grabbed one end of the cart.

'Elevator,' Cash said as I pulled the cart towards the stairs.

'What?' I looked over my shoulder at him.

'The elevator,' he repeated, gesturing to our left. 'You know there is one right here, don't you?'

'Um, yes,' I said slowly. Of course I knew. I was here all the time. I knew the place like the back of my hand. 'But it's awful. It takes forever just to get to the first floor.'

'Maybe,' Cash said. 'But that cart is going to be a bitch to get up the stairs. It looks really heavy. Let's just use the elevator.'

As much as I hated to admit it – and to spend any amount of time stuck in an enclosed space with Cash – it really would be easier to move the books upstairs in the elevator. And who knew? Maybe they'd fixed it. I hadn't used the thing in months.

'Fine,' I agreed.

Cash helped me roll the cart into the ancient, microscopic elevator. Now that I was inside again, with the doors closing, I remembered why I'd hated it the first time. Aside from being slow, it was also kind of creepy.

My fingers tightened around the handle of the cart as the elevator trembled, making horrific scraping sounds as it slid upwards at a snail's pace. Of course, my anxiousness wasn't helped by the fact that Cash was standing just centimetres away from me, the limited room forcing us uncomfortably close to each other.

'So . . . you and Jenna have a lot in common, huh?'

I looked up from the titles on the cart, narrowing my eyes at him. 'What?'

'Jenna,' Cash repeated, as if I'd misunderstood him the first time. 'She reminds me of you.'

'How?'

'I don't know. She just reminds me of you. You're both kind of control freaks – not in a bad way or anything, but . . . You haven't noticed?'

'No.'

'Huh.' he shrugged. 'Maybe it's just me, then. But she really reminds me of you. I just remember when we were talking at that party over the summer, you said you had a thing about order and . . .' He trailed off. I could feel the heat rising on my face when he mentioned that night. 'Anyway,' he continued, 'she seems like she's a lot like you.'

I focused hard on keeping my reply cool, free of any emotion.

'You just met her,' I reminded him. 'And really, you don't know me that well, so you can't make comparisons. Especially not between me and Jenna. I'm nothing like Jenna.'

'You sure about that?' he teased, elbowing me playfully. Flirting, the way he did with every girl.

Despite his romance-novel-worthy name, Cash Sterling was anything but a leading man. We'd gone to the same school since kindergarten, and in all those years, he'd never once had a girlfriend. Hell, as far as I knew, he'd never even hooked up with a girl. But he was a flirt. Chloe called him 'the ultimate tease' because he was good-looking, friendly and charming, and he led all the girls on but never pursued any of them.

I didn't understand why it was OK for Cash to flirt

71

with every girl he met and never commit to any of them when, if a girl did the same thing, the guys would call her a cock tease. Guys were such jerks.

'I'm sure,' I replied, probably with more of an edge to my voice than was fair, but it bugged me that he was comparing me to my worst enemy, and it bugged me even more that he had the gall to flirt with me.

The elevator didn't seem to be moving any more, but the doors hadn't opened either. I jabbed the button again, and we lurched upwards, as if the contraption had stopped between floors, forgetting to move on. This could not be safe.

'You OK?' Cash asked.

'Yes. I just want to get off this thing.'

Suddenly his hand was over mine, and I realized that I'd been tapping my knuckles against the cart of books. 'Don't be nervous,' he said, squeezing lightly.

I stared up at him, surprised to find concern in his green eyes.

'I should have asked you if you were claustrophobic.'

'I— What?'

'Isn't that why you're such a stressball right now and didn't want to use the lift? My cousin's the same way.'

'Um . . . yes. Right. That's it.'

'I'm sorry. I shouldn't have talked you into this.'

'I'll be OK,' I said, and despite everything, I couldn't help letting out a little laugh.

'Well, it's almost over,' Cash said. 'Looks like the doors are about to open.'

And sure enough, they did. The noisy elevator screeched as it finally halted on the first floor and the metal doors slid aside. Cash removed his hand from mine – it felt like a little jab at my chest – and we pushed the cart out on to the floor.

'All right, start shelving,' I said, trying to regain my composure. 'Someone might be looking for one of these.'

'Like *The Velveteen Rabbit*?' Cash grinned and picked up one of the picture books.

I opened my mouth to argue that I was so not like Jenna, but Cash turned those green eyes on me and I felt myself start to melt a little. I shook my head, laughing against my better judgment.

'Touché,' I said.

He grabbed a few books and walked over to one of the shelves, smiling at me as he passed.

I smiled back, then scolded myself for it. It had taken me nearly a year to relax around Randy, and sometimes it was still a challenge. It shouldn't have been so easy with Cash.

As quickly as it had appeared, my smile slipped away.

73

7

Randy and I'd had our first big fight this past June, right after school was out. We'd broken up, and I was devastated. But on a hot night in July, Chloe decided to get me out of my funk and drag me to a party at Vikki McPhee's house.

'Come on,' she'd said, pulling me from my bedroom that night. 'You'll never get over Randy if you don't put yourself out there. A few meaningless hook-ups are exactly what you need right now.'

When we'd arrived at the party, Chloe gave me a once-over and sighed. 'I still can't believe you're wearing that. You have some sexy clothes. Why aren't you rocking them?'

I rolled my eyes and edged past her into the house. The place already smelled like beer and pot, and the walls were practically shuddering against the pounding bass of the stereo. I wrapped my arms around myself and moved towards the perimeter of the room, staying close to the wall. I wanted to fall through the floor. This kind of chaos wasn't what I needed right then. Or ever.

Chloe ran up beside me. 'Let's get something to drink.'

'You know I don't drink,' I said.

'For once in your life, can't you just let go? Lose control a little? You might actually enjoy not agonizing over every little thing.'

I shook my head.

'Have it your way,' she said, shrugging. 'But please, promise me you'll go talk to people? Have a little bit of fun tonight, OK?'

'Fine.'

She squeezed my shoulder before hurrying off towards Vikki's kitchen. I pressed my back against the wall and looked around. More people were arriving, and many were already dancing and shouting along with the music. In the corner, I saw a side table topple over when a boy fell backwards on to it. I cringed. I had to get out of there.

Keeping my word to Chloe, I said a quick, 'Hey, how are you?' to Kelsey as she passed me, wearing an expensive-looking white sundress. She gave an annoyed glance – probably deciding that she didn't want to talk to anyone dressed as badly as I was – and moved on. Just like I'd hoped.

With my task complete, I edged around the living room and headed towards the back door. Leaving the party wasn't an option, since Chloe was my ride – as usual – but I could at least get out of this room.

The sun had just set when I pushed open the door to the back porch. But instead of finding the backyard empty, I discovered Cash Sterling sitting on the steps.

'Oh, sorry,' I muttered, my hand still on the door. 'I'll leave.'

He was sitting on the top step of the wooden porch, one of his legs pulled up to his chest while the other stretched out towards the steps below him. His chin had been resting thoughtfully in his hand, but when he heard me, his head turned in my direction.

'Hey,' he said. And I thought I saw his eyes light up a little, though it could have just been the flickering porch light playing tricks. 'No. Stay. I don't mind.'

Even though I'd wanted to be alone, I decided that Cash would be better company than the crowd inside Vikki's living room. I shut the door and walked over to sit beside him on the steps. The smile he gave me was so sweet, so warm, that even in my bad mood, I couldn't help smiling back at him.

I didn't really know Cash that well. We'd had a few classes together, and back before Ellen and I had stopped talking I would see him hanging out with Adam, her boyfriend. We'd talked maybe twice, but we'd never been alone together. Until now.

'So what are you doing out here?' I asked. 'Already tired of the party?'

Cash laughed. 'I guess you could say that. It's not really my thing. A few of the guys from the soccer team asked me to play designated driver, though. So I agreed to help out. How about you?'

'My best friend made me come.'

'Why? I mean, if you don't want to be here . . .'

'She thinks it'll be good for me,' I explained. 'My boyfriend and I . . . Well, we just split up, and she decided it would be good for me to be social.'

Cash looked away, and I watched as his sneaker scuffed against the wooden step a few feet below us. 'So you and Randy aren't together now?'

I almost asked how he knew who my boyfriend was, but I stopped myself. The answer was obvious. Randy was the quarterback, one of the most popular boys in school. Everyone knew who he was dating. Not to mention, Hamilton boasted only about a hundred students per graduating class. It was almost difficult not to be aware of who dated whom.

'Yes.'

'How long ago?'

'Three weeks.'

'I'm sorry.'

He didn't sound sorry, though. I couldn't read his tone – caught somewhere between indifference and smugness. I almost stood up and walked back inside then. Almost ran away from his insensitivity.

But before I could move, he turned to face me again, freezing me on the spot with his gorgeous eyes. 'Have you ever played the Star Game?'

I just blinked at him.

Cash's cheeks turned just the slightest bit red before he elaborated. 'You have to be here because of your friend, and I'm driving home guys who won't want to leave until the keg is empty. We're going to be out here awhile, so we might as well find some way to entertain ourselves, you know? So have you ever played the Star Game?'

'What's the Star Game?' I asked.

'Well . . . technically, it's this thing I saw Russell Crowe do in a movie once, but I just kind of turned it into a way to pass the time.' He looked up at the sky, which had now become dark enough to make out the vast number of summer stars. 'OK, pick a shape,' he said.

'A . . . What are we doing?'

'You're picking a shape,' he said. 'Anything. It could even be an object. Or an animal, but sometimes those are harder.'

'Cash, I don't—'

'Just pick one.'

'Fine. A triangle.'

He sighed. 'That is way too easy.' Then, without warning, he reached between us and picked up my hand. I was startled, and I almost pulled back, but then our eyes met.

'Relax,' he said.

And, for once, I did.

His fingers were warm and callused against mine. He uncoiled my hand and gently forced me to extend my index finger. He made me point to a cluster of stars over our heads, and I watched as he drew a triangle with my finger, using three stars as the points. 'See? That's the Star Game.'

'Oh,' I said. 'Wow . . . A triangle *was* too easy.'

'Your turn,' he said. 'I tell you a shape and you have to find it in the stars.'

I admit, the game was kind of cheesy, but I thought it

was sweet of him to try to entertain me when I was so clearly having a bad night. So I played along.

'All right, what shape?'

'An elephant.'

'Are you joking?' I cried. 'You said animals were the hardest. You can't give me an elephant.'

'That's what makes it a game,' Cash teased, grinning and looking at me out of the corner of his eye. 'The first person unable to piece together the image loses. I like winning. So I give you an elephant.'

'Jerk.'

'Clock's ticking.'

'There's a time limit, too?' I asked, panicked.

'No,' he laughed. 'Now I'm really just messing with you.'

I sighed and looked up at the stars. At least there were a lot out tonight. That made finding the shapes easier. But an elephant? There was no way I could find an elephant in the sky. Just as I was thinking this, though, the lines began to form in my brain, connecting one star to another in a somewhat animal-like shape.

I picked up Cash's hand and he extended his index finger, willing me to draw through him. Slowly, I traced the stick-figure outline of the elephant. I started with each leg, then did the back, but when I got to the head, I halted. These stars would make a better dog or cat, because I couldn't find the trunk. My eyes scoured the tiny lights, hoping to find some way to connect the final pieces, just as Cash began to hum the *Jeopardy!* theme song in my ear.

Then his wrist began to move without my guiding it, and Cash connected a few stars jutting upwards, making a trunk pointing towards the air instead of at the elephant's feet, as I'd been imagining. He drew his finger back down, making the animal whole. Lopsided and irregularly shaped but whole.

'Nice job,' he said, as if I'd figured out how to finish the constellation myself.

'You let me win,' I said.

He shrugged and gave me a small smile. 'It was your first time.'

'Well, thanks for being gentle.'

Cash cracked up, and when I realized what I'd just said, my cheeks flamed.

'I-I mean—'

'It's no problem,' Cash choked out between laughs. 'Any good guy would have made it special for you.'

I buried my face in my hands. 'Oh, God.' But I was laughing, too. With anyone else, I would have been mortified. But in that context, it really was funny.

'All right,' he said, taking my hand again as his laughter eased. It felt so natural, so normal, that it didn't even faze me to have him hold my hand. 'So do you think you can win on your own next time?'

'Of course I can.'

He smirked and leaned against my arm just a bit, his fingers still wrapped around mine. 'Prove it,' he said.

'I will,' I said defiantly. 'But you have to go first. And this time, you have to make an . . . an octopus.'

Cash hesitated, then looked up at the sky before turning back to me. 'Game on.'

Cash and I played the Star Game for hours, talking between each challenge. He explained his position in soccer to me – though the explanation really flew right over my head – and, after he caught me counting the seconds as I waited for him to complete my newest constellation assignment (Santa Claus), I'd been forced to confess my control-freak neuroses. Which, shockingly, didn't send him running back into the party.

'So when you're nervous, you count?'

'Not just when I'm nervous,' I said. 'It's . . . all the time. I count the seconds during pauses in conversations. I count the minutes when I'm waiting on something. Sometimes, when I'm kind of panicked or anxious, I count my heartbeats. Something about counting makes me feel like . . . like I have the power. Like knowing how much time has passed or how many steps I've taken from one place to another will somehow keep me in control of the situation.' My hands twisted in my lap. I couldn't believe I was telling Cash this. It wasn't something I'd shared with anyone besides Chloe. 'I know it's crazy.'

'I don't think you're crazy,' Cash said. 'I think you're . . .'

I looked up at him just as he trailed off. It was too dark to tell, but I thought he was blushing.

'I'm what?'

He cleared his throat and ran a hand over his hair. I wanted to touch it, feel the short, dark strands. 'I think you're kind of amazing.'

One, two . . .

I was holding my breath, my whole body tense as I waited for his next words. Then I realized, with a little bit of a shock, that it was the first time I'd been anxious in a few hours. He'd had me so relaxed, so at ease – until now.

Three, four . . .

What was he going to say? What did I want him to say?

'I mean,' he added, 'you are surprisingly good at the

Star Game. Until tonight, I'd never found anyone who could compete with me.'

'Do you, um, play with many other people?'

'Well . . . no. Honestly, you're the only other person I've played with besides my mum. We played when we'd go camping when I was a kid, but that's been years. I usually just do this on my own. So . . . you're the first person to be able to compete with me. No lie.'

'So . . . your mom really sucks at the game, huh?'

Cash laughed. 'She couldn't even make a triangle . . . but I was nine, so she may have been letting me win.'

'The way you're letting me win right now?'

'Yeah . . . just much more subtle. I never would have guessed back then that she was helping me.'

Before I could respond, I felt Cash's hand wrap around mine. He nudged my index finger out and pointed it to the sky.

'What are you doing?' I asked. 'I haven't challenged you yet.'

'No,' he said. 'But I just saw one on my own. Look at this.'

And I watched as Cash traced my finger along a line of stars, following a few more into a curve, and then another, until a long line connected them all at a point.

'A heart,' I murmured.

And my own skipped a beat.

I cleared my throat. 'You know, that's, um, a little cheesy.'

'Yeah, maybe.'

I turned towards Cash just as he turned towards me. I closed my hand over his, and then he was leaning and I was leaning and it felt like a gravitational pull. Like moving towards Cash was the most natural thing in the world.

And that's the way the kiss felt, too. Natural. Like I'd been kissing him forever. Like we were supposed to be kissing each other at that moment. Maybe for every moment after.

My phone buzzed in my back pocket just as Cash's free hand moved up to cup my cheek.

'Sorry,' I murmured into his mouth as I pulled away. 'It might be an emergency . . . or something.'

He nodded and turned away, running a hand over his head again.

When I flipped open my phone, I found a text from Chloe.

Going back 2 shanes place. Can u get another ride or want me 2 take u back now?

I glanced over at Cash and felt the butterflies beating their wings against my rib cage. Four hours ago, I would have given anything to leave this place. But now, as it approached midnight, I wanted nothing more than to stay here. Or be wherever Cash was, anyway.

'Um, hey,' I said, summoning all of my nerve. 'Do . . . do you think you can give me a ride home when you take your friends?'

He turned to look at me. 'Yeah, of course. There'll be room in my car.'

'Great. Thank you. My ride is leaving and . . . well, let me text her.'

I replied to Chloe and shoved my phone into my pocket. I turned back to Cash, and he smiled.

And kissed me again.

I gave Cash directions to my place after he drove his drunk friends home about an hour later. It was with some regret that I watched my house draw nearer. I didn't want the night to end. I didn't want to be away from Cash.

Everything about Cash made me melt. The smell of his cologne. The way he said my name. The constant spark in his green eyes. And knowing that no girl had got this far with him – knowing that I had kissed Mr Unattainable and that he'd called me amazing – made me feel special and real and giddy.

We'd spent only a few hours together, but I already

felt so connected to Cash. Being myself with him, relaxing around him, came so easily. More easily than it did with anyone else.

We made out in his car for a few minutes after we pulled into my driveway. Slow and easy. He didn't push me further than I wanted, and I was grateful. I was still getting over Randy, after all. I didn't want to rush anything new.

But then he was pulling away from me. His thumb traced along my lower lip as he said, "You should go inside. You don't want to worry your parents.'

'Just my dad,' I murmured, wanting to keep kissing him but knowing he was right. If Dad woke up and found the door still unlocked, waiting for me, he'd be angry. I was already an hour past curfew – banking on the fact that he'd go to bed early and never know the difference.

'Give me your phone,' I said.

Cash handed me his phone, an old-school Nokia like they'd had when I was in sixth grade. I couldn't help smiling as I programmed my number in for him. He grinned at me when I handed it back, and he kissed me one last time. Quick. Smooth. Leaving me longing for more.

'I'll turn on the headlights so you can see to get in,' he said.

'Thank you.'

The lights flicked on, illuminating the driveway and glaring off the back of Dad's van.

'Football fans, huh?' Cash said.

'Oh, yeah,' I said. 'Well, you know. My brother used to play, and they supported Randy, of course.'

I wasn't thinking about the rivalry then. I wasn't thinking about sports at all. It was summer. I was free from it all. Or so I thought. But Cash's face darkened just a little at the mention of football, and I quickly realized my mistake.

'Give me a call,' I said, reaching for the door handle. 'I had a great time tonight. Really.'

He turned to face me, and I thought his eyes still looked a little guarded. Or maybe he was just tired. Or maybe I was, and my vision wasn't what it usually is. Because his voice sounded normal.

'I had a great time, too,' he said. 'Good night, Lissa.'

'Good night.'

I climbed out of his car and ran up the sidewalk. I stopped on the porch and watched as Cash's car disappeared around the corner. When the last glow of his tail lights had gone, I walked inside.

But the joy of that night faded pretty fast.

Even after everything I thought we shared, Cash never

called me. I waited for three weeks, and not a peep. Not even a text message. It was like that night had never happened – and sometimes I wondered if maybe it hadn't. If I'd imagined it. Dreamed it up as a way to get over Randy. Like an idiot, I hadn't got Cash's number for myself.

Not that it would have mattered. He'd rejected me. That much was clear.

In the long run, though, it was for the best. At the start of August, Randy crashed his Cougar. Despite that night with Cash, I was still in love with Randy, and I was just so happy he hadn't got hurt that when he called me to apologize for our fight, I ran back to him.

And I was lucky, too. Because we'd both realized that breaking up was the biggest mistake ever. So we got back together that night, and I decided to put Cash behind me.

Easier said than done.

Isn't that how it always works?

8

I was really excited for my date with Randy that Friday night, until I opened the front door and got a good look at his face.

'Oh, God. Randy, what happened?' I asked, grabbing his arm and pulling him into the bathroom. He sat on the edge of the sink while I opened the medicine cabinet and located my extensively stocked first-aid kit.

'I'm fine, really,' he said, putting a hand to the thin cut running along his left cheekbone. 'Kyle threw a rock at me in the parking lot after practice. I think he meant to hit the back of my head, but I turned around and—'

'Kyle, the soccer goalie?'

Randy nodded as I cleaned a little dried blood off his cheek with a cloth. 'Asshole,' he hissed. 'I planned to come over here right after I showered and changed. I didn't get blood on my shirt, did I?'

90

'I don't think so. It's not a deep cut. Here, this might sting a bit.' I dabbed peroxide along his cheekbone with a cotton ball.

'Well, at least it makes me look all rugged and sexy,' he said with a grin when I'd finished cleaning up the little cut.

'Yeah,' I said, pressing a Spider-Man Band-Aid on to his cheek. 'Real sexy.'

He laughed, but I didn't. Randy was hurt. Not severely, but he'd spilled blood because of this stupid, ridiculous feud. How many more boys would suffer because of this rivalry?

None, I decided. Because the strike started tonight. Officially.

'Ready to go?' Randy asked, squeezing my hand as he slid off the sink. 'The movie starts in half an hour, and we still have to drive out to Oak Hill. I figured we'd eat dinner afterwards.'

'Sure. Let's go,' I said once I'd put away the first-aid kit. I was already impressed. He'd actually taken the time to plan out the date and everything.

He smiled and put an arm around my shoulders, leading me towards the front door. 'I'm surprising you, by the way. You're going to love the restaurant.'

I flinched. 'You know I hate surprises.'

'Trust me. You'll love this one,' he said, opening the car door for me. 'I hate to brag, but I did awesome tonight.'

To tell you the truth, he really had done a great job. Instead of taking me to see some gory action movie, like I'd expected, he actually picked a romantic comedy. Granted, the movie as a whole kind of sucked, but the fact that he'd tried that hard really said something.

To top it off, he even took me to Giovanni's, an expensive little Italian restaurant a few blocks from the theatre. Despite his insistence on surprising me (surprises always made me uneasy), it was the nicest date Randy had taken me on since we'd started dating last year.

And not a soccer player in sight to ruin the evening.

After dinner, Randy took me back to his house, just like he'd planned. It was only ten thirty and I didn't have to be home until midnight, so we had plenty of time to do whatever we wanted.

Of course, I knew what Randy wanted to do.

We walked up to his room and just sat on his bed for a while, talking about how bad the movie had been.

'But the actress – she was pretty hot,' he said. 'That shower sex scene was . . . wow.'

I rolled my eyes. Tonight, after such a great date, I was totally loosened up. 'She had a butt double. You know, where someone stands in as the actress's butt? It wasn't even edited well.'

Randy grinned at me. 'Jealous?'

'Of her butt double? No.'

He leaned forward, putting his hands flat on the bed, one on either side of my waist. 'You're really hot when you're jealous,' he told me. 'But there's no need to be. Because, to tell you the truth, you know what I was thinking during that scene?'

'Do I want to know?' I asked.

'I was thinking about how much I wanted to re-enact that part in the shower with my hot' – he kissed my cheek – 'sexy' – he kissed my neck – 'gorgeous girlfriend.' He kissed my lips gently at first, then pulled away just a little. 'And how she wouldn't need a butt double because she's perfect already.'

'You smooth talker, you.'

'I was also thinking how much sexier I am than that guy she was screwing in the shower.'

I laughed.

'I am, aren't I?'

Instead of answering – because, to be honest, the actor in the movie was pretty fine – I closed the gap between us and kissed Randy again. We sat there on his bed making out for a while, but after a few minutes I felt

Randy's hand on the small of my back as he tried to ease me backward.

I pulled away, putting a hand on his chest. 'No – I mean, not tonight.'

For a second I felt guilty, as Randy's hands dropped away from me and he turned to stare in the other direction. We'd really had a wonderful night, and I hated to ruin it by upsetting him.

But I'd taken an oath, and it would be worth it in the end. The rivalry would be over soon, and Randy and I could have many more perfect dates just like this one.

'You want to watch a movie or something?' I asked, standing up and straightening my skirt over my thighs.

'I don't understand,' he said. 'The night has been so great – you had a good time, right?'

'Yes. Of course I did.'

'Then why not end it on a good note? Make it special?'

'I just . . . don't feel like it tonight. But we can watch a movie or something, and that will end it on a good note, too.'

'We just watched a movie.'

'We can watch another one.'

'Lissa,' he whined, giving me puppy-dog eyes, 'please? If you don't want to, we can, like, do other stuff.' His suggestive smirk made it clear that 'other stuff' didn't mean watching a movie.

I stared down at the carpet, fiddling with the hem of my skirt. 'I told you. I just don't feel like it tonight.'

He tilted his head to one side and stuck out his lip like a pouting toddler. 'Come on. I'll do anything. I'll beg.' He flopped on to his back, sticking his hands in the air like a dog waiting for his belly to be rubbed. He even made whimpering pup noises.

'Stop it,' I said. 'You're silly.'

'You love me.'

'I do.'

He sat up and looked at me seriously. 'Then why not?'

I could have told him about the strike then, about our demands that the rivalry end, but I couldn't force the words out. After the good date, I didn't want to upset Randy more than I had to – and I knew that finding out about the strike wouldn't exactly lighten his mood.

'I'm kind of tired,' I told him. 'I got up early this morning to finish some homework and I'm just exhausted. I'm sorry. But you don't have to take me home yet. We can just curl up on the couch . . . What do you say?'

Randy sighed and stood up. 'Yeah, I guess that sounds OK. This night is supposed to be all about you, after all.' He kissed me on the cheek. 'But this means we have to have a night all about me soon, where everything goes my way.' He grinned and squeezed my shoulder before heading out of the room and walking downstairs.

That won't be happening any time soon, I thought guiltily, before following him down to the living room, where we ended our date with a little couch cuddling and a Leonardo DiCaprio movie.

9

'Hey, Lissa!'

I was on my way to AP US history the next Tuesday afternoon when Susan Port, girlfriend of Luther, a linebacker, caught my arm. Before I could jerk away, she dragged me into the closest girls' bathroom.

'You,' she began, letting go of my arm and spinning to face me. I flinched, thinking I was in trouble. Like maybe she was mad at me for some reason – and that wouldn't have boded well for me. Susan was on the girls' basketball team. She was, like, five-eleven and built. If she wanted to, she could have really hurt me.

But when our eyes met, a huge grin spread across her face.

'You, Lissa Daniels, are a fucking genius.'

I sighed with relief, and Susan laughed.

'For real,' she said. 'Luther and I went out on Saturday

night. We went to the Nest, and I looked good. I mean, Beyoncé good. He wanted to take me up to Lyndway Hill for a little fun afterwards, but I totally made him drive me home instead. He was so confused. He would have done anything.'

'I'm glad it's working,' I said, tugging on the bottom of my shirt. I was also glad that her reservations about the ethicality of using sex seemed to have faded. 'I knew it would work, of course, but it's nice to hear other people are, uh, having success.'

'I know what you mean.'

She moved to face the mirror, searching for non-existent blemishes on her perfect complexion. I was sure she was right about how she'd looked Saturday night. Even in her sweatpants and oversized T-shirt, Susan looked like a queen, her black hair pulled up into a simple ponytail at the top of her head, accenting her high cheekbones. Poor Luther.

'Actually,' Susan said after a moment, 'I was thinking: maybe the other girls would feel the same way. Like, it might make them more confident if they heard everyone else's stories.'

'Maybe,' I said. 'Oh, we could email our stories to one another through the email chain I set up. That would be—'

'I was actually thinking more along the lines of slumber parties,' she cut in, turning back to me. 'With all twelve of us, plus whatever soccer girlfriends joined. It'll be crowded as hell, but it might still be fun. I can host the first one. This weekend? Like, after the game on Friday?'

I hesitated. Images of pillows being tossed and furniture being overturned coursed through my mind. I wasn't exactly a slumber-party expert, but I could just picture the chaos of twelve-plus girls piled into one room. I mean, I could barely sleep sharing a room with just Chloe. Twelve girls? It wasn't something I thought I'd particularly enjoy.

But the other girls would. Susan was looking at me with such excitement, such certainty that this would help the others. I had to put the cause before my own control issues. I had to think of Randy and Pete and the other boys who had been hurt in this feud.

Knowing I would likely regret it later, I said, "That sounds like a great idea, Susan.'

So that afternoon I sent out an email to all the girls who had taken the oath in the library last Tuesday, instructing them to be at Susan's house on Cherry Drive no later than nine on Friday night, once the football game ended. After double- and triple-checking the email for spelling and punctuation, I wrote a postscript to

Ellen that she should forward the message to the soccer players' girlfriends she'd convinced to join us. Then I clicked send.

'You OK?' Cash asked when I'd shut off the library computer from which I'd sent the email. Our shift was about to start, and this time, he'd arrived early.

'Yes. Why wouldn't I be?' I asked a little too harshly.

Cash shrugged his shoulders. 'I don't know,' he said. 'You just look really stressed.'

'I always look stressed,' I told him.

'Well, we should do something about that,' he said, giving me a smile as he brushed past me, carrying a stack of autobiographies.

'Oh, yeah?' I asked. 'And how do we plan on doing that?'

He looked over his shoulder at me. 'I could think of a few ways.'

I gaped, shocked that he was being so suggestive.

Cash's face shifted into an expression of horror and he spun around to face me. 'Oh – I didn't mean it like that.' He shook his head and adjusted the books in his arms. 'I was going to say, like, yoga or blogging or whatever it is people do to relieve . . . Yeah. Sorry.'

But I was laughing now. I couldn't help it – he just looked so abashed. 'Don't worry about it. I'll be gentle.'

The words slipped out of my mouth before I remembered that I was referencing our night over the summer – the night I was pretending never happened.

Cash chuckled and winked at me. 'How do you know I don't want it rough?'

OK, that time it definitely wasn't an accident.

But Cash walked away towards the bookshelves, leaving me with my eyes clenched shut in embarrassment. It wasn't like I could tell him off for flirting with me when, admittedly, I'd kind of started it.

I grabbed a few children's books and ran upstairs to shelve them, putting an entire floor between Cash and me. Unfortunately, less than ten minutes later, Jenna found me hiding out.

'What are you doing?' she asked, raising an eyebrow at me.

'Nothing,' I said, pretending to re-alphabetize the shelf in front of me. 'My job. Why?'

'That shelf is fine,' she said. 'But Cash needs your help downstairs. I just checked in a bunch of books and I need you two to put them away.'

I sighed. I'd hoped to avoid him for the rest of the afternoon. I should have known it wouldn't work.

I started to walk towards the stairs, but Jenna called after me. 'Hey, Lissa?'

'Yes?' I was hoping she would change her mind, assign me to do something away from Cash.

'Is, um . . . Is your brother picking you up tonight?'

'Yeah. Why?'

'No reason . . . OK, what are you waiting for? Chop, chop. Cash is waiting for you.'

I rolled my eyes and kept walking. Oh, God, Jenna had a thing for Logan. I so didn't need to know that.

Cash smiled at me when I reached the first floor. 'Hey,' he said. 'I've already piled the returned books here.' He gestured to the cart. 'Now we just need to put them away.'

I nodded, not trusting myself to say anything. It seemed like every time I opened my mouth around Cash, I said things I shouldn't. I had a boyfriend, after all. One I really loved. I didn't know what it was about Cash, either. I wasn't normally the flirting type – far from it. And I didn't even like him. Not any more.

I also didn't understand why he was working at the library with me right now. Didn't he have soccer practice? Friends to hang out with? Other girls to reject?

'Why are you here?'

Crap. The words flew out of my mouth before I could stop them. We'd just pushed the cart against the wall of the Fiction section, and I was crouched on the floor, staring up at Cash as he handed me a copy of *It* by Stephen King that needed to go on the bottom shelf.

'Huh?'

I bit my lip, taking the book and putting it on the shelf, making sure the spine was even with those around it. 'I-I mean . . . Why are you working today? Don't you have soccer practice or something?'

'Oh.' Cash laughed. It was a deep, mature laugh. Not like Randy's loud, goofy cackle.

I shouldn't have been comparing the two. God, I was a terrible girlfriend.

'Well,' Cash said, handing me another Stephen King book, "I do technically have practice, but I've talked to Coach Lukavics and he's agreed to let me miss for work on Tuesdays and Thursdays.'

'Why?' I asked. 'Don't you need the practice? I'm not saying you're bad and need practice – you're good at soccer – I mean, when I've seen you play before, which was, like, once when I was passing by the field to get to the concession stand during a football game, so I didn't see much, but . . .' I took a deep breath. I was a babbling idiot. I hated it. 'I just meant, don't you need to go to practice with the other guys?'

Cash grinned at me – a smug, teasing grin, like the one he'd given me when he knew he was winning that cheesy Star Game of his over the summer. I looked away, wishing I could stop thinking about that night.

'I'm actually working here to help out my parents,' he said as I checked to make sure all of the books on the shelf before me were in the correct order. 'My dad just got laid off, so we need a little more money around the house. My mom didn't want me to, but I decided to get a job to help pay the bills and stuff until Dad can get work again.'

I looked up at him, surprised. 'So the money you make here is going to your parents? Wait, sorry, that isn't my business, I guess.'

'You're fine,' he said, reaching down a hand. I took it reluctantly, and he pulled me to my feet. 'But yeah, it will go to them. They'll hate taking it from me, but it's the least I can do to help. I don't make much here – well, I guess you know that – but I plan to cash the cheques and sneak the money into Mom's purse every two weeks. She'll find out I'm doing it, but money's tight, so she can't really afford to fight me.'

'God, Cash, I'm sorry. I didn't mean to pry.'

'It's OK,' he assured me. 'We all have tough times once in a while, right?'

'Yeah. You're right.'

I couldn't help but think of Logan. He'd given up

going to grad school to come home and help take care of Dad and me after Mom died. And Cash was doing the same thing – giving up his time, his practice, to help out his family when they hadn't even asked him to.

Suddenly I realized that my hand was still in his from when he'd pulled me to my feet a few seconds before. I jerked my arm away and stumbled backwards, accidentally ramming my hip bone against the nearly empty cart of books. 'Ouch! Damn it.' I rubbed my hip, hoping it wouldn't bruise.

'You OK there?' Cash was staring at me, looking a little amused, with one eyebrow raised like he was about to laugh at me.

'I'm fine.'

'Careful,' he teased. 'Those carts . . . they can be dangerous.'

'Ha, ha,' I mumbled. 'All right. We should get back to work; we're moving too slowly, and there will be other things to shelve soon.'

'OK, Jenna Junior.'

I buried my face in my hands. God, he was so right. I sounded just like her. 'Ugh, sorry.'

'Don't be,' he said, reaching around me to grab a John Grisham book off the cart. 'To be honest, Lissa, there is no one I'd rather shelve with.'

Right, I thought. That's some consolation there. He liked me enough to work with me but not enough to give me a real chance. Not enough to call me back.

We worked in silence as we put away the remaining sixteen – yes, I counted – books. No matter what I told myself, I knew I couldn't hate Cash, especially now that I knew his reason for working here. The fact was, he was a good guy.

A good guy who just . . . didn't want me the way I'd wanted him.

Even though I loved Randy and didn't want to be with Cash any more, I knew it would be a while before I completely got over his rejection. It was out of my control.

10

'Pass the popcorn over here, Chloe.'

'Keep your panties on. Let me get a handful first.'

'Is there any more Diet Coke?'

'Here you go . . . Don't you dare spill it on my rug, or my mother will kill me!'

Sixteen girls squeezed into Susan's bedroom on Friday night after the Hamilton Panthers lost to the Oak Hill Tigers (I said my boyfriend was a quarterback, not that he was a good one). Sixteen girls in one bedroom – and believe it or not, that wasn't even everyone who'd taken the oath. Ellen reported that she'd got all of the soccer players' girlfriends to join the cause. But, as to be expected, a few girls couldn't make the sleepover for various reasons.

But sixteen of us showed up, and that was more than enough to have me on edge. I found myself on the floor, in the corner of Susan's room, with my knees pulled up to my chest, counting and recounting the girls, the tiles in the ceiling, the Lakers posters on Susan's wall – anything just to relax a bit. But with everyone talking over one another and tossing pillows and carelessly passing around overflowing bowls of food, relaxation seemed pretty far out of the realm of possibility.

I knew that the strike was my idea and that meant I should be the leader here, but I couldn't shake the thought that I would have had a much better time on a nice, quiet date with Randy.

'Hey, listen up!' Chloe shouted over the chatter. Everyone fell silent and turned to look where she was standing, right in the middle of the room. She was dressed in her skimpy pink pyjamas, with her curly brown hair pulled up in an alligator clip. 'All right,' she said. 'So Lissa asked us all here so we could have a little fun and share stories about our scheming and shit, and eat brownies and . . . and what the fuck? Why am I doing this? Lissa, get your ass up here. You're the one running the show.'

She reached over to me, her reassuring smile like a secret between us as she pulled me to my feet. Then she dragged me into the centre of the room.

'Take it away, babe,' she said, plopping down on the

floor and grabbing her fifth brownie from the Tupperware box I'd brought from home.

The girls instantly began forming a circle around me, like first graders during story time. A few sat on Susan's bed. Others were lying on their stomachs or sitting cross-legged on the carpet at my feet, looking up at me expectantly.

'OK,' I said, tapping my fingers against my leg. I could do this. Now that the girls were still and quiet and attentive, I could handle it. 'So Susan thought it would be interesting to share our stories about what has happened so far in our efforts to end the rivalry. Does anyone have a good story?'

'I do,' Kelsey said, raising her hand.

'Bet you ten bucks it's boring as fuck,' Chloe whispered, much too loudly, to Susan.

Kelsey shot her a death glare before turning back to me. I gestured for her to continue.

'So Terry came over on Saturday night unexpectedly. I'd mentioned that my parents weren't going to be home, but I hadn't, like, invited him or anything. So he just shows up out of nowhere with this big goofy grin on his face and a bottle of wine he'd convinced his brother to buy him. He totally thought my saying my parents were out of town was a cue that he was going to get some.

Which, duh, is stupid anyway.' She shook her head. 'Whatever. When I told him no, he looked like a hurt puppy. He just kept asking if I was mad at him. I told him no, but he didn't believe me. So you know what he did next?'

I looked at Chloe, silently begging her not to say anything.

She stayed quiet.

'He totally made me dinner. Like, he went into my kitchen and cooked me a fucking meal. Since when can he cook? But anyway. Yeah. He was so sure I was pissed off that he would do anything to suck up. It was so cute . . . and lame. Mostly cute.'

'So, in other words, Kelsey has a girlfriend now,' Susan joked.

A few girls laughed. Others called out things like, "Lucky! Seth never cooks for me!" Even Chloe smiled and shook her head. I wondered if, like me, she was imagining Terry – a stout, muscular boy with a constant five o'clock shadow – wearing a pink apron and bustling around a kitchen.

'Wow, Kelsey,' Chloe said, grinning at her. 'Your boyfriend becomes a housewife and Lissa's turns into a canine. Interesting transformations for the first week.'

Suddenly everyone was looking at me again, expecting

an explanation. I felt the heat creeping up my neck. I hadn't intended to share my experience. I preferred to keep my private life private, except when I decided to share with Chloe.

'Tell them,' she said. 'Come on. It's hilarious.'

Traitor.

'Randy, um, begged like a dog. Literally.'

The girls laughed, and Chloe nudged my leg, urging me on. I sighed.

'He rolled over on to his back, showed me his belly, gave me doe eyes. He made puppy noises and everything.'

'Gives "doggie style" a whole new meaning, huh?' Chloe said, and everyone busted out laughing again.

Even I cracked a smile.

'I doubted you before, Lissa,' Kelsey said, her usual sneer contorted into a – holy crap, sincere? – smile. 'But now, I think you're right. I bet it'll work, and thank God, because this fight needs to stop. This was a good idea, Lissa. Seriously.'

Coming from Kelsey, that was huge.

And she wasn't the only one with a story to share. I watched as several of the girls stood and told their stories. All of them smiling at me when they reached the end. All of them laughing and proud and confident. All of them really believing that my plan was going to be the one to end the rivalry. Their confidence made me confident.

'I wish I had a story to tell,' Mary murmured to me as we filled up another bowl of popcorn in Susan's kitchen. Since she and I had eaten the last pieces, the other girls decided it was only fair that we make the next bag. I was more relaxed away from the crowd, and the air in the kitchen felt much cooler than it had in Susan's packed bedroom.

'Don't worry about it,' I told her, shaking the hot bag of popped kernels into the orange bowl we'd been using. 'Having stories isn't what really matters.'

'I know. And I haven't kissed Finn since we started the strike, like you told me. But it's just . . .' Mary trailed off, twisting the fingers of her left hand in her chocolate-coloured hair. In her right she gripped the can of Diet Coke Susan's mom had forced on her, knowing Mary would never ask for it.

'Just what?' I asked, picking up my own Diet Coke and taking a sip.

'Am I weird?' she whispered as she glanced over her shoulder towards the living room, where Mrs Port was watching a movie. 'I mean . . . is it weird that Finn and I have never . . . ?'

'No,' I said, then hesitated. 'I mean, I'm sure you're

not the only one. I don't think you're weird.'

Mary shrugged, still twisting her hair. 'I just hear all these stories, and sometimes I feel like I'm the only one who's never done it. I feel like I'm behind or something. Like it makes me a prude.'

'You're not weird, or a prude, or a tease, or any of that,' I assured her. 'Actually, I think it's great that you're waiting. It's sort of refreshing. And sex is a big deal, so you shouldn't rush it just because everyone else is doing it. I think it's a major decision. Honestly, I—'

'Lissa! Mary!'

I jumped, almost spilling my Diet Coke as Chloe's voice rang down the stairs. I'd been so caught up in my conversation with Mary that I'd completely forgotten about the girls in Susan's room.

'What the hell is taking you two so long? I want some popcorn, damn it!'

'I guess she finished all the brownies,' I said with a small laugh.

'Can you girls keep it down a little?' Mrs Port called, without anger, over the back of the living-room couch.

'Come on,' I said to Mary. 'Let's get up there before poor Chloe starves to death.'

Mary giggled and I smiled at her. It had taken a few hours, but after hearing everyone's stories and eating way too much junk food, I had loosened up a little.

'Finally.' Chloe grabbed the popcorn bowl from me as soon as we reached the top step, and she ran into Susan's bedroom. Mary and I glanced at each other. I took a deep breath and smiled at her one last time, and then we walked back into the crowded room.

11

Apparently the girls weren't the only ones swapping gossip about their love lives. The boys had been talking, too. I guess when a bunch of high-school jocks don't get laid, word starts to spread that something is seriously wrong, because by Monday, the guys were worried.

'What's up with all the girls?' Randy asked me during the drive to my house that afternoon. For once, he didn't have football practice, and he'd decided to take my father up on his ever-present dinner invitation and make up for the date we'd missed on Friday.

'What do you mean?'

I knew exactly what he meant, though.

'Like . . . I don't know. I've heard stuff.'

'Such as?'

'Like, you're all distant,' he said. 'Finn's girlfriend won't even kiss him, and ever since last weekend, you've been acting weird. Shane says even Chloe's not putting out, and she's a slut, so we know something's wrong.'

'Don't call my best friend a slut,' I told him. 'Just because people think so doesn't make it true.'

'But it *is* true.'

'It's relative,' I said. 'I'd bet money Shane has slept with more people than Chloe. Correct?'

'Probably. Shane's the man.'

'You don't call him a slut, so please don't call Chloe one.'

'OK, OK.' Randy shrugged and turned the Buick on to my street. 'Sorry. Whatever . . . But you never answered my question.'

'What question?'

'What's up with all the girls?'

Crap, I thought. Changing the subject usually worked with Randy. He got so distracted that he didn't even notice I'd nudged him away from the original topic. That was part of the beauty of dating him; I never had to worry about him cornering me into a conversation I didn't want to have.

Except now.

Naturally, when sex was involved, Randy managed to stay focused.

'We'll talk about it later,' I said as his car slid into my

driveway. Before he could argue, I climbed out of the passenger's seat and started walking towards the front door.

I could have slapped myself. There was a huge hole in my strike plan; we'd never discussed when or how to tell the boys. Eventually we'd have to, obviously, because the whole point was to get them to hear us out, to listen to our demand that they end the rivalry. But now, with Randy asking questions, I was nervous about answering him.

'Hey, honey,' Dad called from the kitchen when I stepped into the house. 'I just got in from work and decided to make a sandwich. You want one?'

'No, thanks,' I said, walking across the carpet towards the kitchen. Behind me, Randy shut the front door and began to follow. 'I brought company. I figured I'd make a real dinner tonight.'

Dad looked over his shoulder and smiled when he saw Randy standing next to me in the kitchen doorway. 'Hey there,' he said. 'No football practice?'

'No, sir,' Randy said. 'Coach gave us the day off – said he couldn't look at our faces after the loss on Friday. But I'm sure he's going to kick our asses tomorrow.'

'Oh, yeah.' Dad grabbed his sandwich from the counter and put it in his lap so he could turn his wheelchair towards us. 'I heard the game was pretty brutal. I couldn't make it – I needed to return some emails and get a situation with a student straightened out – but Logan said Oak Hill has really shaped up this year.'

'Yeah, none of us was expecting it,' Randy agreed. 'So weird. They sucked last year.'

Dad wheeled over to the table and Randy sat down next to him. I let them talk sports for a bit while I sorted through the fridge, trying to decide what to make for dinner. When I realized we didn't have much of anything (living with two adult men meant food never lasted long), I decided to call and leave Logan a voice mail, asking him to stop by the grocery on his way home and pick up the stuff I'd need to make pasta.

When I hung up the phone, I heard Randy ask, 'So how's work going, Mr Daniels?'

I smiled as I walked over to the round wooden table and sat down beside my boyfriend. He reached over and put an arm around my shoulders. I glanced self-consciously at my dad, and stiffened a bit at the contact. But Randy didn't seem to notice – or maybe he was just used to it by now.

'Work's good,' Dad said. 'Been a bit crazy this week. There's a student having some pretty sudden behavioural issues. I think she's having a difficult time at home, but she won't say. Poor kid. She's never had problems before.'

When I was little, he'd worked construction, building houses in the newer part of town. After the accident, he decided to go in a different direction. That's how he ended up as the guidance counsellor at Hamilton Elementary.

'You're so patient,' Randy said. 'I can't stand kids. I'd get so frustrated. I never want to be a parent.'

'You'll change your mind,' Dad told him. 'Especially if you and Lissa end up getting married. You two would have to give me some grandkids.'

'Logan can do that.' Randy laughed. 'Lissa and I aren't going to have kids. Maybe a few dogs, though.'

I cleared my throat, reminding them that I was sitting right there. I hated when Randy planned my future for me.

'Logan's going to pick up a few things at the store on his way back from work,' I said. 'It'll be an hour or so if you two want to go and watch TV.'

In an instant, Randy was on his feet, pushing Dad's wheelchair into the living room as they bickered over which of our six ESPN networks to watch.

When they were gone, I pulled out my phone to text Chloe.

Randys asking questions. I think he knows

Within seconds, she replied.

What r u gonna tell him???

I glanced into the living room. Some sports talk show was on the TV, and I could hear Dad and Randy laughing as they disagreed with the commentators. I smiled to myself. Randy was already a part of my family. Part of me. I shouldn't be afraid to be honest with him.

Without even looking at the screen, I moved my thumbs across the keypad and texted Chloe back.

The truth.

By the time dinner was on the table, I was on the verge of pulling my hair out. Logan came home almost an hour late and refused to tell me where he'd been. Dad had to make me stop asking him. And, of course, my brother had picked up the wrong kind of pasta. I mean, I guess the pasta didn't really matter – it all tastes the same – but it was the principle of the thing.

I'd been able to relax a little at the dinner table, though. Logan gave Randy a hard time about Friday's game, everyone complimented my cooking (not that pasta was difficult, but it was still nice to hear), and no one mentioned the soccer team.

After we left the table, still smiling from a joke Dad had told us, Randy offered to help me wash dishes.

'Why don't you use the dishwasher?' he asked.

'Pipes are messed up,' I said. 'Have been for weeks. The plumber hasn't come by to fix it yet.'

'That sucks.' He set a stack of plates on the counter as I filled the sink with water. 'I might be able to fix them. I've helped my uncle fix the ones in his house before. I can give them a look when I come over this weekend, if you want. Then you don't have to pay a plumber.'

'That'd be great,' I said. 'Randy Vincent, pro-bono plumber.'

'Pro what-o?'

'Never mind. Just bring your wrench and your saggy plumber pants on Saturday.'

Randy grinned. 'Saggy plumber pants, huh? Lissa, are your pipes really messed up, or is this just your way of trying to see my ass?'

'Hardly,' I said, flinging a little water at him. 'Only if you hire a butt double.'

Randy stuck his tongue out at me and flung some water in my direction.

I had to admit, I was pretty impressed that he was helping me clean up. I figured he'd be running back to the TV the second his plate was clear, the way he usually did.

'So back to what we were talking about earlier,' he said after a pause. 'What's up with the girls?'

Of course he had an ulterior motive. I was on my guard again instantly. I shut off the tap just as the bubbles from the dish detergent began to ease over the rim of the sink.

'Do you really want to know?' I asked quietly, gesturing for Randy to move the plates into the soapy water.

'Yeah.'

'All right. We're on a sex strike.'

Randy, God bless him, just sort of blinked at me, confused.

I reached into the top drawer and pulled out a sponge and a dishcloth. 'OK,' I said, handing the cloth to him. 'The girls are tired of the rivalry. It's been going on for too long, and you guys don't even have a reason to fight.'

'Like hell,' Randy argued. 'We have a ton of reasons to hate those—'

'Randy, can you even tell me how the fight started in the first place?' I asked.

He opened his mouth to answer, then paused, lips still gaping. 'Uh . . .' he swallowed, and I passed him a plate I'd just cleaned so he could dry it while he thought. 'It started . . . It started because . . .'

'If it takes you this long to remember,' I said, dunking another marinara-covered plate into the foamy, bubbly water, 'then the fight isn't really worth it.'

'OK, so what does this have to do with all you girls being weird?'

'I told you,' I said. 'We want the rivalry to end. So we've decided that none of the boys on the teams are getting any action until the fighting ends. A sex strike.'

Randy stopped drying the dish I'd just handed him. 'You're shitting me.'

'No.'

'Like . . . just no sex?'

'Shhh.' I tensed and looked over my shoulder to make sure Dad and Logan were still safely in the living room, TV blasting. 'Not just sex. It could be anything.'

'Like fooling around, hand jobs, BJs. All of it?'

I cringed and glanced over my shoulder again.

'Yes,' I hissed through gritted teeth. 'All of it. Keep your voice down. If Dad hears us . . .'

'Right, sorry. So this will last until the teams stop fighting?'

I nodded and handed him another clean plate. He took it, but he didn't start to dry it immediately. Instead, he just shook his head back and forth, lips tight like he was holding back a laugh.

'What?' I asked.

'Sorry, but do you really expect something that stupid to work?'

'It's not stupid,' I said. 'What's stupid is your little rivalry with the soccer team. It happens every fall, and it's getting worse. People are getting hurt – you got hurt. My plan to end it is genius. If there's one thing we can withhold that'll make you do anything, it's sexual favours.'

'It'll never work,' Randy said, finally drying the plate he'd been holding for the past thirteen seconds and placing it on top of the growing stack of clean dishes. 'The girls will never last.'

'Why do you say that?'

'Because we're not going to stop fighting with the soccer team, and I know you girls can't last forever. Hell, I bet if I tried hard enough, you wouldn't be able to resist me right now.' He gave me an exaggerated version of a seductive smile, batting his eyes and everything, as he leaned over to kiss me.

I shrugged him off, annoyed. 'Don't you want the rivalry to end?'

'Not really.'

'You know, Randy . . .' I hesitated, then said, "When we got back together, you promised you'd grow up and behave like an adult.'

He stiffened. 'Well, Lissa, we both made some promises we didn't keep, huh?'

One second.

Two seconds.

I couldn't believe he'd just said that. Couldn't believe

he'd brought it up. We turned to face each other, my jaw dropped and his set firm. He'd been teasing before, but he was mad now, and so was I.

Three seconds.

Four seconds.

My fists clenched at my sides as, with every second, the tension grew between us. The air thickened and I forced myself to steady my breathing. This was the closest we'd come to a fight in a long time – and less than a minute ago, it wasn't even a fight.

The worst part was that, logically, we should have been on the same side. He should have wanted this to end as much as I did. Or maybe he didn't see himself as the victim at all. Maybe he enjoyed the chaos.

The idea made my head spin.

Five seconds.

Six seconds.

I was beginning to think we'd never move again when my brother's voice penetrated the silence.

'Yo, Lissa! Randy!'

I turned my head, pulling my gaze away from Randy's, just as Logan appeared in the doorway. For a second, his eyes darted between us, and I knew he could tell something was up. Logan wasn't as dense as Randy. Or as compassionate as my father. Instead of asking about it, though, he just shook his head, as if shaking the knowledge of all tension out of his mind.

'Dad wants ice cream,' he said, running his hand over his short black hair. 'I'm heading out to get some. You want any?'

I glanced at Randy. He was still watching me, but the look on his face was unreadable.

'We do,' I told Logan. 'Strawberry with sprinkles for me. And make sure Dad's is low-fat, OK?'

'Yeah, yeah, I know,' Logan said. 'What about you, Randy?'

'Um . . .' Slowly, he turned to look at my brother. 'Chocolate. With chocolate syrup.'

Logan laughed. 'Now that's my kind of ice cream. All right. I'll be back.' He swiped the keys off the counter and walked out of the kitchen.

'Look, Randy,' I whispered when Logan was gone, 'the girls are on a sex strike. It's going to be this way until the rivalry is over.'

'It'll never happen,' Randy told me.

I didn't reply. Instead, I turned and walked into the living room, where Randy wouldn't dare return to this conversation in front of my father, and sat down to watch some crappy sports show and wait for my ice cream.

12

'So you've been reading Aristophanes, huh?'

I jumped, and the book I was trying to shelve slipped from my hand and thudded to the floor. My empty fingers groped for the stability of the wooden shelves as the ladder wobbled beneath me, my feet scurrying to regain their balance.

'Whoa,' Cash said.

His hands were on my hips then, steadying me. My T-shirt had ridden up slightly as I'd stretched my arms to the highest shelves, so his fingers made direct contact with the exposed skin just above the waistband of my jeans. A small burst of fire pulsed through me, starting at the places where he was touching me and spreading to the rest of my body.

'Sorry,' he said. 'I didn't mean to scare you. You OK?'

'Fine.'

His hands were still on me.

I wondered why he didn't let me go. I was fine now; he could have pulled his hands back. But he didn't. And I wanted him to keep touching me. I knew I shouldn't – if my own boyfriend's touch made me stiffen, Cash's should revolt me – but my body hummed in stark disagreement with my brain.

His hands stayed on my hips as I climbed down the ladder, guiding me to safety on the floor in front of him. Once my sneakers hit the thin brown carpet, he let me go, his fists moving instantly into his pockets.

'You OK?' he repeated, as if I hadn't answered.

'Fine,' I said again. 'God, are you taking a class in sneaking up on people or what?'

Cash shrugged a shoulder. 'Natural talent, I guess.'

'A natural talent that is going to get me killed one day. Can you please not do that? I could have fallen off the ladder and broken my neck. Or at the very least my leg or my ankle or something. Or my wrist, and then shelving books would have been hard, and Jenna would have yelled at me – and at you for making me fall, and . . .' I trailed off. I should have just shut up after 'Fine'.

'I'll work on it,' Cash said with a sheepish smile.

'Right. Good.'

'So,' he said. 'Aristophanes?'

'What?'

'I was trying to ask if you'd been reading Aristophanes,' he repeated. 'You know, the Greek playwright? One of the forerunners of satire?'

'I've never heard of him,' I admitted, a little ashamed. 'Who is he? What has he written?'

'Oh, uh, well,' Cash said, his cheeks turning just a touch red. 'His most famous play is probably *The Clouds*. They don't really teach him in high school, though – too racy. I guess the fact that I know who he is really proves what a dork I am, huh?' He laughed, scuffing the toe of his sneaker against the floor.

Great. He was a hottie, a good kisser and a literature buff. God really must have had a sense of humour, because if I had to name my biggest turn-on, it was literature. And he had just recommended a book that I didn't know, that wasn't taught in school. If I were single, there would be no better pick-up line.

Suddenly, I found myself thinking back to *Atonement* – you know, the scene in the book where the two main characters have sex in the library? Even though Chloe said doing it against bookshelves would be really uncomfortable (and she'd probably know), it was still a fantasy of mine. Like, what's more romantic than a quiet place full of books?

But I shouldn't have been thinking about my library fantasies.

Especially while I was staring at Cash.

In the middle of a library.

'So,' I said, clearing my throat and trying to sound cool and detached. Instead, what came out was pretty flirtatious. What was it about this guy that always made me do that? "It's funny. You can't do geometry but you read Greek plays?'

Cash's blush deepened. 'Yeah . . . I know it's a little lame. But you're sure you've never read anything by Aristophanes? Not even one play?'

'It's not lame,' I said quickly. Too quickly. 'I love the Greeks. I've read *Antigone* and *Medea* and *Oedipus* and—'

'Wow,' Cash teased. 'No wonder you seem so tense sometimes; all you read are tragedies. Do you have something against smiling?'

'No, I just . . . always end up reading the tragedies, I guess.'

He leaned a little closer. 'Maybe reading a comedy would be just the thing to help you loosen up a bit. You have a great smile – I'd like to see it more often.'

I looked down, smoothing my hair behind my ear. 'Thank you.' Then we were staring at each other and I felt my heart speed up and I knew this wasn't the situation I

wanted to be in, so I said, 'Anyway, yes. I mean, I'm sure
– I haven't read anything by Aristophanes.'

I turned and knelt down to pick up the book I'd
dropped off the ladder, needing to look at anything
besides Cash. Why did I always fall into his trap?

Maybe if I ignored him, he would walk away. I could
go back to shelving and Jenna could give him something
to do and I wouldn't have to look at him for the rest of
the day. Ignore, ignore, ignore.

'He wrote about a sex strike, you know.'

'What?'

I looked up and found Cash grinning down at me.
So much for ignoring him. Quickly, I shifted back into
a standing position, hugging the retrieved book to
my chest.

'Aristophanes,' Cash said, moving a little closer to me.
'He wrote a play about a group of women in Athens going
on a sex strike to convince their husbands to end a war.
I figured maybe that was where you got the idea.'

I felt the heat rise into my cheeks. 'You know about
the . . . ?'

'Everyone does,' Cash said. 'All the guys on the team
are talking about it.'

'Oh.'

'So,' he said, leaning against the bookshelves beside

me, keeping his eyes trained on mine. 'Why are you doing it?'

'To end the rivalry.'

'No. I know that part. I mean . . .' He hesitated, running a hand over his head and smoothing his short brown hair. 'I mean, what made you decide to do it now? Like, what pushed you over the edge or whatever?'

I bit my lip and looked over at the books to my left. We were in the Ds. The spine of *A Tale of Two Cities* jumped out at me from the shelf, golden letters popping off the black binding.

I wasn't going to tell Cash the truth. No way. I wasn't going to tell him about my boyfriend putting the fights before me, or about the booty call. He was the last person I wanted to know about my problems with Randy. Not that we had many. Just this stupid feud.

Instead, I needed him to know that I was perfectly happy with my relationship. Maybe if he got the message, he'd stop flirting with me. Stop reminding me of his rejection.

'I got really upset when that kid tore his ligament,' I said, deciding to tell part of the truth. 'When you told Randy about it in the cafeteria, I realized that the fighting had gone too far. And then Randy got a little banged up, too, and I just . . . I knew the war wouldn't end until both sides called it quits, so I came up with the plan to have a strike. The girls all loved it.'

'Yeah, poor Pete.' Cash sighed. His flirty smile melted for an instant into a softer, more natural one. 'I think he'll be able to play next season. I told him I'd practise with him in the spring so he doesn't lose his place on the team.'

'That's nice of you.'

'He's a good kid. He deserves a shot.' He hesitated for a second, glancing away from me when he asked, 'So how does Randy feel about this sex-strike thing? I'm sure he hates it.'

'Why do you say that?' I asked, shifting a little so we weren't standing so close.

'I don't, uh – I just know it's hard on a lot of us guys,' he said quickly. 'Just wondering how he's coping.'

'Randy's cool with it,' I said, which wasn't really a lie. He hadn't taken me seriously enough to be unhappy about the strike. 'I mean, he's got hurt in this rivalry. I'm sure he'll be grateful once it's all over.'

'Uh-huh. Well, that's nice.' For a second, Cash looked annoyed. Or at least I thought he did. Because I blinked and the expression had left his face. He was smiling again, and I was sure I'd imagined the whole thing. 'I should get back to work,' he said. 'See you around, Lissa.'

Then he turned and left me between the stacks, not as happy to see him go as I'd hoped I'd be.

Logan was five minutes and sixteen seconds late to pick me up. I didn't even bother asking where he'd been, because I was sure he'd been at home since right after five, when his shift finished at the auto parts store. Most likely, he'd just lost track of time. I didn't quite understand how anyone could do that. I was always aware of what time it was. Constantly. How did someone let seconds or minutes or hours just slip away from them?

I don't know. But Logan was the master of it.

We were about to head out of the door when I heard Cash call to me from across the room. I turned and found him hurrying towards me.

'Here,' he said, handing a thin paperback to me. 'I checked it out for you earlier.'

'What is it?' I asked.

'*Lysistrata*,' he said. 'The Aristophanes play I told you about. I thought you might find it interesting. Considering your plans and all.'

'Oh, um . . . thanks.'

'No problem. Let me know what you think.' He smirked and touched my shoulder playfully. 'Who knows? Maybe you'll like getting away from the tragedies.'

'Maybe.'

'Well, I'll let you get going. See you later, Lissa.'

'All right. See you,' I said, moving toward the library door, holding the copy of *Lysistrata* to my chest. I was sort of curious to read it. 'OK, Logan, let's go . . . Logan?'

I glanced over my shoulder. Logan was talking to Jenna at the front desk, and she was totally chatting him up. Flipping her hair, batting her eyes, smiling. Ugh. My skin crawled. Jenna didn't smile. Not unless she really wanted something.

Like my brother, apparently.

'Logan,' I said too loudly. 'Hey, come on. Let's go.'

'All right, all right,' he sighed, stepping away from the desk.

I squeezed my eyes shut and took a deep breath, trying to erase from my memory the image of Jenna and my brother flirting.

'You don't have to be so demanding, you know,' Logan said, walking out to his Jeep with me at his side. 'It really isn't very attractive.'

'Thank you,' I said. 'I appreciate it. Now can we just get out of here?'

I took a look back at the library as we drove away. I could see Cash walking across the parking lot, a streetlight casting his shadow across the pavement. When I looked away, I realized I was hugging the copy of *Lysistrata* like it was a prized possession.

Quickly, I stuffed the book into my backpack and, before Logan could notice anything was up, I started commandeering the radio dial.

13

I dreamed about Cash that night.

Not a prophetic dream where he died in a fiery car accident, or a goofy dream where we walked on Mars and ate cotton candy or something stupid like that. No, this dream was . . . Well, it involved me, Cash and that library sex scene from *Atonement* that I wasn't supposed to be thinking about whenever Cash was around – even though I couldn't help it. And in my dream, there was nothing uncomfortable about the bookshelves.

I rolled over and slapped the snooze button, but lying there, as the dream flooded into my conscious brain, I discovered that the extra seven minutes of sleep wouldn't do me any good this morning. The shame would keep me awake instead.

I climbed out of bed and headed for the bathroom, turning off my alarm clock along the way. I couldn't get my mind out of the dream. Even after I was done showering and getting dressed, or when I ran downstairs to catch the bus.

Somehow, having a dream like that about Cash made me feel . . . guilty.

'Why would you feel bad about that?' Chloe asked in our first-block computer applications class after I confided in her. 'It's not like you can help what you dream about. And damn, the boy is hot. Who doesn't have raunchy dreams about him? Too bad he's such a tease. He could be the ultimate stud if he wanted, but he won't even move beyond the flirty stage with girls. Maybe he's part of some crazy religion or something.'

I blushed and opened up an Excel spreadsheet to start the project we'd been assigned. I always told Chloe everything. About my family, my relationship with Randy (the parts that weren't too private, at least), my college plans, and even my dirty dreams. But there was something she didn't know about: what happened between Cash and me at Vikki McPhee's party over the summer.

'Seriously, though,' she pressed, leaning over to see what buttons I was clicking to start the arithmetic functions on the spreadsheet. 'Why do you feel guilty?'

'I don't know . . . Because I have a boyfriend?' I offered, not mentioning the fact that I'd never had that

138

kind of dream about Randy. 'Doesn't that make it sort of wrong?'

'No,' Chloe said flatly. 'It doesn't. You can't help who or what you dream about. It's not like you're cheating on him. Besides, boys can do it.'

'What do you mean?'

'I mean,' she said, checking my screen again to figure out how I'd created the assigned bar graph, "boys check out girls, talk about girls, and totally dream about girls they aren't dating, and it's cool as long as they don't actually act on it. But when a girl like you does the same thing, she feels dirty or guilty or whatever.

'I don't get that.'

'Yeah,' I murmured. 'I guess I don't, either.'

There were a lot of things I wasn't getting lately. Like how it wasn't OK to like sex too much because then you were a slut, but not having it made a girl weird. Or how boys like Cash could get away with flirting too much but a girl would get trash-talked for doing the same thing. Or how my boyfriend seemed to think it was OK for him to put me second to this rivalry crap, but when I decided to do something about it, he wouldn't take me seriously.

I was starting to think I just didn't understand anything. Like there was some handbook to adolescence and dating and boys that was passed out in middle school on a day when I was absent or something. I wondered if other girls were as clueless about all this stuff as I was.

'Lissa, I'm clueless,' Chloe whispered as our computer teacher, Mrs Moulton, walked past. For a second, I was really weirded out, totally thinking she'd heard my thoughts, but then she added, "What's the difference between a bar graph and a line graph? And why does it even fucking matter? Help me over here!'

I laughed, relieved, and leaned over to help her with the assignment.

Things between Randy and me had been off since Monday night, when I'd told him about the sex strike. He wasn't giving me the silent treatment or avoiding me, exactly. He was just being . . . distant. He wasn't quite as touchy-feely as usual, maybe because he'd finally realized it wouldn't work, and he didn't talk as much as he normally did when I was around.

It hurt to have Randy act so coldly towards me, but I hoped that meant the strike was working. That he was finally getting frustrated enough to do something about it. That all the boys were, and the war would end soon.

But at the moment, sitting next to him at lunch was becoming unnecessarily awkward – though I'm sure my behaviour that day was no warmer; I could barely look Randy in the eye after the dream I'd had about Cash.

So after thirteen minutes of uneasy conversation had passed at the lunch table, I decided I'd had enough.

'So, Homecoming,' I said loudly, interrupting a conversation Randy was having with Shane. I was sure it wasn't important, anyway. 'It's this Friday. We should make sure our plans are set.'

Randy looked at me, confused. 'What plans?' he asked. 'I mean . . . you have your dress or whatever, and I have the clothes you made me buy for it. What else is there to plan?'

'I think we should go to dinner first,' I told him. 'Just you and me. Quiet and romantic, you know? We can eat and then head to the dance.'

'Sure,' Randy said. 'Whatever you want. Just tell me where to take you when I pick you up. Your call.'

I scowled. Yeah, I thought. Because that's romantic.

'Why don't you pick?' I suggested. 'And then surprise me.'

'Nah,' he said, poking his fork at a disgusting-looking pile of macaroni and cheese. 'You said you don't like surprises.'

'I don't . . . But you did a great job last time.'

'You just pick. I wouldn't want to choose the wrong one and then piss you off or something.'

It'll be over soon, I told myself, knowing the strike

141

was the cause of Randy's distance. The boys had figured out the plan. They knew there would be no action until the rivalry was over. The girls had the advantage. We had the power.

We were in control.

With a sweet smile and a chipper voice, I said, 'Fine. I'll pick a place in Oak Hill and get us a reservation for eight o'clock. It'll be a great night.'

'I'm sure it will be,' he murmured, his voice right on the verge of sarcasm in a way that made me sure he was mentally adding, *Even if I won't get any.*

That's right, I thought back, as if he could hear me. *You won't.*

Chloe came over later that day to help me plan the next sleepover while I made dinner.

'You think we need another one?' Chloe asked as she painted her nails at the kitchen table. I'd shoved a towel under her hands, worried she'd spill the polish. She'd selected an electric blue colour that I would never be brave enough to wear. 'I mean, we just had one, so why do we have to do it again?'

'I think we should have them on a regular basis,' I told her. 'It'll keep things consistent and organized. The other girls really enjoyed it. I think the unity may help us win.'

'Whatever.' Chloe sighed. 'Just as long as we win soon.

It's been two weeks already, and I'm seriously not a fan of this whole celibacy thing.'

'I know you're not.' I plucked one of my mother's old cookbooks from the stack on top of the fridge and sat down across from her. 'But I'm glad you're helping me.'

'Yeah, well, you owe me.'

I flipped open the cookbook and started looking for a recipe I might actually have a shot at concocting successfully. I was a decent cook, but not like my mother. She could whip up anything without even looking at a book. She was the type of person who followed the recipe once and then found ways to tweak it, make it her own, and make it better.

Unfortunately, she hadn't had time to pass that knowledge on to me.

And God forbid my father or brother attempt to use the stove. The house would be in flames within moments. The idea of either of them making anything more complex than a tuna sandwich gave me nightmares.

'So you gonna have it here?' Chloe asked.

I cringed at the thought, and she laughed.

'Oh, come on. You're supposed to be the leader here, Little Miss Bossy Pants. Step up.'

'Fine. I guess I could. But what about Dad and Logan?'

'I'm sure there will be some sort of sporting event on

TV to keep your dad occupied,' she said. 'And Logan . . . Well, I can distract him if you'd like.'

I gave Chloe a sharp look.

'I'm kidding. Sort of. I mean, yeah, your brother is hot, but I wouldn't do anything with him you wouldn't approve of . . . unless I knew for sure we'd get away with it and you'd never have to find out and—'

'Chloe!'

'That time I really was kidding. Chill.'

'Not funny.'

'What? I can't help who I fantasize about. You can't help that you have kinky dreams involving unattainable soccer studs, so it isn't my fault that my deep dark fantasy involves me, your brother and a—'

'Stop, stop, stop!' I cried, covering my ears. 'I don't want to hear the end of that sentence! It's bad enough that he's flirting with my co-worker.'

'He's flirting with Cash? Now that's hot.'

'What? No! Jenna, not Cash. Geez, Chloe.'

'Whoa,' she said. 'Logan has a thing for the Wicked Witch of the Library? No fucking way.'

'He's been flirting with her lately . . . and she definitely likes him.'

'Weird . . . Maybe that means he has a thing for dominatrices. Whips and spiky heels and all that.'

I buried my face in my hands. 'Why do you like torturing me?'

'Because you are torturing me with this whole no-sex thing.' Chloe sighed. 'Lissa, I'm sexually frustrated.'

'Are you even old enough to know what sexual frustration feels like?'

'Now I am. And thanks to this strike, I know that when I'm sexually frustrated, I like to punish others. You are the logical target here.'

'You're evil.'

'That's why you love me.'

'Sometimes,' I muttered.

She blew me a kiss across the table and winked. 'Seriously, though, it'll be fine. Throwing the sleepover here, I mean. I'll come over early on Saturday and help you set up before and clean up afterwards, OK?'

'Really? Thanks.'

'Whatever. It gives me a good reason to get away from my mother. She's decided to quit smoking again, so she's crabby as hell.' Chloe stood up and walked around the table to stand behind me. 'Now,' she said, leaning over my shoulder, 'let's figure out what you're making for dinner. I'm starved, and I've decided you're feeding me, too.'

14

On Thursday, I was taking my break in the back room of the library, eating an apple and reading, when Cash walked in. I kept my eyes on the page as heat crept up my neck. I'd been trying to avoid him since our shift started – it was almost impossible to look at him after that dream I'd had a couple of nights earlier.

'Hey, Lissa,' he said, sitting down on the other side of the couch. 'What are you reading?'

I didn't answer, just lifted my book a few inches so he could see the title.

'HP Lovecraft's short stories,' he said. 'Nice. I didn't know you were into sci-fi.'

I nodded. 'Sometimes. I try to read every genre.'

'Cool. Have you got around to *Lysistrata* yet?'

'No,' I said, flipping the page. 'Sorry. I wanted to finish this collection first.'

'All right,' Cash said, sounding a little disappointed. 'I'm just curious to see what you think about it.'

'I'll let you know.'

'OK.'

I peeked over the top of my book and watched as Cash unwrapped a Snickers bar. He was just wearing a maroon T-shirt and faded blue jeans, but he still looked amazing. Feeling guilty for ogling him, I hurriedly turned my attention back to the book. Don't think about him, I told myself, keeping my eyes trained on the page as I picked up my red pen. Don't think about him . . . Just keep reading . . .

'Lissa,' Cash said slowly, drawing out the A at the end of my name. 'Correct me if I'm wrong, but . . . Did you just mark a typo in your book?'

I bit my lip. 'No. Of course not. Why would you say that?'

'Because you just marked the page with a red ink pen – like the ones teachers use to check papers.'

'No, I didn't.'

'Lissa.'

'What?' I asked, ducking my head. 'You're imagining things.'

'Let me see,' he said, not bothering to hide his laughter. 'I don't believe you.'

'Cash, stop it!' I cried. He was already leaning over me, pulling the book gently from my hands. I tugged back, and we wrestled over it for a few minutes. Then Cash poked me in the side and I let out a burst of laughter. In my momentary distraction, he swiped the book from me.

'Cash,' I whined.

He shook his head, staring at page 124. 'I can't believe it! You circled a misspelling. And you keep a red pen on you whenever you read?'

I ducked my head again and didn't answer. Cash was sitting very close to me, his shoulder leaning against mine, our fingers nearly touching where we both held the book. My heart raced – from struggling to get the book back or his proximity, I wasn't sure which.

Cash started flipping through the pages. 'Damn,' he said. 'This thing is covered in red.'

'It's a newer edition,' I said, yanking the book back towards me. 'It happens sometimes.'

'You should be a copy editor,' he said, letting go of the book. 'I think you'd be good at it.'

'Maybe,' I muttered. Honestly, correcting spelling and punctuation errors for a living was more than a little appealing to me.

He leaned away from me and settled into his side of

the couch again. 'So,' he asked, smirking, "were you born this neurotic, or did it develop over time?'

'I actually took a class. Anal-Retentive 101.' Cash laughed, and I smiled back, shaking my head. 'No. It, um, started after my mother died.'

Cash's face fell. 'Oh, shit. I'm sorry. I shouldn't have asked. You don't have to talk about it if you—'

'It's fine,' I said, realizing as I said it that it was true. 'It was a long time ago. But after the accident, I just got so freaked out, so scared of something else bad happening, that I wanted to be in control of everything. That started with me being bossy and then the counting started, and that spawned a whole slew of idiosyncrasies. It's silly, I know, but—'

'It's not silly,' he said. 'What's silly is my deep-seated and unreasonable fear of fish.'

I frowned. 'Fish? Like food?'

'No, that doesn't bother me so much. Fish that are alive. I can't swim in lakes or rivers or anything besides a swimming pool because I'm always convinced the fish are swimming all over me . . . all slimy and . . . ugh.'

I laughed, and Cash smiled.

'We all have our quirks,' he said. 'This is yours. You wouldn't be you without it.'

'Thanks,' I said, looking away, feeling embarrassed.

'All of that said,' he continued, and when I turned back to face him I realized he'd leaned close again. We weren't touching, but he was definitely crossing the personal-bubble line. 'I do think you should loosen up every once in a while. For your own sake.'

'Easier said than done.'

'I know.'

He was so close, and his green eyes were looking right into mine. In that moment, I felt anything but uptight. I was completely relaxed. Completely comfortable.

Too comfortable, I realized, as the break room door swung open and I jumped away from him.

'Lissa,' Jenna said from the doorway, 'your break ended almost a minute ago. Come on, I can't have you slacking off when you're on the clock.'

'Right,' I said, scrambling to my feet. 'Sorry. I'll get back to work.'

'Good,' she said. 'There are some magazines that need to be reorganized. And when you're done with that, can you put away the books I just checked back in?'

I nodded, and Jenna walked away.

'My guess,' Cash said, smiling up at me, 'is that she was just born that way.'

'Yeah, probably,' I said quickly, grabbing my book

150

and tossing my apple into the trash. 'See you, Cash.'

I forced myself to think of Randy while I worked in the magazine room. Despite our current issues, I had a great boyfriend. One who didn't deserve a girlfriend with a wandering eye. Or mind.

But Homecoming was the next night, and I was determined to have a good time with my friends and my boyfriend and no Cash interfering with my thoughts.

15

Hamilton High had two Homecomings a year – one for football in September and another for basketball in January. When you're a freshman it's exciting because two Homecomings means two opportunities to dance with boys in a dark gymnasium (which, for some reason, seems glamorous when you're fourteen) and have TV show–like high school experiences – or so you hope.

By senior year, the whole thing was far less glamorous, but if you had good friends to hang with, it could still be pretty fun.

I was having a decent time this year, despite my awkward, unromantic dinner with Randy before the dance. I'd picked a Thai restaurant in Oak Hill, the next town over, that I knew served great food and had a nice, dim, romantic atmosphere. But that atmosphere had been kind of crushed by Randy's attitude. He'd barely talked to me, shrugged his shoulders in response to almost everything I said, and sent text messages throughout the meal.

'Who are you texting?' I asked playfully.

'Shane,' he grunted.

'Who's he going to Homecoming with?'

'No one.'

'Why not?'

'You know why not.'

I frowned and poked my fork at a piece of shrimp on my plate. Yes, I knew why Shane didn't have a date. It's because Shane wasn't really the 'dating' type. He was essentially the male version of Chloe. Neither of them would willingly spend an evening attached to a member of the opposite gender unless it ended with sex. Which, tonight, it clearly wouldn't.

When the waiter brought the bill, Randy paid for both our meals, though he didn't seem to do it with pleasure.

Again, I tried to tell myself that this was a good thing. That his annoyance with the sex strike was a positive sign. That the girls would have their victory soon and the rivalry would be over and we'd get along again. I convinced myself that I should be happy he was pissed off with me. It still didn't feel good, though.

It struck me then that Randy and I were sort of playing the same game. I was withholding sexual activities and he was withholding . . . well, everything else. By avoiding conversation and being so distant, he was leaving me feeling frustrated and unfulfilled, too.

Whether I liked it or not, I didn't complain about the way our paths separated once we got to the gymnasium. We needed a break from each other, so he went off to talk to his teammates – none of whom seemed to understand that dances were meant for dancing – and I found Chloe at our usual place by the refreshment table.

'I still cannot believe Kelsey is wearing that,' she said after we'd been hanging out and eating pretzels for about an hour. 'Someone should tell her that yellow isn't her colour. Oh, and I think that someone should be me. Be right back—'

I grabbed her elbow and held her in place. 'Leave her alone.'

'Party pooper.' Chloe took a sip of her Diet Coke and scanned the dance floor again. 'At least Susan had the sense to wear something cute. Oh, and Mary's dress is so pretty. I wonder where she got that? It's probably expensive, though. Damn it. And – hey, looky there.'

'What?' I looked up from the plate of cupcakes I had been examining on the table, trying to decide between chocolate-on-chocolate or chocolate-on-vanilla. 'Look at what, Chloe?'

'Your lover boy is standing over there,' she said, gesturing across the dark gymnasium.

I squinted, thinking I'd see Randy standing there. Thinking he'd be looking at me. Thinking he'd walk over, take me in his arms and tell me he was sorry for not taking me seriously and that he wanted the feud to end, too. Thinking we'd dance until midnight when they finally kicked us out and for once I wouldn't care who was watching and—

No.

No, it wasn't Randy at all. It was Cash. Cash was the one standing across the dance floor, and he wasn't looking at me. He was leaning against the wall, arms folded loosely over his chest as he talked animatedly to a pretty sophomore in a dress so short I wondered if it was meant to be a shirt instead. He was flirting with her, and the girl was inching closer and closer, touching his arm when she laughed.

'That's not funny,' I told Chloe, forcing my eyes off Cash and continuing my mental cupcake debate. I reminded myself that I had no reason to be upset. I was with Randy. I shouldn't care about Cash at all.

Still, I couldn't fight that nagging feeling in my stomach. That irrational possessiveness over Cash. I just wanted to march over there and pull him away, keep him to myself and hide him from all the other girls.

Crap. Cash wasn't supposed to be on my mind tonight. I'd promised myself.

'I think it's funny,' she teased. 'Randy might not, though.'

I groaned. If only she knew.

'Speaking of Randy,' Chloe continued, 'you should probably go and find him. It's almost time for the Homecoming Court announcements.'

'Yeah.' I sighed. 'All right. I'll be back.'

I grabbed a chocolate-on-chocolate cupcake and headed off in search of Randy. Really, there was no important reason for me to find him, but I did want to be next to him when they announced that he'd won. It was just good girlfriend behaviour. I should be there to smile and cheer and hug him when the 'unexpected' announcement came – whether he liked it or not.

When I finally reached the other side of the gym, I found Shane leaning against the wall, sipping a Coke that was probably spiked with something. Knowing Shane, something strong.

'Hi,' I said.

'Hey there, Lissa Daniels,' he said. He raised his Coke. 'Would you like to say hello to your distant cousin, Jack?'

'No, thank you.'

Shane shrugged and took a swig of his Jack and Coke. 'So what's up?'

'Not much,' I said. 'Where's Randy?'

And right then – when Shane's big blue eyes darted towards me and away so fast I barely noticed, and his free hand shoved forcefully into his jeans pocket – right then I knew something was wrong.

'Shane?' I asked slowly.

'He's, uh, in the bathroom. He'll be out in a minute.'

I thought back to when I had been standing with Chloe next to the refreshments table. It had been a good ten minutes since I'd noticed Randy over here with Shane – way, way more time than he needed in the bathroom.

'Thanks,' I said, moving around Shane and heading towards the boys' bathroom.

'What?' Shane sounded terrified as he reached for my arm with one hand while struggling to hold on to his bottle of Coke with the other. 'Lissa, wait a sec. You can't go into the boys' bathroom.'

I sidestepped his attempts to reach me. I wasn't just going to wait around to find out what was going on.

'Lissa, wait. You really don't want to do that—'

And I knew he was hiding something from me.

As fast as my heels allowed me to move, I shoved through the freshmen, towards the bathrooms. I pushed

157

against the heavy wooden door of the boys' room – a door that was supposed to be propped open by a doorstop at all times. As soon as I stepped into the tiny hallway, separated from the rest of the large bathroom by a tiled wall, I heard the noises.

A suction-y noise mixed with heavy breathing and one very female giggle.

I skirted around the wall as fast as I could, daring myself to see who was on the other side. Even though, really, I already knew.

Sure enough, there was Randy. He was with some leggy blond girl (or maybe she only looked leggy because of the way Randy had her skirt hiked up to her hips, exposing a string of her thong). They were leaning against the wall opposite the urinals – classy – with her back pressed against the tiles and his front pressing into her. They were making out in the most vulgar way possible, and by the way her fingers were scurrying across his zipper, it appeared as though the scene was about to turn into a lot more than just making out.

'Oh my fucking God.'

'Lissa,' Randy gasped, his mouth still only inches from the Blonde's. I hated that he said my name so close to her lips. Hated that he said my name at all. It wasn't his to say. Not any more.

I turned and hurried out of the bathroom, back into the gymnasium.

'Lissa, hold up!'

I don't know how Randy managed to disentangle himself from the Blonde so quickly, but suddenly he was there behind me, grabbing my arm and turning me to face him.

'Don't touch me,' I said, jerking out of his grip. 'Just leave me alone, Randy.'

'Lissa, don't be mad.'

'I don't want to talk about this here,' I hissed, knowing we'd already attracted the attention of a few bystanders. Deep down, I wanted to scream, How could you? What the fuck is wrong with you? But my instincts kicked in before I could do anything so dramatic. Instead, I was stiff, cut off. Chloe called me Little Miss Ice Queen, and that's how I felt. Emotionless. I was safer that way.

'You brought this on yourself, you know. I didn't have a choice,' Randy snapped, not letting me go. 'What was I supposed to do? Keep waiting for you? Been there, done that.'

'Randy, stop.'

But he didn't. He was in a rage now. Whether at me for catching him or at himself for getting caught, I don't know, but while I closed myself off, he exploded.

'You promised,' Randy reminded me. I was painfully

aware of how loudly he was speaking. 'When we got back together at the end of the summer, you promised you'd stop being such a prude. That we'd do it. And then you went and started this stupid-ass sex strike, and what am I supposed to do? Keep waiting?'

I felt my cheeks burning, but my tongue was stuck to the roof of my mouth. I couldn't believe he was saying this. Saying it in front of everyone.

'Hey,' Randy called, looking away from me, his eyes searching the group around us, 'just so all you girls know' – his eyes focused on me again, steely and meaner than I'd ever seen them – 'your ringleader here is a hypocrite. She's making all of you give up sex, but really, she's not giving up anything. Lissa is a virgin.' It was the most spiteful look he had ever given me.

I expected there to be an audible gasp – like in movies – but there wasn't. The only sounds were the fading pulse of a techno song and a screech of feedback as the Spanish teacher, Mrs Romali, took the stage. 'Time to announce the winners of this year's Homecoming Court!' she yelled cheerfully, unaware of the humiliation I was facing.

I turned slowly away from Randy, hoping only freshmen and sophomores had gathered to witness my embarrassment. Not my friends. Not the girls. Not people I knew.

But of course I'd never get that lucky.

Among the faces staring back at me were Ellen, Kelsey, Susan, Mary, Chloe . . . and Cash. They'd all heard. They all knew that I was a liar.

Like I was playing Red Rover on the playground, I hurtled through the wall of people in front of me.

Red Rover, Red Rover, send Virgin right over.

This time, Randy didn't stop me. He was done embarrassing me for the night. I ran despite my heels. Despite the crowd. Despite the pain searing my calves. I ran out of the gym and through the empty hall and out the blue-and-orange double doors into the warm, welcoming arms of the parking lot.

Only it wasn't warm or welcoming. Not at all. The parking lot was chilly, a cool September breeze wafting past me, and it was empty and dark. It looked like the set of a horror film. In the dark with all the abandoned cars, it seemed like the kind of place you'd find a dead body.

And what made it worse?

Randy had been my ride.

'Damn it,' I muttered.

Then, slowly, the ice around me melted. I slammed a fist into the brick wall of the school building and choked back a burst of tears as all the emotions I'd pushed away burned through me like a wildfire.

161

'Lissa?'

I looked over at the exit, expecting to find Randy coming after me again, to apologize or grovel or maybe just to hurt me some more.

Instead, it was Cash.

'Leave me alone,' I said automatically. 'I don't want to talk about it.'

'I know,' he said. He looked so nice in his semi-formal clothes – black dress pants and a red button-up – and I knew that his appearance wasn't what I should have been thinking about at that moment.

'What do you want?' I asked.

He hesitated. I watched as he ran a nervous hand over his cropped brown hair. 'Do you need a ride home?'

I stared at him for a moment. He'd just seen an epic, soap opera-esque reveal about my love life and one of the most public break-ups in Hamilton High history, yet all he could say was, Do you need a ride home?

'No.'

'Lissa,' he said doubtfully.

'I'll walk.'

'You live six miles from here.'

'How do you know that?' I asked.

'I took you home after Vikki's party this summer . . .'

I stared at him in the dim light of the parking lot,

waiting for him to finish that thought. He'd almost brought it up once before, in the library elevator, but he'd never really crossed into that territory. I wondered if he would now, if maybe he'd bring it up and I'd get the answers I'd been waiting for.

Cash cleared his throat. 'I'm ready to get out of here, anyway.'

I sighed. It was probably better that I didn't get my answers. I couldn't take more hurt tonight.

'Lissa? Come on. Seriously, I'll drive you.'

I thought about arguing with him again, but I was too tired, too angry and too lost to even try. He was right; I couldn't walk home, and who could I ask for a ride? I was sure Chloe and the other girls were pissed off with me for how I'd misled them about my sex life, and there was no way I'd let Randy drive me home after what I'd seen.

'Fine,' I muttered. 'A ride home would be nice . . . thank you.'

'No problem,' he said. 'My car's on the back side of the lot.'

As we crossed the parking lot, I heard a muffled round of cheers go up from inside the gymnasium, and I was sure Mrs Romali had just crowned Randy Homecoming King.

16

'Look,' Cash said as we pulled away from the high school. 'I know you don't want to talk about it. That's understandable. But . . . But just so you know, he's a jackass. Any decent guy wouldn't have done that to you.'

If I'd had the nerve, I would have reminded him that a decent guy wouldn't have kissed me, acted like I was special and then forgotten about me, either.

Instead, I just ran my fingers through my hair and said, 'Thanks.'

We went along in silence as Cash's Toyota turned through the dark, curving roads of Hamilton towards my house. The dream I'd had on Tuesday night slithered into my thoughts. The feel of his hands on my hips, his breath on my neck, my head leaning back against the bookshelves as his lips traced a line between my jaw and shoulder. It had been so private, had felt so real and good. Sitting

164

beside him now, in the dim glow of the speedometer's light, with only a foot or less space separating us – I felt claustrophobic and . . . guilty.

I wasn't sure why. I mean, Chloe was right. I couldn't control whom my dreams were about, and it wasn't like I'd cheated on Randy.

It wasn't like he felt guilty for cheating on me.

I glanced at Cash out of the corner of my eye. He was facing out towards the road ahead of us, and I watched as the passing streetlamps cast the silhouette of his profile across the car. Strong jaw, straight nose, broad shoulders. It felt strangely intimate to watch him drive, his eyes on the road instead of looking back at me.

I wanted to kiss Cash again. Right now. I wanted him to pull the car over and make out with me right there on the side of the road. I don't know if I wanted to spite Randy or just lose myself. Either one sounded good. I could still remember the way Cash's lips had felt on mine – in real life, not just in my dream – and how much I'd liked it. How special it had made me feel.

But Cash had rejected me once already, and after what had just happened with Randy, I knew I couldn't take it again.

'Do you want me to walk you in?'

'What?' I blinked and realized the car had come to a

165

stop and Cash was looking at me – he'd caught me watching him. Embarrassed, I turned away. We were in front of my house. 'N-no,' I stammered, scrambling for the door handle.

'You sure?'

'Positive.' I shoved the door open and slid out of the car, glanced over my shoulder once to mumble 'Thank you,' shut the door, and hurried away from the car before I could change my mind.

The first time Randy and I broke up was at the end of June, and it was because I wouldn't sleep with him. Not that either of us advertised that little detail. Instead, I skirted around the truth when people asked, saying, 'things just weren't working out,' and trusting, of course, that Randy wouldn't tell anyone the real reason for our break-up – it would make him look like less of a man to his testosterone-crazed friends, after all, if they knew that he couldn't get into my pants.

The hardest part of that break-up, though, was telling Dad and Logan. They were devastated. They tried not to show it, but all summer long they said things like, 'I'm sure you two will work it out' and 'I wonder how Randy's doing – I bet he misses you.' Little hints that I should call him or give things another shot.

They were thrilled when we got back together after the car accident. Little did they know I'd promised to sleep with Randy when we reconciled – a promise I never kept.

So here I was, barely two months later, walking down the stairs in my Rainbow Brite pyjamas, preparing to tell them that we'd split up again – for good this time.

Dad was sitting at the table eating a bowl of Raisin Bran when I came into the kitchen. 'Morning, sunshine,' he said cheerfully. 'How was the dance? I didn't even notice you come in last night, but when Logan got home he peeped into your room and you were in there, fast asleep.'

'Yeah,' I said, sitting down across from him and pouring my own bowl of cereal. 'You were watching a game when I got home. I didn't want to bother you.'

'Aw, that's all right. My team lost, anyway. So how was the dance?'

'Um.' I took a bite of cereal, chewing slowly to put this off as long as I could. 'Actually, we should talk . . . Where's Logan?'

'Sleeping, I assume. He got in late last night.'

'Really? Why? Where was he?'

'Date.'

I narrowed my eyes at Dad. 'With who?'

Dad sighed. 'Logan's a grown-up, remember? He doesn't have to tell us whom he is going out with.'

'Fine,' I said, hoping it wasn't Jenna, and poked my spoon at a raisin floating in my milk. 'OK, then I'll just tell you alone, I guess.'

'Tell me what, sweetheart?'

Deep breath. One, two, three . . .

'Randy and I broke up last night.'

'Oh.' Dad hesitated before putting his spoon down on the table and focusing all his attention on me. I could already see the cloud of disappointment in his eyes. 'Well, I know things can get dramatic at school dances. Maybe you'll see him at school on Monday and you two will talk it over and—'

I shook my head. 'No, Dad. It's over. I'm not getting back together with him this time.' I pushed my bowl of cereal away from me, my appetite gone. 'Sorry. I'm really sorry; I know you and Logan love him, and I know he's like part of the family, but after last night . . . I'm sorry, Dad.'

'Lissa, honey, don't apologize to me.' He reached across the table and took my hand in his. 'What happened?'

I rubbed at the corners of my eyes with my free hand, feeling tears begin to spring up. 'Last night at the dance, I caught him kissing another girl.' No need to go into the dirty details about the bathroom and the girl's thong. 'I'm sorry, Dad.'

'Hey, I said stop apologizing.' Dad squeezed my hand. 'Listen, honey, Logan and I . . . We do think a lot of Randy. But if he doesn't respect you, then he has lost our respect, OK?'

The tears were actually slipping down my cheeks now. So embarrassing. Maybe I had just been in too much shock last night to really cry, and sitting here, talking to Dad, it was finally hitting me. I hated it, though. I didn't want to cry over Randy.

'But he was like a second son to you,' I reminded Dad. 'He played football and watched games with you. He made you happy.'

'But making you this upset does not make me happy,' Dad said. 'Lissa, what made me happiest about Randy was that, as far as I knew, he made you happy. Sure, it was nice that we had things in common, but that doesn't matter in the long run. Who you date is your decision. If you want to date an unshaven, sports-loathing vegetarian poet, I'll still be happy for you – just as long as you're happy with it.'

I managed a crooked smile. 'Even a soccer player?'

Dad laughed. 'Even a soccer player . . . though Logan may disagree on that one.'

'Well, he won't even tell us who he's dating, so he can just deal.'

Dad smiled and patted my hand before pulling his away and returning to his bowl of cereal. 'I love you,' he said. 'And I'll welcome any boy you date with open arms. And if they hurt you, I'll . . . Well, I'll make Logan think of some way to make them pay, because I'm pretty useless.'

'No, you're not.'

'You're right. I do leave some mean shin bruises.'

I laughed and stood up to walk around the table. I wrapped my arms around Dad's neck from behind and rested my chin on his shoulder. 'Thank you, Dad. I just wish it hadn't worked out this way. I know you loved him. You don't have to deny it.'

'I'll love the next one even more.'

I released Dad. 'There may not be a next one. I'm giving up on boys.'

'Don't get my hopes up.' Dad looked over his shoulder at me. 'But you'll have another one in no time. I'm sure of it.'

'We'll see.' I picked up my half-eaten bowl of cereal and took it to the sink. 'But thanks. For being so sweet, I'll let you have dessert after dinner tonight. What would you like me to make?'

'You're making dinner?' Dad asked. 'I thought your friends were coming over for a girl-slumber-over-sleep-party thing.'

I rinsed out my bowl. 'Slumber party. And no. I have a feeling no one will show up tonight. Some other stuff happened after I caught Randy . . . Anyway, I don't want to talk about it, but I don't think they'll be talking to me for a while.'

'Even Chloe?'

'Especially Chloe.'

Just as the words left my mouth, the doorbell rang. I finished cleaning my bowl, wiped my hands on the tea towel and headed into the living room. 'Coming!' I shouted as the doorbell rang again.

'Rainbow Brite? Really, Lissa? How old are you?'

'Chloe?' I stared at her standing in the open doorway. 'What are you doing here? Aren't you supposed to be—?'

'Pissed off with you? Yeah, but I wanted to talk to you, too. Why haven't you been answering your phone? I called it, like, a gazillion times.'

'I haven't heard it ring,' I told her, stepping aside so she could walk in. 'I didn't charge it when I came in last night, so it might be dead. I honestly wasn't expecting anyone to call me today – except maybe Randy, and I don't want to talk to him.'

'Ugh. Who would?' Chloe slipped off her sandals and positioned them neatly on the front mat, just the way I liked. 'But whatever. Enough chitchat. You have, like, twenty girls showing up here in about four hours, and we have a lot to talk about and work to do before they get here.'

'Wait. What? Twenty girls? You mean they're still coming?'

But Chloe was already halfway up the stairs to my bedroom.

I glanced at Dad, who'd wheeled his chair into the doorway between the kitchen and the living room. I shrugged my shoulders, and he just smiled at me. 'I'll order pizza tonight,' he said. 'Go have fun.'

'Thanks, Dad.' And I ran upstairs after Chloe.

17

'So why didn't you tell me?' Chloe asked, perching on the edge of my bed as I folded a fresh load of laundry and put the clothes into my drawers.

'How was I supposed to tell you? I didn't know he was cheating on me, either.'

'That's not what I'm talking about.'

I knew that, but I didn't want to answer her real question.

'Lissa, how could you be a virgin? I mean, like . . . I thought you and Randy had been banging forever.'

'You make it sound so romantic.'

'Stop avoiding the question,' she insisted. 'I'm dead serious. How could you lie to me?'

'I didn't exactly lie,' I told her, bumping the open drawer shut with my hip. 'I just never elaborated on the details of my sex life. I mean, we did other stuff.'

I had to fight off a blush so Chloe wouldn't make fun of me. 'And anyway, I didn't want to catch hell about it. I didn't want anyone else to know that I was . . . scared. And I figured my secret was safe with Randy because he'd be embarrassed about the fact that he couldn't get into my pants or whatever . . . So much for that plan.'

'You're scared? Like . . . of sex?'

I wondered if my cheeks were as red as they felt now. 'Yes, I guess I am.'

Chloe cocked her head to one side and stared at me the same way you'd stare at a three-legged lion in the zoo.

'God, Chloe, don't look at me like that. See, this is why I didn't tell you.'

'Sorry,' she said. 'I'm just . . . surprised. It's weird. Sex was never scary to me.' She paused. 'So what about it do you find scary? Like, penises? Because I can see how those might be a little scary. Or is it the idea that the first time hurts? Or—'

'Oh, please stop,' I said, moving to sit down beside her on the bed. 'No. Nothing like that. It's . . . it's letting someone that close to me. Physically and emotionally. Randy and I got close a few times, but . . . I chickened out. I'm afraid of letting someone have that kind of power over me. Not being in control is what scares me.'

'Wow,' Chloe said. 'I'd never thought about it like that. See, for me, it's the opposite.'

'What do you mean?'

'It makes me feel like I am in control,' she explained. 'Like, I don't know. I started fooling around a lot after my dad moved out, which makes me sound like I have lame daddy issues, but whatever. I wasn't looking for pity; I was looking for something I could do on my own. Something I could own. My parents were dividing up all of their shit and fighting over stuff, and I couldn't do a thing about it. Then Mom and I had to move into our shitty apartment, and I felt like I had nothing. Nothing but my body. It's the one thing I can control. For me, sex is my way of taking control of my body. I'm in charge. Don't psychoanalyze me on all that or say you're sorry about my family or anything. That's not what I want. I just . . . I think it's kind of interesting how we look at it so differently.'

'It is, I guess.' I sighed and leaned my head on her shoulder. 'I hate boys.'

'I miss boys.'

Chloe helped me get the house ready for the next few hours. Once my room was clean, we dug out the chips and sodas I'd bought a few days earlier. I organized the cans of soda on my desk: diet to the left, caffeine-free in

175

the middle and regular on the right. I also wanted to arrange the chips, which Chloe had spread out on top of my dresser, but she restrained me.

'So I asked around about the Blonde,' she said, sitting down on my bed once the room was completely slumber-party ready. 'She's a sophomore. Her name is Autumn Elliot. What the hell kind of name is Autumn? Why don't they just call her Fall or the Depressing Season When Everything Starts To Die.'

'It's a pretty name, Chloe.'

'Fine,' she huffed. 'But getting your freak on in a public bathroom? Who does that?'

'Um, Chloe . . .'

'OK, fine. I've done that.' She flicked her hair over her shoulder. 'Jesus, Lissa, help me out here. I'm trying to console you, but you're making it difficult.'

'It's all right,' I told her. 'You don't have to say anything. Especially not about her. I don't hate her. She's not the one who betrayed me.'

'True . . . But her dress was really, really ugly.'

'Chloe!' I laughed.

'I'm just saying. The whole plunging-neckline thing did not flatter her figure. You looked way hotter.'

'Well, yeah. That's true,' I said, smiling.

Just then, the doorbell rang downstairs. 'That'll be the

girls,' she said, hopping off the bed.

'How did you get them to come, anyway?' I asked, standing up and following her out of my bedroom. 'I just assumed they'd all skip out.'

'Oh, it was easy,' Chloe said. 'I hacked your email and sent them a pleading, grovelling message begging them to come and promising them ice cream. You should go and order some of that, by the way. Sorry, forgot to warn you.'

I stopped in the middle of the stairs, but Chloe kept walking. 'How did you get my password?' I asked.

She turned around at the bottom and smiled up at me. 'Lissa, I'm your best friend. I know you well enough to know your password would be atonement. The book's constantly under your pillow with the dirty pages dog-eared. I'm not stupid.' She winked and scampered off to the door to let in the guests.

I hated her and loved her at the same time.

'All right. So what's the deal?' Susan asked, sitting on my bed and crossing her legs. She arrived last of all the girls – twenty-one this time. My room was sweltering, and I couldn't crank the AC up any higher. This had not been a good idea.

And neither was letting Kelsey into my house.

She plopped down on the bed beside Susan, after

Chloe told her off for stalking around the room, glaring at me and making snarky remarks. I think Chloe's exact words were sit down and shut your ugly mouth or I'll find a much, much more painful method of silencing you.

'I cannot believe this bullshit,' she snapped, apparently not taking Chloe's threat seriously. 'Who do you think you are, Lissa?'

I could feel myself getting nervous, shaking as I counted all the girls in my head, over and over again. There were too many. If they got mad or started yelling . . . Images of the chaos flashed through my brain, causing a knot to form in my chest. What if they made a mess of my room?

'Kelsey, do you have a point?' Susan asked, sounding bored.

'The point,' Kelsey said, "is that Lissa's a hypocrite. She's not even having sex, but she thinks she can tell us we should stop? And it's all to solve her problems.'

'Kelsey, I'm sorry, but can you shut the hell up?'

I turned and was shocked to find that Ellen was the speaker. Our eyes met, and Ellen gave me a small, imperceptible nod before focusing her attention back on the mortified Kelsey.

'It's not just Lissa's problem,' she said. 'It's all of ours.

You've complained about the rivalry, too, in case you forgot. And last week, you were singing Lissa's praises. So stop acting all high and mighty. We're all sick of your shit, and frankly, Lissa needs friends right now. We'd all be there for you if your boyfriend turned out to be a dickhead. So do you mind showing the same courtesy?'

There was a long silence – which, considering there were so many girls in the room, was pretty impressive.

Kelsey took a deep breath, and we all waited to see what she'd do next. I was about to throw myself in front of Ellen to protect her from the pointed, claw-like fingernails I was sure Kelsey would be attacking her with when Kelsey spoke and made the moment even more bizarre.

'Yeah, you're right, Ellen. I'm sorry.'

'Holy shit . . . Is that . . . Did hell just freeze over?' Chloe asked, clasping a hand to her heart.

'Shut up,' Kelsey snapped. Then she looked at me. 'I'm sorry, Lissa. For the way Randy treated you and for the way I acted. It wasn't cool.'

'Um . . . thanks.' I took a deep breath. 'And honestly, you may be right. It was wrong of me to keep that detail from you guys. I just didn't want you to judge me. I felt like I was abnormal or whatever because I hadn't done it. Then you guys freaked out about Mary waiting, and even after she'd been brave enough to admit it, I just couldn't . . . Still, I shouldn't have lied, considering what I asked all of you to do. Not that it matters now. I think the strike is over.'

A rustle of surprised whispers ran around the room.

'What are you talking about?' Ellen asked. 'The boys are still fighting, aren't they? Adam's car got vandalized last night, so the rivalry definitely isn't over. We can't end the strike.'

'One of the things you guys worried about was cheating,' I reminded the room. 'That if we cut the boys off from sex, they'd cheat. Well, that's what happened to me, so you were right. We should have never done this.'

'Oh hells no,' Chloe said. 'Don't go there. I said it at the first meeting and I'll say it again – if any boy cheats on you just because you won't fuck him, he's the prick and you shouldn't be with him, anyway. If anything, Lissa, this was a good plan. It showed you what an ass Randy really is, and at least you're done with him now.'

I flinched. I knew she was right, but the idea that this was better – that having him chase other girls was best for me – still stung, and it probably would for a while.

'Let's be fair about this,' Susan said, getting to her feet,

180

which wasn't easy since every inch of floor was filled by the bodies of teenage girls. 'All in favour of ending the strike prematurely, raise your hand.'

No hands.

Not even Kelsey's.

'Excellent. And all those in favour of continuing as planned with Lissa at the lead?'

All around the room, hands shot up.

'Seriously?' I asked, surprised.

'It actually might be better,' Ellen said. 'You know, for you to be in charge without a boyfriend and all. It gives you a clearer perception, maybe. You aren't biased by the pressure anyone is putting on you any more.'

'Well, except me,' Chloe said, leaning against me and running a teasing hand up my thigh. 'Can you resist me, Lissa? I don't think you can.'

I bumped her hand off my leg, laughing. I was overcome with emotion, so awed by the girls' support, that I forgot to be on edge. Even with twenty-one girls piled into my room, I found myself suddenly relaxing, trusting all of them more than I'd ever expected to.

'Wow, Chloe is getting desperate.' Mary giggled.

'No shit,' Susan said. 'But we all knew she'd be dying inside without some booty.'

Chloe clutched a hand to her chest, made a few

gagging noises, and then fell back onto the carpet, playing dead.

'So how about it, Lissa?' Ellen said, calling back my attention. 'You still with us?'

'Yes,' I said, beaming. 'I'm still with you. The strike continues.'

'Awesome,' Chloe said, using my shoulder to pull herself back into a sitting position, apparently no longer dead. 'Now, where the fuck is my ice cream?'

'Can I tell you something?'

I was standing at the kitchen sink, washing a few of the bowls that had been used for ice cream, unable to stand the idea of letting them sit around for more than a few minutes. I could still hear the chaos upstairs, where the others waited. I was just trying to figure out the sleeping arrangements – there was no way they were all staying in my bedroom – when I heard Kelsey's voice behind me.

I glanced over my shoulder and found her standing in the doorway to the kitchen, looking way more nervous than I'd ever seen her look before.

'Sure,' I said. 'What's up?'

'The thing is, I . . .' She stopped and turned to look into the living room.

'My dad isn't here,' I said, knowing instantly what she was doing. 'My brother decided at the last minute that he wanted to drive to the lake and go fishing in the morning, and Dad wanted to go with him. It's just us here. Which is a good thing, you know? It opens up some rooms for everyone to sleep in . . . sorry. What were you going to tell me?'

Kelsey stepped into the kitchen, easing up to the counter, her keen eyes watching as I put away the clean bowls. 'OK,' she said, "this is going to sound weird, but . . . I don't like sex.'

I dried my hands on the tea towel and turned to face her, confused. 'You . . . What?'

'Don't tell anyone,' she insisted. 'Please. It's embarrassing. But I really don't enjoy it. It's just kind of . . . underwhelming. I only do it because it makes Terry happy, and I love him, but . . . I don't know. I don't know why I'm telling you this. It's just, you felt like you had to lie about being a virgin and I feel like I have to lie about this, and . . . I'm so weird.'

I remembered standing in Susan's kitchen with Mary and how she'd asked if she was weird for being a virgin. I'd almost told her the truth about me that night. That she wasn't weird, because I was a virgin, too. Or, rather, that we were weird together. This moment with Kelsey felt like intense déjà vu. Only this time, I couldn't relate quite as much. Still, I said the same thing.

'You're not weird.'

'How would you know?'

'I guess I don't,' I admitted. 'I don't know if I'll like it or not once I do it. If I ever do it. Because I may not.' I shrugged. 'But why does not liking it have to make you weird?'

'Because everyone else seems to like it so much.'

'Maybe some of them are just pretending,' I said. 'So no one thinks they're weird.'

'Maybe,' Kelsey murmured. 'God, why am I even telling you this? It's so weird.'

'Stop saying it's weird.'

Kelsey shook her head, laughing slightly. 'Don't repeat this,' she said, "but that's part of the reason I hate Chloe. I'm jealous. She obviously enjoys it. I wish I liked it that much.'

'Well, Chloe gets hell for liking it too much. From you and others.'

'So she's the weird one for liking it,' Kelsey suggested.

'Or it could be that no one is weird,' I offered. 'I mean, Mary and I thought we were weird because we hadn't done it at all.'

'Maybe we're all weird, then,' Kelsey said.

'If that's the case, then why does it matter?'

'Because I want to know what's normal.' She hesitated and then looked down at her bare feet on the tiles. 'I want to be normal, but no one talks about sex, so how should I know what normal is?'

I considered this for a second. She was asking the same questions that had been running through my head for weeks: What's normal? What is expected of us?

'You know,' I said quietly, "I don't think normal exists.'

18

The next day, after all the girls had left, I decided to spend the afternoon cleaning up. Dad and Logan wouldn't be home until dinner, so there was no one to get in my way while I vacuumed and dusted and sanitized nearly everything in the house – my version of a relaxing Sunday. I was in the middle of reorganizing my closet by colour – Chloe had decided to raid it during the sleepover – when the doorbell rang.

'Just a second,' I yelled down the stairs. I ran into the bathroom to check my reflection. Part of me expected it to be Randy, coming to grovel and beg for forgiveness, and while I had no intention of taking him back I still wanted to look good, to show him I wasn't suffering without him.

Once I was certain that none of my hair was sticking up in the back and that no stress acne had popped up

overnight, I ran down to the living room. 'Coming! Sorry.'
I tugged once at the hem of my tank top before opening
the door.

But Randy wasn't on my front porch.

Cash was.

'Hey.'

'Um . . . hi.'

The surprise must have shown on my face, because he
glanced over his shoulder before turning back to me. 'Are
you expecting someone?'

'No, I just . . . I thought maybe you were Randy.'

'Oh.' There was an awkward pause and Cash ran a
hand over his cropped hair, shifting his weight from one
foot to the other. 'Sorry I'm not who you were hoping for.
I can go if you—'

'No!' I exclaimed. I blushed and glanced down at my
feet. 'No, I . . . I wasn't hoping to see him. I just kind of
expected to. He hasn't come to apologize yet, so . . . But
I'm glad it's you and not him. I don't think I'm ready to
see him yet – I mean, I guess I should get over it, since
he'll be at school tomorrow, but I'm hoping I can avoid
him, since we don't have classes together, or maybe he'll
avoid me, and now he has the Blonde, so . . . ugh, sorry.
I'm rambling. Why are you here?'

Cash shoved his hands into his pockets. 'I wanted to

check on you,' he said. 'To make sure you're doing OK after everything that happened Friday night.'

'Oh . . . Yeah, I'm fine.'

He raised an eyebrow at me. 'Really?'

I opened my mouth to say, Yes, really. Why do you care? But the way he was looking at me, so genuine and warm – I knew he did care. Somewhere along the way, Cash and I had become friends. I knew that should bother me, that I should be wary of getting close to anyone after what Randy had done to me, but I couldn't fight the feeling of calm that washed over me when my eyes locked with Cash's.

'Do you want to go for a walk?' I asked.

'Yeah – sure.'

'Great. Give me a second.' I stepped into the house and slipped on my sandals. I grabbed the house keys off the hook and joined Cash on the porch again, locking the door behind me. I double- and triple-checked the lock before shoving the keys into the back pocket of my jeans. 'OK, let's go.'

We started walking down the street in silence. My arm brushed against his, but I didn't move away, and neither did he. We were on the corner, turning to follow the sidewalk, when I finally decided to speak.

'I'm better than I thought I'd be.' I could feel his eyes

on me, but I just kept walking. 'After Homecoming, I expected to be a wreck. I expected to cry or be locked in my room or something . . . I expected to miss him more, I guess. And I do – miss him, I mean – but it's not as bad as I'd thought. Some of my friends came over last night, and they really helped me. They made me realize that I could do better, you know?'

I glanced over and saw Cash nod.

'I thought I'd miss him more, but . . . that's not the problem.'

'What is?'

'It's just . . . I keep asking myself, Why? Why wasn't I good enough to wait for? What's so wrong with me that he could just throw everything away for one night? Why was sex so damn important?' I felt the heat rise into my cheeks. 'Oh, God, sorry. I shouldn't be talking to you about this.'

'About what?'

'My, um, sex life . . . or, as everyone now knows, my lack thereof.'

'Oh.'

I took a deep breath and let it out slowly. 'Sometimes I wish Mom was still around to talk to me about this stuff. She'd be able to tell me what to do.'

'What do you think she'd say?'

I smiled, remembering her voice. Soft but stern. 'She'd probably say something like, "Melissa Anne, stop questioning yourself. You're smart and beautiful, and that boy is a fool. Never, never let anyone pressure you . . . and please get your shoes off the couch."'

'I'm going to assume you take after your mother.'

I laughed. 'That's what I'm told.'

'Well, you know,' Cash said tentatively, "she may not be around to tell you in person, but it seems like the advice you think she'd give is good.'

'I know. But it's not the same.'

'I'm sorry. We don't have to talk about her if it makes you uncomfortable.'

It did, usually. I never let Randy talk about my mom, but with Cash, it was OK. It was easy. Still, I said, 'Let's change the subject.'

So for the next few minutes, we talked about nothing important – television, a book he'd just finished, our mutual belief that the lunch ladies were trying to poison us. Then, after a while, we fell quiet.

As we walked along Levitt Avenue, a few mothers pushed strollers past us and, across the street, two middle school–aged girls walked side by side, both holding leashes attached to Labrador puppies. It was a beautiful Sunday afternoon, and for a moment I marvelled at the fact that I'd planned to spend the day cleaning instead of walking around the neighbourhood. Hamilton really was a nice place – a generic suburb, sure, but pretty and friendly. Usually, I was too worried about other things to notice.

I didn't even notice that Cash had taken my hand until we'd reached the next corner. We were almost back to my house, having walked around the whole block, and he'd been holding my hand half the time without my even realizing.

'Lissa,' he said slowly. 'Look, about Randy and the whole sex thing—'

'Cash, please, it's embarrassing. Let's not—'

'No, just listen for a second.' We were standing in front of my house again, and Cash had stopped, using our entwined hands to turn me towards him. 'I know you don't want to talk about your . . .' He cleared his throat. 'About what Randy said at Homecoming. But you should know this. The other night, I told you a decent guy wouldn't have done that to you. I didn't just mean embarrassing you in public like that. I meant . . .'

I stared up at him, our palms still pressed together.

He sighed. 'I meant that a decent guy – a smart guy – wouldn't have let something like sex ruin a good thing. A guy with half a brain wouldn't have screwed things up with a girl like you.'

'Thanks. That's sweet of you to say.'

'I'm serious, Lissa.' He lifted his free hand and brushed my cheek, tucking a few strands of hair behind my ear. Both of his hands were touching me, and I didn't miss the way my heart sped up just a little. 'You're amazing – and he really fucked up.'

Amazing. He'd said that at Vikki's party, too. Right before he'd kissed me. Right before he'd broken my heart. I wondered if he meant it this time. If maybe he was trying to tell me something – that he'd been wrong, that he'd made a mistake, that he liked me after all.

'Thank you,' I said. 'That means a lot.'

Cash smiled down at me. Then, after a long moment, he let go of my hand and took a step back. 'Well . . . I should get going. We have a game in an hour – Coach wants us there early.'

'Right. I'm glad you came by.'

He looked at me a little sceptically. 'Really?'

I laughed and smacked him on the arm. 'Of course. We're friends, aren't we?'

Cash grinned – that sweet, flirty grin he gave me in the library sometimes when our banter went a little further than I'd intended it to. 'I'll see you tomorrow,

192

then.' He touched my cheek one last time before turning and walking towards his car.

I tried not to think too much about what Cash had said once I was back inside. I didn't want to get my hopes up. Still, I could feel joy bubbling in my chest, thinking that maybe, just maybe, he'd realized what a mistake he'd made by letting me go.

19

'Cock tease.'

I felt my cheeks flush as one of Randy's football buddies brushed past me in the hall, his words hissing in my ear.

'Hey, assclown,' Chloe snapped, whirling around at my side to face the guy's retreating form. 'Learn some manners or I'll email the whole high school about how small your dick is – because we both know that I'm aware of exactly how small it is.'

'Whore,' he muttered, shooting Chloe a filthy glare over his shoulder.

'Ha. You might have better luck with a whore, actually. Me? You couldn't pay me to bang you again. Dick's too minuscule to keep a lady satisfied. Come on, Lissa.' She took hold of my wrist and pulled me towards the cafeteria.

It was Monday, my first day back at school since I'd caught Randy with the Blonde, and I wasn't sure how I was going to deal with the lunch situation. I obviously couldn't sit with Randy and Shane and the others. But where would I go? That's where I'd been sitting for more than a year. That's where my friends were.

When we walked into the cafeteria, I seriously considered turning around and going to the library. The Blonde was sitting in Randy's lap at our usual table, and she was grinning from ear to ear – and who could blame her? She was getting attention from the coolest people in the school. From the cutest boy.

From the boy who was supposed to be mine.

'Boys suck,' I muttered.

'Not all of them are so bad,' Chloe said, dragging me along behind her. 'There are a few good ones, I swear.'

'Well, introduce me to them, then. Oh, and where are we sitting?'

'Right here.'

I glanced around at the occupants of the table Chloe had just led me to. Ellen was beaming up at me, sitting in a chair beside Adam, her boyfriend. I felt my cheeks flush as I counted the people at the table – they were all soccer players or soccer players' girlfriends.

'What are we doing?' I asked Chloe through gritted teeth.

'Neither of us is dating a football player any more, Lissa. So we don't have to worry about pissing anyone off. Ellen invited us.' My new best friend tossed a smile at my old best friend, and a nice full-circle feeling overwhelmed me. Just for an instant.

'Take a seat,' Adam said, grinning at me. 'Anyone who makes an ass out of Randy Vincent is a friend of mine.'

'Actually,' I said stiffly, sliding into the chair on the other side of Ellen's, "I think he made the ass out of me.'

'Au contraire,' Adam argued, pointing a plastic fork in my direction. 'While it may have seemed that way in the moment, in the long run, Randy will be the one to suffer. He revealed to half the female population that he cheats on girls and divulges intimate secrets about his girlfriend to the school at large. So even though it sucked for you, consider your scene at Homecoming a fair and kind warning to the rest of the world. Oh, and most likely, it will keep him from getting laid.'

While I doubted that last bit, based on the way the Blonde had been wiggling in Randy's lap when I passed, I didn't argue.

Chloe plopped into the seat on my other side. 'Anyone

going up to get food?' she asked, jerking her head towards the lunch line.

'I'll go with you,' I said, feeling silly about standing up when I'd barely been sitting for five seconds. 'Come on.'

'Oh, go ahead,' Chloe said. 'I was just seeing if anyone else was going. Can you get me a Diet Coke? Thanks.'

I swatted her arm with the back of my hand. 'Lazy ass.'

'You love my ass. Don't lie.'

'I'll go with you, Lissa,' Ellen said, getting to her feet. 'I'm actually craving those gross, soggy French fries. I must be losing it.'

I laughed a little nervously before following her towards the lunch line. Honestly, I wasn't quite sure why I was still so anxious around her. I mean, we'd attended two slumber parties together in the past two weeks, and we'd talked . . . a few times. But then again, this was the first time we'd been near each other without Chloe and Kelsey between us, screaming obscenities at each other.

'Hmm. Maybe I'll get a hamburger instead,' Ellen was saying. 'They're obnoxiously greasy, but sometimes greasy can be good, right? What do you think?'

'I'm sorry.' It came out of my mouth before I could stop it. I tucked my hair behind my ear and cleared my throat. 'I mean, not about the hamburgers.

197

I'm sorry about us. How we stopped hanging out and stuff, and—'

'I know. Me too.'

'It was my fault,' I said. 'I let having a boyfriend and the whole football–soccer drama come between us.'

'Yeah . . . You did mess up pretty bad,' Ellen said, reaching down and squeezing my hand. 'But whatever. I'm over it, and we're hanging out now. We're cool.'

I beamed at her. 'I'm glad.'

'Me too.'

We chatted for a few more minutes as we inched forward in the line, catching up on the things we'd missed in the last year – apparently, Ellen's brother had got kicked out of middle school for fighting and was now going to a private school. I couldn't believe I hadn't been with her through that. But it was like she'd said – I was there now, and that's what mattered.

'You know,' she said after we'd loaded our trays with food and I'd grabbed Chloe's Diet Coke, 'I knew. Even before Randy said anything at Homecoming, I knew you were . . . Well, I knew you hadn't slept with him.'

I blushed. 'Um . . . thank you?'

'No, seriously,' she said as she handed the cranky-looking cashier the money for her lunch. 'I mean, I second-guessed myself a few times, but when you started the strike I just thought . . . I thought I still knew you, and the you I knew wouldn't have slept with him, if that makes sense.'

'I thought about it a few times. We got close.'

'I know, I know. Don't get me wrong, he's hot and I know you loved him, but . . .' she hesitated, watching as I paid for my meal. 'As much of a control freak as you are, I knew it couldn't have happened. Not with an idiot like Randy, at least. It's nice to know I still know you.'

'Better than anyone,' I told her.

'Except Chloe,' she said, walking back to the table with me. 'You two are insanely cute together. It's almost ridiculous.'

I was about to respond when we reached the table and Chloe – speak of the devil – leaped from her chair and swiped her Diet Coke off my tray so fast that I jumped, startled, and a few fries fell off the plate and on to the floor.

'Right.' I sighed. 'Really cute.'

Chloe took a swig of her drink and wiped her mouth with the back of her hand. 'Sorry,' she said. 'I was dying of thirst. You guys took forever.'

'Sorry to keep you waiting, Your Highness.'

'You're forgiven.'

Ellen laughed as she reclaimed her seat next to Adam.

I sighed and sat down, only just then realizing that there was now someone sitting in the seat across from me.

'So, Cash, what happened to you on Friday night?' Adam asked. 'At Homecoming. Did you bail or what?'

Cash's green eyes met mine across the table before he looked at Adam. 'Yeah, I left early. Wasn't really feeling it this year.'

'You're never feeling it,' Adam said. 'You never take a date, and sometimes you don't even show up. Don't get me wrong, I appreciate the whole Mr Unattainable tactic, but usually a dude does that as a means to an end. You're sort of missing the point here, Cash.'

For a second, I thought I saw Cash turn red.

'I don't know, man,' he told Adam. 'I'm just too busy to date right now. Between soccer, working and keeping the grades up so I can get this scholarship . . . I just need to stay focused, you know?'

Adam snorted. 'All right,' he said. 'But you know we're talking about a date, right? Like, just asking a chick to Homecoming. Not planning a wedding.'

'You're breaking the heart of every girl in Hamilton,' Ellen teased him, throwing a French fry in his direction. 'The way you flirt with them. They all think they have a shot, and then you go and say things like, "Oh, I have to stay focused."' Her imitation of Cash sounded more like a deep-voiced caveman than anything.

'It's so true,' Chloe chimed in. 'You're really going to give Lissa a run for her money as school tease.'

I felt my cheeks heat up as everyone – Cash in particular – turned their eyes on me. I took a deep breath and clenched my fists in my lap to keep from tapping on the table.

'Sorry,' Chloe said after taking a sip of her drink. 'That sounded better in my head.' She looked imploringly at me. 'I didn't mean to—'

'It's cool,' I said quickly. I looked across the table at Cash, and I felt the tension ease up a bit. 'I mean . . . really, there's no comparison. Unless Cash has his tease status formally announced at prom, I think the crown is safe with me.'

'I'll get on that – having it announced at prom,' Cash replied. 'But anyway, it'll be hard to get a date now. With this sex strike going on. Might as well just wait.'

'Hold up,' Adam said, and his attention was back on me. 'You mean the strike isn't over? Even now that you and the buffoon are done?'

I shook my head. 'No. the strike doesn't end until the rivalry does.'

'You're kidding.' Adam groaned.

'Why would you think it was over?' Ellen questioned. 'You didn't ask me about it.'

'I just assumed now that Lissa doesn't have to put up with Randy's shit, everything would go back to normal. Isn't that why this whole thing started? Because he's a douche bag?'

'Actually,' Ellen said before I could respond, '"it's not just about Randy. We've been over this a thousand times before, Adam. It's about everyone. I got pissed off when you guys shoved Luther into his locker and left him there for a whole block. I wasn't cool with that, and I'm not cool with this, either. None of the girls are. So, like Lissa said, it's not over until the rivalry is over.'

Adam rolled his eyes. 'Sure. We'll see how much longer it lasts.'

'At least our efforts are organized,' I said. I was beginning to lose the affection for him that I'd felt upon first approaching the table. 'We're supporting one another and talking to one another and helping one another through this. All the boys do is sit around and wait for us to change our minds, but that's not going to happen. The strike doesn't end until the rivalry does.'

Adam frowned at me, and he started to say something, but Chloe cut him off.

'Look, can we not fight right now?' she asked.

'Normally, I'd be all about the drama – watching it, not taking part in it, of course – but after Friday night, I'm on overload. So can we skip the debate here, kids?'

Adam slouched into his seat. 'Whatever.'

'For the record,' Ellen added, turning to Cash, "nothing in the oath the girls made says we can't date. Besides, only the current girlfriends of the teammates made the oath to begin with. There's no reason for you to use that as an excuse.'

Cash smiled at her. That winning, charming, perfect smile that won me over time and again. 'You're right,' he said. 'Strike or not, I'm not really looking for a girlfriend . . . But' – and I swear his eyes locked on mine – 'if someone special came along, I wouldn't be stupid enough to let her get away.'

'Well, that's good to hear,' Ellen said. 'As long as you're keeping your options open.'

But I didn't think it was good to hear at all. Cash had basically just told me that I wasn't worth his time. He'd let me go before, so clearly I wasn't special enough for him to date. The hope I'd carried after his visit yesterday was crushed. The way he'd looked at me when he said it left no room for misinterpretation.

'Oh, well, that's a dick move,' I blurted out. 'You basically just said that every girl you've ever flirted with wasn't worth it. And since pretty much the entire female population here has thrown themselves at you at one time or another, you're implying that you're too good for all of us.' I scrambled hastily to my feet when I saw the barely contained shock on the faces around the table.

'Lissa—' Cash began.

But I was already stumbling away.

'Where are you going?' Chloe asked.

'I'm, um, not feeling well,' I said. 'I'll see you in class later.'

Before she could ask again or I could convince myself to chance a look at Cash, I grabbed my bag and hurried towards the cafeteria door, wondering how I'd been stupid enough to think he liked me, and why it was so hard not to fall for him.

20

'Did you really think I was going to let you get away without explaining that one?'

I blinked at my reflection in the bathroom mirror, surprised to see Ellen standing behind me. She smiled and walked over to the sink next to mine.

'Chloe wanted to come,' she said. 'But I told her I hadn't been on a Lissa-in-crisis mission in a while, so she let me take this one. So what was that about?'

'Nothing.'

'Lissa, I've known you for eleven years. I can tell when you're lying. Something freaked you out enough to make you run out of the cafeteria like that. Was it Randy? Are you upset about him being with that girl?'

I shook my head. 'No . . . I mean, yeah, I am, but that's not it. It's . . . it's Cash.'

I don't know what made me decide to tell her the

truth. Maybe I was just sick of holding it in, or maybe it was the nostalgia effect, missing the days when Ellen and I would share our darkest secrets with each other. Either way, I spilled my guts to her right there in the girls' bathroom. I told her about the party over the summer, how Cash had never called me, how I couldn't fight the feelings I still had for him even though, especially after what he'd just said at the lunch table, he clearly didn't have those feelings for me. By the time I'd told her everything, we were late for class.

'Screw him,' Ellen said.

I stared at her. 'What?'

'Don't get me wrong, I like Cash. He's friends with Adam, and he's a nice guy, but if he can't see how special you are, then he doesn't deserve you. Screw him.'

'Oh.' My brain was in the gutter, because that wasn't how I'd thought she meant it at first.

'The last thing you need right now is boy drama,' Ellen said, picking my bag up off the bathroom floor and handing it to me. 'So don't bother. You're awesome no matter what he thinks, OK? Just relax a little.'

She didn't understand that that was part of the problem – I was too relaxed around Cash. It was too easy to say things I shouldn't. Like what I'd blurted out at the lunch table.

'Maybe use the extra energy to focus on taking care of the rest of us,' Ellen continued as we walked out of the bathroom. 'This strike has gone on longer than we'd anticipated. We all thought it would be two weeks, but it's been almost three, and I know they didn't show it, but a few of the girls are getting antsy. Instead of worrying about the stupid boys, why not focus on finding a way to lift morale? How does that sound?'

'Right,' I said. 'The strike. I'll focus on the strike and stop worrying about Cash and Randy. That shouldn't be too hard.'

She gave me a reassuring smile and squeezed my arm before we separated in the hallway.

But the whole idea of not thinking about Cash got overturned the next night at work. I was doing well there for about five seconds. It was hard not to notice certain things, though. Like the way he seemed to be staring at me more than normal.

I worried that he was going to confront me about what I'd said at lunch the day before, about how no one was good enough for him. But when he decided to strike up a conversation in the Religion section, I was relieved that he'd chosen a different subject.

'So have you been reading *Lysistrata* at all?' he asked, walking up behind me as I reorganized the shelf of Bibles.

'What?'

'That book I told you to read. The Greek play about the sex strike.'

'Oh, right.' Stop blushing, I told myself. I shouldn't be embarrassed to talk about this. 'No, I haven't yet. Sorry.'

'Too bad,' he said. 'I'd love to hear your take on the battle-of-the-sexes aspect, since that's kind of what's happening in real life.'

I laughed. 'It's not really a battle,' I told him, readjusting the last Bible on the shelf so that the spine faced properly outwards. It struck me how inappropriate it was to have this conversation in front of so many Bibles. 'If anything, the battle is one-sided, since the boys aren't really doing much about it.'

'That's about to change.'

I turned around, and my breath caught in my chest when I realized just how close he was standing to me. My back was pressed into the shelves, but our chests were almost touching. I had to tilt my head to look up at Cash, he was so close, and I was surprised when he didn't back away from me. Instead, he held his ground and grinned down at me.

'W-what do you mean?' I stammered, trying to stop my heart from beating out of my chest. I cleared my throat and inched to one side.

Cash blinked and stepped back a little, shoving his hands into his pockets. 'Sorry. Personal bubble, radii, all that.'

'It's OK,' I said, trying not to think about a dream that had started with us in a very similar position to the one we'd just been standing in. 'But, um . . . What do you mean about that changing? The battle-of-the-sexes thing.'

'Well, I thought about what you said yesterday, that stuff about the boys not being organized. You're right. We aren't, but that's changing.'

'How?'

'I've decided to take over,' he said. 'The same way you're leading the girls, I'm going to lead the boys.'

I blinked, stunned. Stunned and . . . hurt? Somehow, despite the weirdness between us, I'd thought Cash was on my side with this whole thing. He'd given me that play to read, after all, like it might help me. Besides, he didn't seem like the kind of guy who cared so much about getting laid. Not like Randy. Cash didn't even date.

'Why?'

'I have my reasons.' He grinned and stepped closer again. 'I'm the perfect choice, though, don't you think? Because like you, I can be focused without getting distracted.'

'I can't believe this.'

'Believe it.' Then he took a step towards me, closer than he'd been before, close enough that he could have bent down and kissed me. For a second I thought he was going to. He was so close that our knees almost touched, and I could smell his cologne, feel his breath near my ear as his head lowered just a little. One of his hands was moving towards my hip when he said, 'Because now that we're organized, this will be over before you can say "surrender."'

I hadn't even had time to take another breath when his hand reached behind me and removed a copy of the Children's Bible. 'Someone up front is looking for this,' Cash said, backing away from me. 'See you later, Lissa.' He winked, turned and walked off.

21

I was making dinner on Wednesday night – just over three weeks since the start of the strike – when I finally heard from Randy.

I'd seen him in the cafeteria and passed him in the hallway, but every time he got close, Chloe would yank me into the girls' bathroom out of sight or I'd duck into a classroom on my own, not sure whether I wanted him to apologize or just leave me alone for good. The fact was, I did miss him. We'd been together for more than a year, so it was kind of impossible not to. And I noticed that after that first day in the cafeteria, the Blonde never seemed to be with him. I wondered if he'd dropped her. Or if she'd dropped him.

I'd half expected and half hoped Randy would show up to apologize the day after Homecoming, but after the weekend passed, I assumed it wouldn't happen.

So I wasn't prepared for him to show up at my house that night.

I'd just checked on the roast when the doorbell rang. I'd started to take off my oven mitts to go and answer it when Dad called, 'I'll get it!'

I heard his wheels roll across the carpet and, a second later, the door creaked open.

The silence didn't get my attention at first – I figured it was just someone trying to sell something – and I went on setting the table. But then Dad's voice, low and tired, caught my ear.

'Randy. Can I help you?'

'Hey, Mr Daniels.' His voice sounded so upbeat. So relaxed and normal. It put a spear through my chest to hear him so happy when he'd left me so miserable. 'Is Lissa around?'

Dad sighed. 'She is, but I don't think she should see you.'

'Listen, sir,' Randy said a little more seriously. 'I just need to—'

'I know what happened at Homecoming, Randy,' Dad said. 'She told me. And I think it's best if you go.'

'But – OK. Can you just . . .'

One, two, three, four . . .

Randy let out a long breath. 'Can you just tell her that

I'm sorry? I know I screwed up, but I love her.'

'Sure thing.'

A second later the door closed. I put a plate down at Logan's usual seat and turned towards the living room. Dad was sitting in the doorway, watching me. 'I guess you heard the message.'

'I did. Thanks.'

'You didn't want to see him, did you? I should have asked.'

'No. It's fine.'

'Do you miss him?' Dad asked.

I walked over to the silverware drawer and took out the knives and forks we'd need that night. 'Yes,' I admitted. 'I miss the way he could make me laugh and his stupid grin and how sweet he could be. I just don't know if that's enough to forgive him.'

'Yeah.' Dad sighed. 'I understand that. I miss him a little, too. But seeing him just now and remembering how upset you were this weekend . . . Even if you two worked things out, I don't know that I could ever look at him the same again.'

'Well, you don't have to worry about that,' I told him, walking back to the table and putting on the finishing touches. 'I'm joining a convent after high school. No more boys.'

'Don't tease me that way,' Dad said. 'I might actually start to believe you.'

'I mean it.'

'You don't.'

I shook my head and sank down into one of the chairs. 'The roast will be done in about half an hour,' I said. 'Hopefully it's good.'

'It will be.'

I smiled, and Dad rolled back into the living room, understanding without my saying it that I needed to be alone for a minute.

It hadn't felt as good as I'd hoped to hear Randy's apology. I wasn't quite tempted to run back into his embrace, the way I'd feared I would be. Instead, I just kept imagining him kissing the Blonde and wondering, for the thousandth time, why I hadn't been good enough. Why I was only worth keeping if I'd sleep with him. He hadn't just broken my heart – he'd humiliated me in front of our friends.

I loved Randy. I knew that. But I could never trust him again.

So, sitting in my kitchen, I made myself a promise. No matter what happened, I would never take Randy back again. Not a second time. Not ever. This time, as hard as it was to accept, our relationship was really over.

By Thursday night, I'd decided that I officially hated the entire male population. As if Randy, Cash and the boys at school tormenting me about my sex life weren't enough, I also had to deal with my brother, who, it was clear, truly enjoyed torturing me.

I was already having a bad night. It started when Jenna announced that she was clocking out early – which sounds like a good thing, right? Wrong.

'That means you two have to close up together,' she told Cash and me as she grabbed her jacket off the back of her chair at the front desk. 'Finish shelving the returned books, turn off all the lights and be sure to power down the computer. And lock the doors, for God's sake.'

'Jenna, I've locked up before,' I told her. 'I know what to do.'

She narrowed her eyes at me and flipped her red hair over her shoulder. 'Just don't get distracted,' she said, tossing a not-so-subtle glance at Cash, who was standing a few feet behind me. She lowered her voice when she turned back to me and added, 'I've seen the way you look at him, and let me just tell you, workplace romances, while incredibly hot, never work out.'

Had Jenna just called my non-relationship with Cash 'incredibly hot'? Ew, ew, ew.

'There's nothing going on between—'

'Whatever you say,' she said, waving me away. But even before Jenna cut me off, I knew it was sort of a lie. Clearly there was something up between Cash and me; I just wasn't sure what. 'Just do your job. I've got to go, and I don't want to clean up after you tomorrow.'

'We'll take care of it,' Cash said, coming up beside me. I felt heat rise in my cheeks, wondering how much of my conversation with Jenna he'd heard. 'You have nothing to worry about.'

'We'll see about that.' She grabbed her bag and, without a goodbye, walked out of the library.

And I was left alone with Cash.

But that wasn't the end of it. After my shift was over I called Logan, who was already running late to pick me up.

He answered after four rings.

'Shit, Lissa, I forgot.'

'Hello to you, too, dearest brother.'

'Can you get another ride?' Logan asked.

'Why? Where are you?'

'I've got a date tonight,' he said. 'I'm driving to meet her right now. I'm sorry, Lissa. I totally forgot it was a Thursday.'

'Are you kidding me?' I asked, hoping it was just a

coincidence that Jenna had left early tonight. 'Logan, come on.'

'Sorry, Lissa. Call someone to come and get you,' he said. 'I'll make it up to you later. Gotta go. 'Bye.'

Click.

'Damn it,' I muttered, shoving my phone in the back pocket of my jeans.

'Hey,' Cash said, brushing past me (deliberately, I was sure) on his way to the exit. 'Everything OK? Do you need a ride?'

I sighed, knowing I didn't have much of a choice. 'Yeah, I do. Do you mind?'

'Not at all.' He reached up and flipped the light switch by the door, plunging us into darkness. I gasped, startled by my sudden blindness, and Cash said, "Sorry. Should I turn it back on?'

'No, it's fine,' I said. I was only a few yards from the door. I'd have to be a real klutz not to be able to successfully close that space in the dark.

I took a few fumbling steps towards Cash and the exit, but right before I made it to the door, my sandal snagged on a wrinkle in the rug, sending me stumbling forward. Naturally, I fell right into Cash's arms. God, he was good. This was clearly arranged to make me crazy. Now that he was leading the boys' side, distracting

217

me would obviously be his goal. And he knew just how to do it, too.

'You OK?' he asked, his lips only a few inches above my left ear, sending a chill down my spine.

'You're doing this on purpose!' I snapped. I don't think I really meant to say it out loud, but as always, the words just seemed to spill out when I was around Cash.

'Doing what on purpose?'

Torturing me.

Teasing me.

Trying to trick me into ending the strike.

'Nothing,' I said stiffly, shrugging out of his arms and scrambling away. I found the door and pushed it open. 'Lock up from the inside and go out the employee exit. I'll meet you at your car.' I paused and cleared my throat before adding, 'Um, please?'

'All right.' I could just make out the green of his eyes, and for a moment I considered moving back to him, letting his arms wrap around me again, and acting on a few impulses I could only excuse in the dark.

But I didn't. Instead, I hurried out of the door and went to wait in front of Cash's car.

A few minutes later he walked out of the side door and crossed the parking lot to meet me. He smiled as he unlocked the car and opened the passenger door for me. 'Here you go,' he said.

'Thanks,' I mumbled, sliding in. This was all Logan's fault, and Cash was just being a jerk, toying with me this way. I hated boys. All of them.

I was more determined than ever to lead the girls to victory over the rivalry and the guys who broke our hearts and messed with our heads. We had to win.

That night, after dinner, I went upstairs to do my homework. I was halfway through my physics assignment when I caught sight of the copy of *Lysistrata* Cash had lent me, lying on my night-stand, untouched.

I hurried through the rest of my work without double-checking my answers the way I usually did – when was I going to use physics in real life, anyway? I wanted to major in English, not build roller coasters – and reached for the book. Cash had said there was a battle of the sexes involved. I needed to know which side won.

22

The third slumber party was held that Saturday night at Kelsey's house. A few girls made excuses not to come because, well, they couldn't stand Kelsey and didn't want to be anywhere near her 'fortress of evil'. But I managed to convince Chloe not to bail, and we headed over together at around eight.

By that point, I wasn't getting nearly so anxious about the slumber parties. I'd got to know all the girls pretty well, and I was even getting used to the crowded bedrooms. That night, I was actually looking forward to the sleepover.

Turns out, Kelsey probably should have been throwing the slumber parties all along. Her place was huge. Especially her bedroom. It was as big as my living room and featured a giant wall-to-wall window looking out over her backyard, where there was an Olympic-size swimming pool and a swing set – the latter, I'm guessing, belonged to Kelsey's little brothers.

'Rich bitch,' Chloe muttered when we walked into the room.

'Be nice,' I hissed. Part of me wanted to tell her what Kelsey had told me in my kitchen – that she only hated Chloe because she was jealous. But Kelsey wouldn't want her to know that, so I kept my mouth shut. Maybe they'd be happier hating each other, anyway. It kept both of them from getting bored.

We took our places on a small love seat across from Kelsey's bed. Kelsey had just run down to let in a few more girls, but we'd arrived a little early, so hardly anyone was there yet.

'Why does anyone need a bedroom this big?' Chloe asked. 'Seriously.'

'I don't know, but I'm not complaining. We won't be so crammed in tonight. Please be nice, OK? I really don't want her to kick you out, and you know she'll be on the lookout for any excuse to do it.'

Chloe sighed dramatically. 'Fine. I'll be on my best behaviour.'

'Thank you.'

Just then, Kelsey walked back into the room with Ellen, Susan, Mary and a few of the soccer players' girlfriends. 'Take a seat wherever you're comfortable,' Kelsey said. 'Just don't make a mess.'

'She treats us like we're five,' Chloe growled.

'I do the same thing,' I reminded her in a whisper. 'And you don't complain.'

'Yeah, but I like you. That's the difference.'

I nudged her foot with mine and she fell silent.

Ten minutes later the rest of the girls had arrived, and Kelsey was playing hostess, passing around a plate of mini-cupcakes and retrieving extra pillows for people to sit on. It was a side of her I'd never seen, and it amused me. I think Chloe was getting a kick out of it, too, because she kept glancing at me and giggling between cupcakes.

'So let's get started,' Kelsey said after the cupcakes had been passed around. She sat on her bed and crossed her legs. 'What's on the agenda for tonight?'

'Dude, it's a slumber party, not a student council meeting,' Chloe said.

'But we usually do have something planned to talk about,' Susan argued, stretching out on her stomach on the floor. 'The first week it was funny stories about making the boys miserable. Last week it was Lissa's virginity.'

'That sounds so awkward when you say it out loud,' Ellen joked.

'We could tell funny stories again.'

'Yeah, that could be fun.'

I nodded at the suggestions tossed out by a few of the girls. This time, though, I wouldn't be sharing. Catching your boyfriend cheating on you at Homecoming isn't that funny, really.

Apparently Mary was thinking the same thing, because she asked, 'Does anyone have stories, though? I don't, really.'

'Yeah, me neither.'

'Not me.'

Chloe and I exchanged a 'the ship is sinking' look, and across the room, I could see a crestfallen expression on Kelsey's face. She must have had high hopes for the first slumber party she'd hosted. I felt bad, but I didn't know what to do. I started feeling nervous, that out-of-control feeling I got when I didn't have a plan or a routine to follow, and I had the sudden urge to declare a game of hide-and-seek, the way I had at Ellen's twelfth birthday party when things had started going wrong. Somehow, I didn't think that would work this time.

'Hey,' someone said from across the room, "why are the boys outside?'

'What?'

Everyone scrambled across the room to look out the window, saving me the effort of finding something for us to do. I leaned against the sill, wedged between Chloe and Ellen, and looked down at Kelsey's swimming pool, where a group of boys huddled, as if making a plan before a football play.

'What are they doing?' Kelsey asked.

No one had a chance to hypothesize before we got our answer. The huddle broke and one by one the boys approached the edge of the pool. We were only on the second floor, so I could make out the faces of the boys – especially when they started looking up at Kelsey's window, where I was sure they could see all of us gawking down at them.

The group was a mix of football and soccer players. I could see Shane, and Susan's boyfriend, Luther, from where I stood. A second later I identified Kelsey's boyfriend, Terry, and then there was Adam. I counted seventeen boys total, including the boyfriends of each of the girls attending the slumber party. No Randy in sight, though.

But at the back of the group, grinning up at me, was Cash.

'Oh, no,' I murmured.

'What the hell is going on?' Chloe asked.

I thought I knew, but I didn't answer. I didn't know how to answer.

On the ground, Cash gave a signal, and the guys all lined up by the pool. In unison, they stripped off their shirts and tossed them on to the grass. An audible sigh – like the ones you hear on a sitcom that is 'filmed in front of a live studio audience' – filled the room. It was almost funny, really. Such a strong reaction to a bunch of shirtless boys.

Not that I was judging. I mean, these were some of the most athletic boys in school, which meant they had some of the best bodies. It was like a museum of muscled arms and six-pack abs on Kelsey's lawn. And, naturally, I caught myself staring at Cash. It was the first time I'd seen him shirtless, and even from a distance – wow.

This was not going to help that whole sexual-tension issue at work.

He gave another signal and the boys slid out of their jeans. I felt myself blush and almost looked away before realizing they were all wearing swimming trunks beneath their clothes.

'Oh my God,' I heard Kelsey whisper. 'We've got to get them out of here. If my parents see this . . .' But she didn't move away from the window.

Stripped down to their trunks, the boys began

jumping into Kelsey's pool. It was nearing the end of September, but the weather was still nice enough to allow for good swimming conditions. The boys bobbed and splashed around the pool, looking up every few minutes, occasionally waving or calling out to us to come join them.

'Maybe we should—' Susan began.

'No,' I said quickly. 'No, no, no. This is just their way of messing with us. They get half-naked and wet and think that'll be enough to make us give up the strike. Well, it won't work.'

'You sure about that?' Chloe asked, cocking her head to the side and clearly ogling Shane, who'd just cannon-balled into the pool. 'You have to admit these boys are pretty fine, Lissa. This was a good move . . . I think I want to go swimming.'

'Yeah,' a few other girls said. 'Me too.'

'It doesn't mean anything has to happen.'

'We don't have to do anything – just swim. We weren't doing anything fun in here anyway, right?'

'No!' I cried again. Quickly, I began shoving the girls away from the window. Violent protests met my efforts, but I pushed them anyway. 'We go down there, and they make another move,' I said. 'This is war, and that's a trap.' A good one, I added mentally, focusing all of my energy on not turning to look out the window again to stare at Cash.

'I know you all want to go down there,' I said. 'But the rivalry isn't over. The boys will just use this to coerce us into breaking our oath. You don't want that, do you?'

But no one answered; they all just kept gazing outside.

Mary gave me a look and hurried to the opposite end of the window to help. For a tiny girl, she could put up a fight. Together we managed to shove all the frustrated girls back, and then Mary immediately closed the blinds.

The girls grumbled and went back to their original seats on Kelsey's bed and floor. Outside, the sounds of the boys calling us back, imploring us to come down and join them, could still be heard.

'This is such a farce,' I muttered to Mary. I felt like I was in the middle of a scene from a teen comedy. I was half expecting an epic action montage of boys trying to get our attention, set to Blondie's 'One Way or Another', to follow this ridiculous moment in my life.

'Hey,' Kelsey said, tapping me on the shoulder and whispering into my ear so the others didn't hear, "I'm going downstairs to make the guys leave before my parents come home and flip their shit.'

'Oh, no, you don't,' I said quickly. 'Don't think—'

'Lissa,' she said, shaking her head. 'Believe me, you

don't have to worry about me being tempted.'

I frowned at her, but I knew she was right. If there was anyone I could trust here, it was Kelsey. Now, that was a crazy thought, but it was true. She'd admitted to me that she didn't really enjoy sex, so why would she be tempted to break the oath? I nodded and she edged out the door quietly while I got the others' attention.

'OK, all of you, listen,' I said. 'The boys are getting organized now. You saw that. They're fighting back because they want sex. The rivalry isn't over, but they want the strike to end. Things are about to get harder for us.'

Mary giggled at me. 'You sound like an army commander.'

'You should see her play hide-and-seek,' Ellen joked.

'Focus,' I snapped. God, I really did sound like I was in the military. But it was necessary now, wasn't it? By making himself the leader of the boys' side, Cash had pretty much turned this into a war. If the boys had tactics, we needed ways to combat them.

'So what do we do?' Ellen asked.

'We've got to turn the tables,' I answered. 'Fight fire with fire. They want to get half-naked and seduce us? I say we do the same. Push them a little, make them want us. They're guys. They'll crack before we do.'

'I thought we weren't going to be teases,' Chloe said. 'That's what you said at the first meeting.'

'That was before the boys decided to make this a fight. They gave us no choice,' I argued. 'I'm not suggesting anything extreme – just wearing shirts that are a little lower-cut than normal, or showing a little leg. That's all it will take.'

'That actually sounds kind of fun,' Ellen said, grinning. 'I have a new dress I've been dying for an excuse to wear. Maybe my date tomorrow night is just the occasion.'

A few other girls smiled and whooped in agreement, planning out their methods of temptation.

After the chatter died down, Susan sighed and glanced at the closed blinds over the window. 'I just feel so . . . dirty. Like, I don't know. Right now, I feel like such a perv.'

'Me, too,' Ellen said. 'God, I never thought I'd miss fooling around this much. It's so embarrassing.'

'Why?' Chloe asked. 'Because the boys got you all hot and bothered?'

Ellen shrugged, not looking at her.

Chloe sighed. 'OK, I don't get you guys. Maybe I'm, like, a bad example of the female race or something, but what is so wrong with thinking about sex? So the fuck what? Guys do it.'

'That's because they're guys,' Ellen said. 'It's normal for them.'

'So if it's OK for them, why do girls have to feel dirty when they think about it?' Chloe demanded. She looked over at me for help, but all I could do was shrug. Clearly, I was just as much in the dark as the others. Only Chloe seemed to know what she was doing here.

'Look. This is stupid,' she said. 'We live in a supposedly equal society, so what's the big deal? I'm not ashamed to think about sex. Or talk about it. Or have it.'

'Yeah, and look at the way people talk about you.' Kelsey was standing in the doorway of her bedroom, arms crossed over her chest. I hadn't even heard her come back upstairs.

'I'm not sorry for who I am,' Chloe said flatly.

Kelsey's arms dropped to her sides, and she stepped into the room. 'Then you're lucky, because not all of us can say that.'

We locked eyes for a second before she looked at the other girls.

'I don't like sex,' Kelsey said, shrugging. 'I used to think that made me weird. Or that if I told anyone, they'd make fun of me or call me a lesbian or something. I'm not; I just don't enjoy it. But if we're being all open and honest . . . Chloe's comfortable with who she is, and

Mary and Lissa came clean, so it's my turn.'

Chloe stared at Kelsey in awe. I wondered if she was in shock, hearing from someone who didn't enjoy sex. But she said, 'Did you just kind of give me a compliment?'

'Don't get used to it.'

'I refuse to go down on Luther,' Susan said. Everyone turned to look at her, but she just tossed her dark braids over one shoulder. 'What? Something about it just freaks me out. There are some places mouths just aren't meant to go, you know?'

'That's the only thing I'll do with my boyfriend,' someone said from the back of the room. 'To me, that's less scary than going all the way.'

I smiled to myself. Mary and I weren't the only virgins in the room – and I hadn't been the only one keeping my lack of experience quiet. It made me feel better, knowing I wasn't alone, but realizing this also made me kind of sad. Why had I been afraid to admit I was a virgin? Why was anyone?

'So, like, do you hate sex with everyone, or just with Terry?' Chloe asked Kelsey.

'I don't hate it. I just don't really enjoy it.'

'OK, but that didn't answer my question. Is it bad with everyone, or just Terry?'

Kelsey shifted uneasily. 'Not that it's any of your business, but I've only ever been with Terry, so . . .'

'So he probably just sucks in bed.'

'Chloe,' I chided. 'Be nice.'

'What?' she asked. 'A lot of teenage boys suck. Believe me, I know. But Kelsey should be thrilled. This means there's hope for her yet.'

'Unless I stay with Terry,' Kelsey replied pointedly.

Chloe scoffed. 'Please. High school sweethearts don't last forever – and if they do, they end up miserable and start having affairs early. Ask my dad.'

'Hey, Kelsey, do you fake it?' Ellen said, changing the subject. Thank God. 'Like . . . orgasms?'

Kelsey turned even redder. 'Yes. Why?'

'Because I have a few times, too,' Ellen admitted. 'Not always, but Adam gets defensive if he thinks I'm not enjoying it, so . . . But anyway, I don't think it's that uncommon, actually. I learned how to fake it because of that Meg Ryan scene in *When Harry Met Sally*.'

'When Harry met who?'

'It's an old eighties movie,' Ellen said, shrugging. 'I saw it on VH1.'

'I can honestly say I have never faked it,' Chloe said, grinning. 'Of course, I'm a bitch, so if I can't get off, I just let the guy know how lame he is.'

'And that,' Susan chirped, 'is why Rod Copland went from a stud to a cracked-out emo kid. Chloe salted his game.'

'Hey, honesty's the best policy,' Chloe said.

Susan looked a little embarrassed. 'Yeah . . . honesty. I kind of suck at that. I told Luther he was my first even though I hooked up with a guy in my brother's frat last year, before we started dating.'

'So he thought you were a virgin?' I asked.

Susan nodded, looking a little ashamed.

'Couldn't he, like, tell, though?' Kelsey asked.

'Not really,' Susan said sheepishly. 'It was his first time, so he didn't exactly know what he was looking for . . . if you know what I mean.'

'But why would you lie?' Mary asked.

'I didn't want him to be embarrassed. Like, I didn't want him to feel bad because I'd done it and he hadn't. Besides, would you be very proud of hooking up with a skeezy frat boy at a costume party?'

'Depends,' Chloe said. 'If he had a cool costume—'

'He was dressed as SpongeBob,' Susan admitted.

'Ugh. OK, yeah. I'd lie too.'

The chatter bubbled over as everyone began swapping experiences and theories and philosophies concerning sex. I was so fascinated by everyone's different takes on the subject that I forgot to be embarrassed. Maybe if we'd discussed this sooner, I wouldn't have been so afraid to admit I was a virgin. Maybe the others wouldn't have given Mary such a hard time about it at our first meeting.

I turned and locked eyes with Mary. She was smiling at me, and I knew she was thinking the same thing. She wasn't weird at all. None of us were.

'It's so screwed up, the standards,' Kelsey said abruptly, tossing a pillow towards the ground. 'You should like it, but you shouldn't like it too much or talk about how much you like it. You should do it, but you shouldn't do it with too many people or talk about how much you're doing it. It's like there are so many rules, but none of them make sense.'

'Then maybe we should make up our own rules?' Mary suggested nervously. 'Like . . . change the game, you know?'

'I think that's what we're doing now,' Chloe said. 'Just by having this conversation. The other rules can go screw themselves.'

'Wow, Chloe,' Ellen said. 'That is so deep.'

'I know, right? I should be a freaking philosopher or something.'

I stretched out on my stomach, elbows pressed into the carpet and chin resting in my hands. 'I like it.

The rules can go screw themselves. It ought to be our group motto.'

'Oh my God.' Mary giggled. 'We need T-shirts.'

As the room erupted into chatter again, I realized just how happy I was that I'd started the strike. Sure, it had started because of the sports feud, but now it was about so much more. It was about independence and confidence and breaking free of stereotypes and labels. Now, win or lose, I had these girls – these friends – who'd proven to me that there was no such thing as normal, and that I had nothing to be ashamed of. Even if the boys won, I'd got something out of this strike. Something important.

Not that the boys had a chance in hell of winning. I was personally going to make sure that didn't happen.

23

'Nice job leading the girls the other night.'

I was crouched down on the floor of the Reference section, alphabetizing the encyclopaedias, when I heard Cash's voice behind me. Startled, I jumped and smacked the top of my head against the shelf with a loud thwack.

'Augh,' I groaned.

'Oh, shit. Lissa, are you OK?' He knelt down and turned me to face him, his eyebrows pinched over concerned green eyes that made me forget the throbbing pain in my skull – but only for a second. 'Do you need me to get an ice pack or something?'

'No, it's fine, but you have got to stop sneaking up on me,' I said through clenched teeth. 'God, that hurt.'

'I'm so sorry,' Cash said. Before I could stop him, he'd reached out and cupped a hand over the back of my head, his fingers gently stroking the place where my skull had collided with the wooden shelf. 'That was an accident.'

Sure it was, I wanted to snap. But of course what came out of my mouth was completely different. 'It's all right.' I cleared my throat. 'Did you need something, Cash?'

He let out a small chuckle. 'Not really. It doesn't matter.'

'Glad to know my pain is in vain.'

'Well, at least you're a poet. That's some consolation.'

I rolled my eyes at him and he grinned. 'So,' he said, still stroking my head in gentle, soothing motions, 'how was your weekend?'

'It was all right – until a bunch of idiot boys decided to crash the slumber party I was attending.'

'Damn, what a shame,' Cash said innocently.

'Uh-huh . . . how was yours?'

'Pretty good . . . except for the part where I got kicked off Kelsey's lawn. Speaking of which, does she really have a Rottweiler trained to attack on command?'

I couldn't help but smile at that. Kelsey did have a Rottweiler – Gidget – but from what I'd witnessed at her house on Saturday, Gidget was a lazy, fat dog who barely left her spot on the living-room floor, let alone attacked people.

'Yes,' I said. 'Yes, she does.'

'Scary.'

'Yeah.'

There was a short pause, and then he said, 'Seriously, though. How have you been? I haven't really asked you since we went for that walk last weekend because I didn't want to upset you or anything, but . . . how are you? With the whole Randy thing, I mean.'

'Oh.' I let out a long breath. 'I'm OK. I've just been avoiding him.'

'I hear he wants you back.'

'He'll have to get over it.'

Cash smiled. 'I take it you're not so interested in rekindling the romance.'

'Definitely not,' I said. 'Don't get me wrong – I miss him sometimes, the good things about him, anyway, but not enough to get back together with him. I can't trust him any more.'

'Well, I'm glad,' Cash said. Then he quickly added, "Not that you can't trust him. I'm sorry about that. I'm just . . . I'm glad you're not getting back with him.'

'Why?' I asked slowly, remembering the awkwardness at the lunch table last week when I'd stormed away, how he'd said he'd only consider dating someone special. Before then, I'd dared to hope that his support, his encouragement for me to stay away from Randy, had been a little selfish on his part. That maybe he liked me. That sour moment at the lunch table had squashed that hope, but maybe . . .

'Because.' Cash's fingers stilled, resting lightly against the back of my head, which didn't hurt any more. He looked down at me for a long second before continuing. 'Because I want to see you with someone better than him. Someone who will see how lucky they are to have you.'

I bit my lip, nervous but determined to ask my next question. 'Do you happen to have someone particular in mind, Cash?'

'Maybe.'

We stared at each other for a long, long time. Then Cash's hand slid down from my head to the back of my neck, and he gently pulled me towards him. It was like a slow-motion scene in a movie. I had plenty of time to turn my head, to jerk away, to say 'stop,' but I didn't move, didn't speak, didn't breathe. Instead, I watched his head lower towards mine and felt his free hand fall on to my knee. My eyes shut, and I managed a quick, anxious gasp of air.

And then Cash Sterling kissed me.

My heart raced as Cash's lips moved over mine. I opened my mouth to his as my arms wrapped around his neck. His hand slid up my thigh and came to rest on my hip. I felt his finger curl into the belt loop of my jeans, tugging me a little closer to him. I moved forward willingly, eagerly, needing to be next to him, to touch him.

My body was riddled with electric shocks as his kisses grew more intense. My fingers grasped at his short brown hair, pulling him to me. I'd never felt like this, like I wanted to climb into another person's skin. Like I wanted every inch of him to touch every inch of me, to twine myself around him and never let go. I'd never kissed anyone this way.

Not even Randy.

I was elated. He'd kissed me. Again. He did still like me. He must have realized what a mistake he'd made by never calling me.

My skin was on fire as we pressed closer to each other. I found myself climbing into Cash's lap, straddling his hips as his hands slid to the small of my back, pulling me towards him.

'Oh my God, are you kidding me?'

Cash's mouth jerked away from mine as Jenna's voice ripped through the heated silence. It took me a minute to catch my breath, but I could already feel my cheeks burning, realizing the delicate position I'd got myself into. I scurried out of Cash's lap, straightening my slightly twisted T-shirt and running my fingers through my hair.

'Nice, Lissa,' she snapped when I tentatively looked up at her. 'Didn't I warn you about this?'

'I'll get back to work,' I said, stumbling to my feet. Cash did the same.

'Yes, please do,' Jenna said. 'There's a little girl here who needs help using the card catalogue. Why don't you do that and let Cash finish with the encyclopaedias. Perhaps you two shouldn't work together from now on, if you'll be distracting each other.'

'M-maybe,' I stammered. 'I'll go help with the, um, catalogue.'

Deliberately avoiding Cash's eyes, I hurried off towards the front of the library.

He caught up with me a few minutes later, though. Our paths crossed when we each came to pick up some of the books that needed to be shelved.

'Hey,' he said, pointing down at the stack of books in his arms. 'Looks like someone else just finished reading *Lysistrata*. Maybe it was one of the other strike girls.'

'It could be,' I said.

He smirked and went on shelving while I walked upstairs to put away some of the children's books. I'd just shelved a copy of *Hop on Pop* when Cash's words hit me.

The strike.

Shit.

I felt sudden tears sting at the corners of my eyes as I realized, with a miserable jolt, that I'd just been used again. That kiss hadn't been Cash telling me he still liked me. He'd been trying to mess with me, to make me break my oath. He was using my feelings against me so that the boys would win.

I was an idiot to keep getting my hopes up.

24

'You OK, sweetheart?'

'Huh?' I looked across the dinner table at Dad. His forehead was creased with concern, his eyes searching my face. I blushed and turned away. Truthfully, I'd been thinking about what had happened with Cash in the library. 'I'm fine, Dad. Why?'

'Nothing. You just seem quieter than usual,' he said. 'I mean, you haven't even asked me what I've eaten today or lectured me about the health risks of this steak I went behind your back and grilled.' He jabbed his fork into a pink, juicy piece of meat and brought it to his lips.

'Sorry.' I sighed. 'I'm just . . . distracted. But you're right. You really shouldn't be eating that. You need to have a salad for dinner most nights. I'll let it slide tonight, I guess.'

Dad chuckled and swallowed the bite of steak. 'Oh,

honey. Something has to be wrong. Normally you'd whisk the plate away and force a salad on me this instant. Is it Randy? Did you run into him at school or something?'

'No,' I said. 'It's . . . I'm just exhausted.' I pushed my plate away, the food barely touched, and got to my feet. 'I'm going to go upstairs and lie down for a while, I think.'

'All right,' Dad said. 'You're sure you're OK? Do you need some Tylenol or—'

'I'm fine,' I assured him. 'I just need to . . . to relax. When Logan gets back from his date with Mystery Girl, can you have him take out the garbage, please?'

'Sure.'

'Thanks.' I walked over and kissed him on the cheek. 'And enjoy the steak while you can. I'm getting back on my guard tomorrow.'

He grinned and took another large bite, clearly savouring it. After he'd chewed, he said, 'Just yell if you need anything.'

I nodded and hurried upstairs. The truth was, I didn't need to lie down, and I wasn't tired. In fact, I was wide awake, my body still on edge from that kiss Cash and I had shared. What I really needed was to talk about it – and not with my father. God, that would have been a whole new level of awkward.

When I got to my bedroom, the first thing I did was

call Chloe. I thought about dialling Ellen's number, since I'd already confessed to her about my and Cash's brief history, but somehow I needed Chloe for this one. After all, she always seemed to have the answers, even when the rest of us were clueless.

'What's up, love?' Chloe asked as soon as she answered the phone.

I took a deep breath. 'OK,' I said. 'I have something to tell you, and don't be mad at me for hiding it because I was too embarrassed to talk about it, but now I need your help.'

'Whoa,' Chloe said. 'Slow down. Is this some kind of freaky soap-opera scandal? Lissa Daniels, are you secretly a man?'

I let out my breath and laughed, and so did she. This was why I loved Chloe.

'OK,' she said. 'I'll try not to get mad. Now, what's the deal?'

'I made out with Cash.'

'Wait – Cash Sterling? Holy shit. How did that happen? He doesn't go that far with anyone, the tease.'

I flinched, remembering the way Randy's friends had barked insults like that at me. *Cock tease* . . .

'I can't believe this,' Chloe continued. 'OK, so when? Where? And, most important, how was it?'

'Today, the library . . . and' – I sighed – 'fantastic. Even better than the first time.'

'The first time? What the fuck, Lissa?'

'Yeah, that's the part I didn't tell you about. Don't be mad, OK?' And I proceeded to tell her about the party over the summer, how he'd kissed me and told me I was amazing, only to reject me in the end. I even told her about the goofy little Star Game.

Chloe listened in silence until I'd finished.

Then she made a thoughtful noise before saying, "But he kissed you again. That's got to mean something.'

'It means he's an asshole.' I flopped on to my bed, stretching out on my back and staring up at the ceiling with my phone tucked between my shoulder and ear. 'I thought it meant something at first, too, but then he mentioned the strike and I realized what he was doing. His plan this weekend didn't work, so he was trying a different strategy. He knows I like him, and he was trying to get me to break my oath.'

'Hmm, maybe,' Chloe said. 'Or maybe he's hot for you and just thought making out with you on the library floor seemed like a good idea.'

'I wish,' I admitted quietly, knowing Chloe could hear me, knowing I could trust her. 'It just makes more sense for it to be tied to the strike, though. Otherwise,

246

why now? Why do this after he's told me he's leading the boys' side? If he really liked me, he would have acted on it this summer. I opened the door for him. We both know I don't do that often. And he left me hanging.'

'Look, Lissa, even if he doesn't like you the way you like him, he's clearly more attracted to you than to any other girl in Hamilton,' she pointed out. 'I don't know of anyone else he's kissed, and he's kissed you twice now. So cheer up, because he has to be attracted to you.'

'Right, he just doesn't think I'm "special" enough to actually date,' I said, thinking back to the awkward moment at the lunch table last week. 'Forget how I feel about him – I just want to win. To show him that his sneaky little plans won't work on me. On any of the girls . . . hey, wait a second.' I bolted upright. 'I've got it. I know how to win.'

'Uh-huh,' Chloe said slowly. 'And what is this shiny new idea?'

'You're right,' I told her. 'Cash is obviously at least physically attracted to me – the way he was all over me today in the Reference section couldn't have entirely been an act. And that's all I need – for him to be physically attracted to me. I don't have to be special. I just have to turn him on.'

Chloe hesitated. 'I think I know where you're

247

going with this, but I'm not sure—'

'It's perfect,' I told her. 'If I can get Cash to want to sleep with me, and then turn him down at the last minute, it'll leave him frustrated and wanting me even more. He doesn't have to want to date me, just to have sex with me. How hard can that be? I'll drag him along until he makes the other boys give up. They lose Cash, they lose their organization. It's almost foolproof.'

'Lissa, listen to me a second,' Chloe said. 'I don't think this is a good idea, OK? When you started this, it was just about ending the rivalry. About making the boys stop acting like idiots. All we were doing was withholding sex. Yeah, sometimes it was funny and a little conniving, but it wasn't cruel. Now some of the other girls are taking it further, like you told them, and that kind of worries me anyway, but what you're considering is . . . Well, it's pretty fucked up. Withholding is one thing; messing with Cash's head that way is a whole new issue. You're not just saying "no", you're playing a serious mind game.'

'I'm just giving him what he deserves. After the way he's screwed with my head, I think I have every right to screw with his.'

'Maybe, but Lissa, this sounds like it's about revenge for your hurt feelings over his rejecting you. Is this

248

really about the rivalry any more?'

'Yes,' I snapped. 'Come on, Chloe. Be on my side here? This is about ending the rivalry and us girls reclaiming our sexual freedom. And the only thing we have to do to win is for me to seduce Cash. No one else can do it, after all. I've already got further with him than anyone in Hamilton.' I kind of felt like laughing maniacally at the sheer simplicity of this plan. 'If I can do this, we win. The war is over.'

She sighed. 'Fine,' she said. 'Just be careful.'

'Trust me,' I told her. 'You have nothing to worry about. If anyone can control this kind of situation, it's me. You're talking to the girl who managed to fight off the horny high school quarterback for over a year. I think I can handle an evening with Cash Sterling.'

I ignored the little voice in the back of my head reminding me that today, in the library, I'd been anything but in control.

But I'll be prepared this time, I told myself. I'll have the power, and Cash will never know what hit him.

I grinned, knowing no one was around to see. 'But, hey, Chloe . . . Can you drive me home from school tomorrow? I think I'll need your help with part of this plan.'

I spent the next day scheming. Chloe came over Wednesday afternoon and helped me plan the outfit

I'd wear on Thursday, when Cash and I would work together again. We decided on a short black skirt that, while covering the tops of my thighs, gave a great look at my long legs – one of my best physical assets. Chloe made me try on a number of tops to go with it, but in the end she told me to wear one of my old T-shirts that was just a little too tight, drawing some attention to my chest without distracting from my legs. She said overdoing it would be too obvious and would make me look a little trashy.

'Have you seen the dress Ellen wore on her date? She texted me a picture. It was cute, but it made her look too much like a stripper,' she said, flicking through my closet. 'And speaking of trashy, did you hear about Susan's plans for this weekend? Her parents are out, so she invited Luther back to her house. Apparently she bought some lingerie at a store in Oak Hill, and she told him she wanted to "model it" for him. Funny, since she's the one who was concerned about how ethical using sex was, right?'

'Kind of,' I said. 'But I'm glad she has some tactics, too. We need all the help we can get now that the boys are trying to bring down the strike.'

Chloe gave me a look that I couldn't quite read – something like disappointment or worry. Before I could ask, she pulled a hanger from my closet and presented me with a baby-pink T-shirt. 'This one. It's a good colour for you.'

After she'd gone, I modelled several different hairstyles in front of the bathroom mirror, trying to decide which made me look the sexiest. Almost everything made me look cute, like an innocent, virginal little girl – the innocent, virginal little girl that, in reality, I guess I was. But that wouldn't work. I needed something hot. I needed to look mature and enticing. Everything about my appearance needed to make Cash want to rip my clothes off.

I watched my reflection redden at the thought of Cash ripping my . . . Well, you know. I reminded myself that it wouldn't get that far, so there wasn't any reason to think about it. Ever. This was just a game.

After an hour and a half in the bathroom, with Logan banging on the door, telling me to hurry up so he could take a shower, I found just the right look. My shoulder-length black hair was pulled back into a high, tight ponytail that showed off my neck and gave me a sharp, mature edge. Great.

The knob rattled on the door. 'Lissa, I'm serious. Get the hell out of there so I can get cleaned up and go to bed! Some of us have work in the morning, you know.'

I opened the door. 'And some of us have to be at

school before you even wake up for work,' I told him. 'The bathroom's all yours.'

Logan rolled his eyes and shoved past me. I could smell the perfume on him just before he nudged me out of the bathroom and slammed the door. He'd been out with his mystery girlfriend almost every night this week. Even last night – he'd picked me up from the library, dropped me off at home, and then sped off to meet her again.

'Are we sure he isn't running an illegal drug operation?' I asked Dad in the kitchen while I poured myself a glass of milk. 'I mean, that would explain the frequency of these so-called dates.'

Dad laughed. 'Or maybe he just likes her a lot and wants to see her every day? Back when I first started dating your mother, I wanted to see her every single night. I couldn't be around her enough. That was how I knew I was in love with her. Even her bad jokes didn't get old.'

I walked over to the kitchen table and sat down across from him. 'But did you keep her a secret? Did you tell people you were with her?'

'Are you kidding?' Dad smiled, remembering. 'I told everyone. I was damn proud a girl like your mother was dating me. I would have shouted it from the rooftops if I could have.'

I nodded and took a sip of my milk. 'I miss her,' I said finally. 'Not as much as I used to – it was harder at first – but I still miss her. Sometimes I just want to walk in after school and talk to her, you know?'

'I know,' he said. 'Believe me, I know. I miss her every day. But you know what helps?'

'What?' I asked.

Dad reached across the table and I took his hand. 'Looking at you,' he said. 'You are just like her, Lissa. Smart and funny and beautiful – and a little bossy, too.' He grinned. 'She'd be proud of you.'

I wondered if he was right. If Mom would be proud of me. What would she think of the sex strike? What would she say about what I was planning on doing to Cash tomorrow? That was one of my biggest regrets about my mother. We'd never had the chance to talk about boys or sex or anything like that. Sometimes I wondered if that was why this whole thing was so confusing, because I didn't have a mother to discuss these issues with.

And there was no way I could talk about it with Dad. Our version of 'the talk' had been him clearing his throat awkwardly for about ten minutes straight as he attempted to explain to me the importance of condoms. I was fourteen, and, needless to say, it was an experience I never wanted to relive.

Sometimes, it made me wish Dad had remarried, that I had a stepmother. Not so much to fill in that empty space Mom had left in our lives – no one could do that – but to talk to me about things only girls could talk about. But I'd always known that would never happen. My father had been too in love with my mother to move on after her death. He'd told me once that dating would never work because he'd compare every woman to Mom – and the truth was, no one could compare.

Still, I wondered what Mom would say to me if she saw me now. Somehow, I worried she wouldn't be quite as proud of me as Dad thought.

'I'm going to bed,' I said, finishing my milk and standing. 'Are you staying up?'

'Just for a little while,' he said, rolling his chair towards the living room. 'I want to watch the news, see the sports report – you know the drill.'

'OK,' I said. 'Don't be up too long, OK? You need plenty of rest. It's a big part of staying healthy.'

Dad smiled at me. 'Good night, Lissa.'

'Night, Dad.'

I walked upstairs, readjusting a slightly crooked picture frame on the wall on my way, and got ready for bed. Tomorrow was game day.

25

I texted Logan from work the next afternoon and told him that I didn't need a ride home that night. I had another plan for what I'd be doing after work.

This time, I was the one to sneak up on Cash. He was in the magazine room at the back of the library, reorganizing a stack of *National Geographics* that some nerdy twelve-year-old had raided early in the afternoon. I stood in the doorway, watching the muscles in his back and arms flex and shift as he reached up to the shelf, right at his eye level, and placed each magazine neatly on top of the stack. The perfect order in which he arranged the magazines made me swoon a little.

I readjusted my posture, ran my hands down my skirt and took a quiet breath before strutting over to him.

'Hey,' I said, leaning against a shelf full of *Newsweek* issues.

Cash jumped.

'Oh, finally. I caught you off guard.'

He turned and grinned at me. 'Score one for Lissa.'

'Yeah, well . . . You didn't almost fall off a ladder or crack your skull on a wooden shelf, so we aren't quite even yet.'

Cash laughed and turned back to the magazines. 'What's up?'

This was the curse of Cash and me. We were doomed to never, ever acknowledge the fact that we'd kissed. I was sensing a pattern here.

'I, um, have a favour to ask,' I said. I could feel the heat rising into my face and neck, but I fought to keep calm. I'd rehearsed this, after all. This was part of the plan.

'OK. What is it?'

'I'm supposed to write a thesis for English.' I said it just like I'd practised in the bathroom mirror that morning. 'I'm working on this paper about how participating in sports affects, um, grades and stuff . . . for teenagers, you know? And, uh, Mrs Perkins says I need firsthand accounts or something to validate my arguments. Would it be OK if I interviewed you?'

Cash looked at me again. 'You want to interview me? Why don't you just interview your brother? He played football in high school, didn't he?'

'Um, yeah . . . But that's only one sport,' I pointed out. 'I need people in different types. So I'd love your point of view on soccer and how it affects your health.'

'You mean my grades?'

Crap. I was already screwing up the story.

'Right. Grades. So can you do an interview for me?' I batted my eyelashes in an attempt to appear seductive, but I was pretty sure I just came off looking ridiculous. 'Please?'

Cash smiled at me as he put away the most recent copy of *National Geographic*, the last that needed to be shelved. 'You sure you want to talk to me?' he asked. 'Won't it be weird with this whole strike thing? We are kind of enemies at the moment, aren't we?'

'Enemies?' I forced a laugh. 'No, of course not. It'll be fine. As long as you don't try any of your battle tactics on me, I'll be good.' I winked at him, and he grinned.

I kind of revelled in my own hypocrisy for a minute. He had no idea what was coming.

'I guess it's cool,' he said. 'But we can't do it here; Jenna will be on us in a heartbeat. When do you need it by? You could just email me the questions.'

'I was thinking in person,' I said a little too fast. God, I needed to calm down. Focus. 'And, um, what about

257

tonight? After work? We could do the interview at your place if it's all right.'

He thought about it for a second, then nodded. 'OK. That'll work. I'll give you a ride home afterwards. Sound good?'

'Perfect,' I said with a grin. 'I'll see you after work.'

When I walked out of the room, I made sure to move my hips in a sexy sort of sway, causing my skirt to swish around my thighs in just the right way to show more leg, but not too much more. I hoped Cash was watching me leave. I didn't look back to check.

Cash drove me to his house that night after work. It was the first time I'd ever been there, and I was eager to see where he lived. The answer surprised me.

The Sterlings lived in a trailer on the east side of town, only a few blocks from the cramped apartment complex where Chloe lived with her mom. Somehow, I expected a guy as handsome and popular as Cash to live in a picket-fence type of house, only nicer and bigger than my home. Not that I was judging or anything. It was just unexpected.

Cash seemed a little embarrassed about letting me see his home. He smiled and opened the car door for me and walked me up to the small porch, but I could tell by the way he didn't meet my eyes that he was uncomfortable.

Did he think I was the type to think less of him for where he lived? I really wasn't, and the fact that he obviously felt that way stung.

'Sorry, the place is kind of a mess,' he said, unlocking the front door. 'I don't bring friends over very often.'

'Oh.'

Or maybe I should just be honoured that he'd agreed to bring me here at all. He could have said no, but instead he'd let me see his home. Maybe that made me special.

Not special enough for him to date, but special in some sort of distant way.

'My parents aren't here,' he said, letting me walk in ahead of him. 'Mom's at the hospital – she's a nurse, and she's got a long shift tonight. And Dad's staying overnight in Chicago, interviewing for a new job. So it's just us. Are you OK with that?'

'Yes, of course.' I could feel my heart pounding in my chest. I was alone with him. No Jenna. No one to break us apart if things got heated. 'I'm OK with that.'

Cash gave me a small grin before gesturing for me to follow him towards the kitchen. It really wasn't as messy as he'd claimed.

The dishes were all washed, just sitting in the drainer, waiting to be put away. Actually, his place seemed almost as clean as mine.

259

'Can I get you anything to drink?' he asked.

'Oh, no, I'm . . . I'm fine.' I could feel myself bouncing, my heel tapping an anxious rhythm on the linoleum. I needed to get this over with before my insides exploded. 'So can I see your room?'

He looked a little startled, and I worried that I'd been a tad too forward, but he just nodded and gestured towards the hallway that led out of the kitchen. I walked down the narrow hall ahead of him, checking out the pictures that had been hung on the walls. Photo upon photo of Cash and his family.

I stopped and smiled at a particular picture that stood out to me. A little boy, presumably Cash, was standing on a soccer field, clutching a black-and-white soccer ball in his small hands. He couldn't have been more than four or five years old. On either side of him stood his parents: a pretty blond woman with her hand on her son's head, pushing long brown bangs from his bright green eyes, and a stocky, kind-faced man with his hand on Cash's shoulder, looking like the proudest father in the world.

'That was taken after my first game,' Cash said, standing next to me and staring at the picture. 'It was a league that played out in Oak Hill. One of the best days of my life.'

'You won the first game?'

He laughed. 'Oh, no. We lost pretty badly, but I didn't care. I was just happy my coach had let me off the bench. I loved the game from the minute I stepped on to the field, even when I was that little . . . You can put that in your interview if you want.'

'Yeah . . . my interview.' I looked at the picture, at little Cash's big, goofy smile. It reminded me of the smile my dad wore whenever he talked about football, the way he remembered playing as a kid.

'Should we get started on that?' Cash asked, nodding towards the door to what I guessed was his bedroom. 'I don't want to get you home too late or anything.'

'Right,' I said. 'OK. Let's get started.'

It was time to set to work on the Plan. It wouldn't be hard, I told myself. All I needed was to get Cash to kiss me again. If I could get him to kiss me, I could make him want more. I could make him want everything, and then rip it away from him. I just had to make him kiss me.

Cash's bedroom was cramped but, thankfully, neat. A small twin-size bed was shoved into the far right corner, and a chest of drawers stood on the opposite wall. There was a desk with a computer and printer on it. A sports calendar hung on the wall, but other than that, the room was pretty blank. Almost . . . lifeless.

'I know it isn't much,' Cash said nervously, watching

me look around. 'We haven't lived here long. After Dad got laid off, we had some money trouble and had to sell the house and move in here.'

'Why don't you decorate?' I asked, dropping my bag on to the floor and sitting down on the bed. I crossed my legs, my heart pounding as I gave Cash a nice view of my upper thigh.

He shrugged and walked over to sit down beside me, his eyes barely turning towards my exposed skin. 'I don't see the point. I'll be moving out for college in less than a year, and Dad will get another job. They'll be able to buy another house. This is just temporary . . . That's what they keep saying, at least.' He sighed and looked away for a moment before letting his eyes meet mine again. 'Honestly, I'm kind of afraid that if I settle in too much, Dad will think I've accepted this place as home. It's like, by not making myself too comfortable here, I'm showing I believe he'll find another job, you know?'

I nodded. I did know. I knew what it was like to smile and pretend to make a parent happy, to protect them. Cash was the kind of person who would do anything to keep his family going, even if it cost him. Just like Logan. Just like me.

No, no, no. I had to stop thinking about Cash in such a favourable way. I needed to keep reminding myself what an asshole he was. How he'd hurt me. Used me to help the boys win. I needed to remember so that my plan could work, so that I could use him right back and feel guiltless.

I edged a little closer to him, my bare knee brushing against his jeans. 'What are your college plans?'

'Is this part of the interview?' he asked.

'No, I'm just curious.'

Cash nodded and rubbed his head, making the short strands stand up. It was getting longer every time I saw him. I wondered if he was going to keep it short. I hoped he'd let it grow out a little. I wanted to see how he'd look with long hair, like he'd had as a kid. I wanted to run my fingers through his soft, brown waves and—

'Well, that's why I have to get a scholarship,' Cash explained, angling his body towards mine. 'My parents can't afford to send me, so I need to keep up my grades and get this soccer scholarship. Coach is worried that my missing practice twice a week for work is going to mess up my chances.'

'Do you think it will?'

He sighed. 'I don't know. I hope not. I'm trying really hard to keep up; I work my ass off at the other practices . . . but it isn't like I'm going to quit my job at the library. My family comes first, and they need me right

263

now, you know? Plus' – he smiled at me – 'I like working there . . . with you.'

I loved the way he smiled at me then. Warm and sweet. It made me forget how he'd hurt me. It was hard to be conniving and deceptive when a boy like Cash Sterling was staring at me with his beautiful green eyes.

'You know,' he said, "this whole strike thing aside, I've liked working with you. I mean, when you aren't avoiding me or bossing me around.' He grinned. 'You kind of fascinate me. You're—'

I never found out what I was. Because I messed up.

The plan was to wait until Cash kissed me. But instead, I leaned forward and pressed my lips to his.

26

'Lissa.'

The taste of my name on his lips was intoxicating. I wanted to hear it again and again.

The kisses had started slow. He'd leaned into me gently as my lips found his, tender, small kisses against my mouth that quickly turned longer and deeper. His hands cupped my face, one slowly sliding down to touch my neck and play with my hair.

As the kisses grew deeper, my own hands began to wander. I explored his biceps and abs, marvelling at the toned, athletic muscles of his upper body.

This went on for a while, Cash keeping it slow and sweet, and I stayed in control. I knew what I was doing. I knew the plan, and then—

And then Cash was murmuring into my mouth, my name on his lips, and I was melting into him, feeling that same need I'd felt in the library two days earlier. The desire to crawl under Cash's skin, to meld my body with his.

I started to feel light-headed and leaned back, pulling him down on to the bed with me. Cash eased away for a moment, his emerald eyes meeting mine, questioning. I nodded quickly and kissed him again, tugging him closer.

His lips moved slowly against mine and his hands stayed near my face, running through my hair or touching my cheek, never pushing the boundaries. I was the one who pushed things further. One of my legs wrapped around his waist, and I could feel Cash's whole body tighten. After a moment, he relaxed and continued to kiss me, his hands becoming braver as they slipped down my arms, one inching under my shirt. I arched my back and his cool fingers slid under me, moving across my spine, tracing the curve between my shoulder blades.

Cash wanted me. I could feel it. Not just through his jeans – though that factor was certainly present – but also in the way he kissed me. It was still slow, but there was a hungry edge to it now. That was all I had needed, when I walked into this. For him to want me, to need me. I could have pushed him away then, left him frustrated with unfulfilled desire. Done what I set out to do in the first place.

266

But I didn't stop.

Instead, I put a hand on Cash's shoulder and rolled him on to his back so that I was on top of him, straddling his waist. I pushed my hands under his shirt, and Cash leaned up so that I could shove it over his head. We were both panting, but we just kept kissing. I couldn't stop touching him, couldn't rip my hands or my mouth away from his skin. Like I was the north pole of a magnet and he was the south. It would have taken an effort to tug us apart.

I didn't have that kind of fight in me.

His hands moved to my hips, holding me against him, our bodies grinding together for a long moment before one of his hands inched up slightly, hesitating at the hem of my shirt.

'Yes,' I murmured into his mouth.

I felt Cash's chest rise beneath mine as he took in a deep breath. His hand carefully lifted my shirt, his knuckles skimming my ribs. He paused with the shirt lifted only a few inches, and he pulled back. His eyes met mine again, questioning, always questioning.

I lifted my arms over my head in answer. He sat up with me still on his lap and tentatively pulled off my T-shirt. The shirt fell to the floor, but Cash stayed frozen, staring at me, taking me in. For a second, I felt self-conscious. Then he touched my face with one hand, trailing a finger down my jaw, neck, and collarbone, stopping on my chest, right over the place where I felt my heart racing.

'God,' he whispered. 'You're beau—'

My lips found his again, silencing him. I pressed myself tighter against him, feeling the newness of his warm skin against mine, and I nudged him back on to the bed.

It was a while later, after many long, tender kisses, that I found myself being eased on to my back, and I took a breath as Cash's mouth left mine and began trailing down my neck and shoulder. 'Lissa,' he mumbled into my ear again. Just my name, and it sounded so wonderful in his deep bass voice. So soothing. So right, but—

But then I felt his hand on my back, fumbling a little with the clasp of my bra, and I remembered myself. The oath, the strike, the plan I was supposed to be fulfilling. None of that made me stop wanting to do what I knew we were about to do – because every hormone in my body screamed that this was exactly what I wanted. But remembering did fill me with a sudden sense of fear.

I was terrified to realize how far I'd let things go.

How much control I had lost.

'No,' I gasped, shoving Cash's shoulder. 'No. Never mind. I-I'm not—'

Cash took his hands off me and rolled away, almost falling off his twin bed as I catapulted myself across the room, away from him.

'Lissa,' he said. 'Lissa, it's OK. We don't have to – I didn't expect—'

'I hate you,' I snapped as I pulled my shirt back on. Quietly at first so that maybe he couldn't hear, and then louder, louder, louder. 'I hate you. Hate you.'

'What?' he asked, sounding surprised.

'I do.' But it was a lie. I didn't hate him. I just hated the way he made me feel. Loved and hated it. Being with him like that was exhilarating, but so, so dangerous. I couldn't control myself with Cash, I never could, and it terrified me.

This had never been a problem before. I'd always, always been able to keep the ball in my court with Randy. But with Cash . . . It was hard to push him away. For the most part, I didn't even want to, despite the fact that I knew I should. Despite the fact that he'd toyed with me before and would again.

'You're an asshole,' I said, spinning to face him. He was sitting on his bed, staring at me with wide,

269

confused eyes, his shirt forgotten. 'You just toy with people! This is all just a game to you, isn't it? Making girls fall for you and then never . . . You play with girls' heads by making them think they're special when, really, you don't give a damn.'

He blinked at me once before finding his T-shirt and pulling it back over his head. 'Lissa,' he said, having regained his breath. His voice was smooth but low. 'What are you talking about?'

'You play mind games,' I said. 'You mess with girls' heads, and you shouldn't. It's wrong and selfish and cruel.'

'Wait – I play mind games?' Cash was suddenly on his feet, looking across the tiny room at me as if I were insane. 'I don't know why you're saying this, but you're being really hypocritical right now. If anyone plays with people's heads, it's you.'

'Excuse me?'

'This whole strike has turned into a way to fuck with people, Lissa,' he snapped. 'It was one thing when you were just boycotting sex, but now . . . Look at you. You're using sex to get what you want – playing with my feelings for your own benefit. That's why you came over, right? I'm not stupid. You're the one who's cruel, Lissa. Not me.'

I sneered at him. 'You're no better – leading the boys' side, trying to seduce us.'

'We're not manipulating anyone,' he said.

'Yes you are!' I shouted.

'Lissa, the boys haven't done anything like this,' he argued. 'Maybe the swimming-pool thing was wrong, but that doesn't even compare to—'

'I'm not talking about the damn swimming pool.'

'We haven't been toying with or teasing anyone the way you are.'

I glared up at him. 'So you agree with the other boys at school? You think I'm a cock tease, right?'

Cash's face softened a little. 'Lissa,' he said quietly, "you choosing not to sleep with Randy doesn't make you a tease. It makes you . . . Well, it makes you smart, but aside from that, it makes you independent. There was nothing wrong with your decision. And there was nothing wrong with the strike in the beginning, when it was just saying no.' He stepped a little closer to me, green eyes pressing into mine. 'But there is something wrong with using other people's feelings against them. Manipulating them. The way some of the strike girls are doing. The way you're trying to manipulate me . . . that's what makes you a tease. Fucking with people's heads to get what you want – to get that control you

271

say you're desperate for – without giving anything in return.'

He was right. When this had started, I'd said we weren't using sex as a weapon. But some of the girls were. I'd even encouraged it.

I could feel tears stinging my eyes. It hurt to hear, hurt to know that I really was a tease. I'd spent weeks discussing and fighting sexual labels with the other girls, but here I was, deliberately tormenting Cash with sex, becoming the stereotype. I was ashamed of myself.

But I just couldn't stop fighting him. 'So I'm a bad person because I won't sleep with you?' I demanded, knowing that wasn't what he meant but needing so badly to hurt him. I needed him to feel as angry as I did. To hate himself as much as I hated myself at that moment. I wanted him to regret every bad moment between us, the same way I did.

Cash flinched. 'I did not say that,' he said. 'And that's not how I meant it. Lissa, I—'

'Good,' I yelled. 'Because . . . Because nothing will ever happen between us again.' I was backing towards the door of his bedroom. I had to get out of there before more stupid things left my mouth. 'We're done. It was just a game, right? This whole thing between us – kissing me in the library the other day, all the flirting – it was a game so you'd win the war. Well, game over. I played, and now I'm done. I can't do this any more.'

'It wasn't a game,' Cash whispered. 'Not to me.'

But I barely heard him as I bolted from the room, clapping a hand over my mouth to keep from saying another word. I didn't let myself stop to think about what he could have meant by that. Didn't let myself hope or dream. I just ran.

I'd lost it. My sanity, my ability to think, my control. I'd let Cash get the better of me, and I'd lost my cool physically and verbally. I was ashamed and embarrassed, and before I even got out of the trailer, I was regretting every word I'd said.

27

I was already outside on the porch before I remembered that Cash had driven me here. 'Fuck,' I wailed, sinking down on to the front steps of the trailer and burying my face in my hands.

I took a deep breath and forced myself to calm down. Freaking out would only make this infinitely worse. I needed to keep my cool. To stay in control. To think and find a way out of here.

I heard the door of the trailer slide open behind me. 'Lissa,' Cash said, his voice gentle as his footsteps shook the loose wooden boards I was sitting on. 'Do you need a ride?'

'No, thank you,' I said in a stiff, polite voice. I self-consciously tucked the hem of my skirt beneath my knees, feeling exposed.

'How will you get home?' he asked.

'I'll call someone.'

'You left your bag inside.' I felt the bag drop to the ground beside me. 'You sure you don't . . . ? I could give you a ride, Lissa. It's not . . . We don't have to talk about this if you don't want to.'

'Thank you,' I said, pulling my bag into my lap. 'But I'm fine. I appreciate the offer.'

That was the truth. I did appreciate it. I appreciated that he came after me even considering how I'd talked to him. Randy never would have chased me like that. He would have waited for me to cool down, waited for me to come back and apologize for the things I'd said. He would have just let me go. Hell, I would have just let me go.

Then again, I had left my bag inside. Cash didn't have much of a choice but to bring it out to me.

I ducked my head and began digging for my phone. I could feel Cash still standing behind me, silently watching. 'You don't have to wait,' I told him after I located the phone.

'I know I don't,' he said. 'But I'm not leaving you out here alone in the dark, either.'

I snorted. 'We live in Hamilton, Cash. Not Detroit. It's not like something scary and dangerous is going to happen to me while I'm waiting.'

He didn't respond.

Part of me wanted him to say, 'Fine,' and stomp back inside, out of my hair and my life. But the other part of me – the louder, more emotional part – was thrilled that he cared enough to stay. To watch out for me. I wanted it to mean something.

I hesitated with my finger over the keypad. I could call Chloe. Hell, I could walk to her place from here. But that wouldn't have been a good idea.

Because she'd been right. So right. She'd told me not to do this, not to play with fire. But I'd argued. I'd said I could handle it even though I obviously could not. I didn't want to hear her gloat at me. I didn't want her to know how right she'd been. Not tonight, anyway.

For that matter, I didn't want to see any of the strike girls. Because if they realized whose house they were picking me up from . . . I didn't even want to know what they'd think had been going on.

So I called the only other person I could think of.

'Lissa, I thought you said you didn't need a ride tonight?'

Logan sounded agitated. On the other end of the line, I could hear the sounds of forks scraping along plates on top of a low hum of conversation.

'Where are you?' I asked. 'Shouldn't you be at home?'

'No,' Logan said, sounding a little annoyed. 'I'm on a

276

date. What's the problem, Lissa? Why did you call?'

'I need a ride.'

'I thought your shift ended, like, two hours ago.'

'It did. I'm not at work. Can you come and get me?' I was all too aware of Cash, so close to me, able to hear everything I said. I cleared my throat. 'I just need to go home. Please, Logan?'

'Are you OK?' He sounded worried.

'I'm fine. I just need you to come and get me. Look, you can bring your date, too. Just get me, drop me off at home, and go back out. I don't care. I just—'

'No, no,' Logan said quickly. 'I'll send her home and be on my way. Where are you?'

I gave Logan the address, and I could sense the tone of suspicion as he read it back to me. I'm sure he was wondering why I was across town in the trailer park. There was no way I was giving him an answer to that.

I hung up the phone and slid it back into my bag. 'My brother is on his way,' I said, as if Cash hadn't just overheard every word. 'So you don't have to worry any more. Thanks.'

'Lissa, I—' Cash began, but then he stopped himself. Finally, he said, "Do you really want me to leave you alone?'

No.

'Yes.'

I wasn't looking at him, so I couldn't see his reaction to this. But I felt the ache of my own disappointment when he said, "All right.' the porch creaked, and a moment later I heard the screen door close behind me. When I turned around, I saw that he'd left the bigger wooden door open, and I wondered if he was still keeping an eye on me from inside, still watching to make sure I was OK.

I wished he'd stayed.

Something was wrong with me. I should have been happy Cash was gone. I hated him. Hated him for making me feel this way. For turning me into a sex-crazed freak. I couldn't believe how willing I'd been. How eager I'd been for things to go further. I was ashamed.

I shouldn't have been; I knew that. If there was one thing this strike had taught me it was that there was no right answer – it was OK to want or not want sex. It wasn't anything to feel guilty about. I knew, I knew, I knew . . .

But I guess sometimes knowing doesn't fix everything. I'd played by the rules of secrecy and shame my entire life. Learning to break them would take time.

It wasn't fair. *Lysistrata* never had this problem. In the play, the other women yearned for their husbands, missed sex, but not her. She stayed strong. Why couldn't I be like that? Why, after a year of being afraid, of avoiding it with Randy, was I suddenly lusting after Cash?

Part of me didn't even want to know the answers.

Seventeen minutes and six seconds later, Logan's car pulled into the driveway. 'Hey,' he said, leaning out the open window as I strolled towards him. 'What is going on? You look . . . Your hair . . . Never mind.'

'My hair what?' I began, but I could see the reddish colour in my brother's cheeks, and I shook my head. Make-out hair.

I climbed into the car and gave the trailer one last look. For a second, I thought I could see Cash's silhouette in the window, but then we were driving away, and there was no way for me to be sure, to know that he'd stayed there, watching to make sure I left all right.

When we got home I ran upstairs, telling Dad I had a lot of homework to do and leaving him and Logan to fend for themselves dinner-wise.

I needed to be alone for a while, so I closed my bedroom door, curled up on my bed and pushed my face into the pillow. The tears I'd been fighting back in Cash's bedroom ached to be released, and this time I didn't fight them.

I was angry – at Cash for making it so easy for me to

lose control, at myself for still wanting him. But I was embarrassed, too. I'd fucked this strike up. I'd taken a good idea and let it get out of hand, encouraging the girls to be cruel, to tease, just so I could beat Cash.

Only one thought offered me any comfort: Cash was wrong as well. The boys had been manipulative. Him, especially. I remembered that kiss in the library, that kiss that should have made me so happy, and how it had hurt to realize it had been a battle tactic. Cash was cruel, too, even if he couldn't admit it.

Which was why I wasn't giving up yet.

I sat up and wiped my eyes. The strike wouldn't end because of this. I'd talk to the girls; I'd tell Susan and Ellen to stop with the seductress acts – and I would stop, too. We could go back to how we started; we could run this strike the right way. We could – we would – still do what we set out to do in the beginning: end the rivalry.

With a little sigh, I climbed off my bed and walked to my desk, where my physics homework waited for me. Tomorrow, I'd fix things. If Cash wanted me to play fair, I would. But the girls were still going to win.

The strike wasn't over.

Chloe called later that night – I knew she would, but it was a phone call I hadn't been looking forward to.

'So how'd it go?' she asked. 'Did you shut him down?'

I let out a breath. 'Um . . . sort of, but not in the way I'd planned.' Before she could ask, I dived into the story of what had happened in Cash's bedroom. She waited in silence, and I talked as fast as I could so I wouldn't get embarrassed and lose my nerve.

'And I know you told me so,' I said.

'Lissa—'

'And I know I messed up,' I said, cutting her off. 'I know what I did was wrong, like you said. I'm sorry.'

'Lissa—'

'Please don't lecture me, Chloe.'

'Lissa!' Her voice was harsh, crackling through my phone, and I flinched. 'Will you let me talk? I wasn't going to lecture you.'

'Oh?'

'No. I was going to ask if you're OK,' Chloe said. 'It sounds kind of . . . intense.'

'Yes, I-I guess that's a good word for it. Intense.'

'So are you? OK, I mean?'

I sighed and pushed away from my desk, where I'd been attempting to do physics homework for the past hour. Attempting and failing. My thoughts were too consumed. With Cash. With the rivalry. With this war between the boys and the girls – the battle of the sexes that had sprung up. Just like in *Lysistrata*.

The girls had won. In *Lysistrata*, the women had won. The war between the Athenians and the Spartans ended, and the women were successful. I'd finished the play a few nights earlier, and I'd decided that if they could win, so could we.

'I will be,' I answered. 'So, slumber party at Ellen's this weekend, right?' I turned to my computer and opened up my email.

Chloe snorted. 'Hell if I know. I stopped reading your emails weeks ago. I just do what you tell me to do, since I have to drive you around anyway.'

I rolled my eyes and checked the calendar I'd set up on my email server. 'Well, you're driving me to Ellen's tomorrow night, then.' I clicked the button to shut down my computer. 'I have to go or I'll never get this homework done.'

'Whoa, you still do homework?' Chloe asked. 'Why? We're seniors. You've already taken your SATs. Why bother?'

I laughed. 'Good night, Chloe.' And I hung up the phone.

28

Being in Ellen's bedroom brought on a little déjà vu. She lived in a nice house about a block from the high school, which made it an easy walk for the girls who wanted to support their boyfriends at the football game before heading to the sleepover.

Ellen's room sent me back to a time before all of this. Before the strike, before Randy, before the stupid rivalry began interfering with our lives. Sitting cross-legged on Ellen's floor, flipping through one of her fashion magazines, made me feel thirteen again. It felt good. Simple.

Boys had ruined that.

Plink.

'What was that?' Kelsey asked in a bored voice, pushing herself up on one elbow where she was stretched out on the floor. Ellen's room wasn't as big as Kelsey's, but it was still big enough that we had room to lounge around – especially since it was the weekend before fall break and almost half the girls had already headed out of town with their families, venturing to places far, far more interesting than Hamilton. Kelsey wasn't one of them, and I could tell she was pissed off about it.

She got up and stepped over the other girls, making her way to the window as another pebble hit the glass. My body tensed as I thought of Randy and the night he'd shimmied up my drainpipe. The night I'd decided to start the strike.

'Um, Mary?' Kelsey said. 'You should come and see this.'

Everyone, not just Mary, made their way to the window then, curious and bored and in need of some sort of entertainment.

And we got entertainment, all right.

Standing in the grass below Ellen's bedroom window was a small group of about seven boys. A few were still wearing football jerseys, and the others were soccer players – Cash among them. The sight of him made my cheeks burn – for several reasons, anger and shame not excluded.

At the front of the group, staring up at us and holding a battered acoustic guitar, was Finn, Mary's boyfriend. He wasn't the kind of guy you'd expect to see with a shy, tiny girl like Mary. Finn was tall, broad and growing a steady beard. Normally, he looked like the intimidating beast that might beat you up and steal your lunch money. But right now, the way he looked up at us, at Mary, with this glow in his eye and the sweetest smile, he looked more like a teddy bear.

'Mary,' he called up to us as Kelsey, against my protests, opened the window. 'Mary, I . . . I miss you. I—'

'Can we get this over with, man?' Shane asked. 'Come on. We came here to do this. Let's get on with it.'

'Right.' Finn cleared his throat. 'Anyway, Mary, I have something I want to say to you, but I never get to be alone with you any more. You won't let me, and . . . and I know this strike is . . . well, anyway.' I'd never seen a boy Finn's size turn into such a blubbering fool. 'You don't have to come down here,' he said. 'But please listen.'

'Shut the window,' I hissed at Kelsey.

She shook her head. 'Let the boy speak.'

Finn began to strum on his guitar, but before he got very far, Shane interrupted again.

'Hold up,' he yelled towards the window. 'Just gotta say – I did not agree to this song selection. This was all Finn and Sterling's idea, all right? I just agreed to help.'

'Are you done yet?' Cash asked. Even though it sounded harsh, I could tell he was half laughing.

'Yeah. Whatever.'

Finn cleared his throat and began to strum again. After a moment, he started to sing.

'It's tearin' up my heart when I'm with you . . .'

'Oh my God,' Ellen said slowly. 'Is that . . . ?'

''Nsync,' Susan said, nodding. 'I haven't heard this song since elementary school.'

The thing was, Finn could not sing. He wasn't horrible or anything – not like the really, really bad people they showcase on the *American Idol* audition episodes. But he wasn't really talented, either. Then again, none of the boys were. They performed as back-up singers while Finn strummed his guitar – something he was talented at.

Cash's eyes locked suddenly with mine as the second verse ended, and my heart thrummed in my chest. I knew this was about Mary and Finn – or, more likely, about the boys sabotaging us. But for a second, I wished he was singing to me. That he was telling me he wanted to be with me. That not being with me was killing him.

And he was killing me.

I looked away and nudged Chloe, who was crouching next to me. 'Dear God,' I said. 'They're like sirens. We've got to close the window and stop listening.'

'Lissa, look at her.' She reached out her hands and forced me to turn and face Mary.

She was standing up, peering out the window with this look on her face like she might swoon. Her eyes were wide, and for a second I worried she was about to burst into tears. She slowly lifted a hand and placed it over her chest, her gaze fixed out the window. It was like a scene out of a romance novel.

'She hasn't kissed him in over a month,' Chloe whispered in my ear. 'She won't even be alone with him. Shane says Finn's afraid it's more than the strike. Like she's lost interest in him.'

I turned my head back to look at her. 'You talk to Shane?'

Chloe shrugged. 'We're kind of friends. Like, we've hooked up enough that we're comfortable with each other. We talk.'

I narrowed my eyes at her. 'Even when you aren't hooking up?'

Chloe gave me a fierce stare. 'Yes, Lissa. Stop being so paranoid. I've stuck to the oath, but . . . but look at her. Mary. And Finn. Look at him, too. You remember how I told you there are some good guys out there? He's one of them. I know I'm not an expert on romance, but they are clearly in love, and this is hurting them.'

287

I opened my mouth to say something, but Susan turned to face me, her palms pressed against the window – her boyfriend, Luther, was one of the boys singing up to us. 'Lissa,' she said, 'when can this whole strike thing be over? It's been, like, a month. I thought it would be done by now.'

'Yeah,' a few of the girls echoed. 'I thought you said two weeks.'

'Stop,' I said, jumping to my feet – I'd been kneeling by the window. 'This is what they want. They want us to give in. But we can't. We have to stay strong. We have to win.' I pushed Kelsey out of the way and positioned myself in front of the window just as the song ended and the last notes of Finn's guitar were carried off by the October wind.

'Go home,' I called down to them. 'This won't work – and you'll wake up the neighbours.'

'Mary!' Finn called, ignoring me.

I felt Mary come up behind me so she could peer over my shoulder out the window.

'I miss you,' he said again. 'I—'

Before he could finish, I slammed the window shut.

'Lissa!' Kelsey snapped, annoyed. 'Why did you do that?'

'It's a trap.' I looked right at Mary then. 'You know

that, right? This is just another attempt by the boys to make us give in. To make us lose. But we can't. We have to win. You know that, right?'

Mary opened her mouth, paused, then closed it again. Slowly, she nodded and turned away, her shoulders slumped as she moved towards Ellen's bed.

Both Kelsey and Chloe were giving me the evil eye.

'What?' I asked. 'I'm right. This is just a trick. Another one of their games. The same thing happened in *Lysistrata*.'

'In . . . what?' Kelsey asked.

'It's this Greek play about a group of women who decide to end the war by going on a sex strike,' I explained to the puzzled-looking group. 'I'd never read it but, um, someone recommended it to me after the strike started. Anyway, the women take over the Acropolis and the men show up and try to lure them out. Just like this.'

'And what happens?' Susan asked.

'They stay strong,' I told her. 'Their leader, Lysistrata, makes them stay inside – just like I'm doing. And they win. We have to win. That's the point.'

'I thought the point was ending the rivalry,' Kelsey said.

'It was – I mean, it is. It still is. And we will. I was wrong before, when I said we should tease them. We'll have to stop that, but if we just stay strong, keeping to the oath, they'll give up.'

I could feel the unsatisfied murmur that rippled around the room, but no one argued with me. Instead, they all just exchanged glances before going back to what they'd been doing before the boys had shown up.

Chloe gave me one last glance – one full of recognizable frustration – before walking across the room and sitting next to Kelsey.

Kelsey? Of all people?

They began to talk in low voices. Like they were friends. Like it was normal for them to speak without screaming at each other. And I knew they were talking about me. It felt like a slap in the face.

But I kept my mouth shut and turned back to the window. I could just make out the boys' retreating backs as they skirted across Ellen's backyard and out towards the gravel back roads of Hamilton. The moonlight framed their silhouettes, and for a moment, one paused. I could see him turning his head back, but he was too far off for me to recognize his face as he looked at the house. At the window. At me.

Somehow, I knew it was Cash.

29

The next morning, Ellen volunteered to drive me home. Logan had texted and asked me to be back by noon because he had something to tell Dad and me over lunch, so I accepted Ellen's offer because, while Chloe would usually give me the lift, I got the vibe that she was still upset with me about last night. Though I wasn't sure what I'd done to upset her so much.

'So,' Ellen said slowly as we drove away from her house. The other girls had left only a few minutes before us, sneaking out as quietly as possible so as not to wake up Ellen's mom, who really liked to sleep in at the weekends. 'We need to talk about this whole strike thing.'

'What about it?' I asked.

'Lissa, I— Look, it was a good idea. Really, I'm glad we did it because . . . Well, honestly, I've learned a lot. About what people expect of me and what I expect from

291

myself. And because it brought us back together.' She gave me a quick smile before focusing her attention on the road again. 'But . . . I think it's time to end it.'

'What? Why? We haven't won yet.'

Ellen sighed and switched on the turn signal. 'What are we winning, exactly?' she asked.

'We . . . the rivalry has to end. That's the point.'

'Is it?' she asked, her voice very serious but not accusatory. 'Think about this, Lissa. Is the rivalry really what the strike is about? Because I don't know if you noticed, but the boys aren't fighting any more. The group at my house last night was made up of football and soccer players. They were working together.'

I didn't say anything.

Didn't know what to say.

But I did know what Ellen was thinking. And then she confirmed my suspicions.

'I think this is about Cash,' she said. 'I think . . . OK, don't get mad at me for saying this, but I think you're using this to get back at him for how he hurt you. It didn't start that way, obviously, but now . . . Lissa, we all see the way you look at him. All of us. Even Kelsey mentioned it to Chloe and me.'

'Wait, you guys talked about me? Behind my back?'

'Not in a bad way,' Ellen said quickly. 'But we're

worried. This strike was a great idea, but it's going too far. They asked me to talk to you about it. They thought you'd listen to me.'

I stared out the window, refusing to look at Ellen. I was more than pissed off. I was hurt. Angry. Betrayed. I thought these girls were on my side. They'd been on my side from the start and now, suddenly, they were against me. Talking about me when I wasn't around. Trying to think of ways to overthrow me.

Ellen must have guessed what I was thinking because she quickly added, "We love you, Lissa. It's not like we're mad. But think about this, OK? The strike is tearing apart the guys and the girls. It's becoming its own rivalry. Even you talk about 'winning' like it's just a game to you. But didn't you start this to end a rivalry? To make peace?'

Yes, I thought, but I didn't respond. I was pushing down all the hurt and anger, falling back into my safe place, the one where I was Little Miss Ice Queen.

'If we let this keep going, it'll turn into another long-lasting rivalry, and no one will know where or why it started,' Ellen continued. 'I know you don't want that. I know because I know you.' She took a breath and let it out slowly. 'The end of *Lysistrata*?'

'What?' I asked coldly. 'What about it?'

'The end. The women won, but how? Do you remember?'

'*Lysistrata* talked to the guy representing the men,' I said. 'He agreed on their behalf to end the war. You've read it?'

Ellen shrugged. 'My mom teaches Greek studies at the community college in Oak Hill. I've learned a lot.' She turned on to my street and continued talking. 'But think about what you just said. She talked to the leader of the guy's side. Have you thought . . . have you tried seriously talking to Cash?'

'Yes – No . . . It's complicated, OK?'

'I know.' She sighed. 'And I'm sorry. I'm sorry things are weird between you two, but you can't let your relationship with Cash run this strike. You need to talk to him so that this can end. So that we can all move on.'

I didn't reply. As much as I hated to admit it, I knew she was right.

Ellen's car stopped in my driveway, and we sat listening to the engine idle for a moment before either of us broke the silence.

'Just promise me you'll think about it,' she said. 'Please. Know that I'll be on your side, no matter what. I'll stand by your decision, but . . . but you owe me this.'

'I know,' I said quietly. 'I owe it to all the girls. They've stuck by me – all of them – through a lot. Through Randy . . .' I swallowed hard, unable to keep the emotions back the way I wanted. 'I'll talk to Cash. Not sure what I'll say, but I'll talk to him.'

I wasn't looking at her, but I felt Ellen's hand slide over the console and squeeze mine. 'Thank you,' she said. 'And remember what I said the other day, OK? If he doesn't see how special you are, he doesn't deserve you.'

'Thanks,' I said. 'I'm going to get going. I just need to think about all of this. I'll call you tonight or something, OK?'

'OK.' She let go of my hand as I slid out of the car.

I paused before slamming the car door shut and poked my head inside for a second. 'Hey, Ellen?'

'Yeah?'

'Thanks . . . for putting up with me.'

She beamed at me. 'No problem,' she said. 'I'm happy to put up with you, even when you're at your craziest. That won't change.'

I didn't deserve her, I realized as I walked up to the front door and let myself into the house. Honestly, I didn't deserve anyone. As much as it killed me to admit it, Ellen was right. I'd been using this strike as a way to fight with Cash. If I hadn't been so blinded, so obsessed with winning and beating him, I might have noticed the way the rivalry had gone dormant.

I was trying to figure out what I'd say to Cash when I confronted him – how I'd start, what arguments I'd make, whether I should lie about how I felt – when I walked into the kitchen, where my family sat waiting for me at the table. Waiting so that Logan could give me the news. Waiting with one extra person.

'Jenna,' I said, not as shocked as I would have liked to be. 'What are you doing here?'

But I could have guessed the answer.

30

'Lissa,' Dad said, a laugh still on his lips. 'Honey, come in and sit down. Logan has something to tell us.'

I was frozen in the kitchen doorway, the bag I'd packed for the night at Ellen's hanging loosely from my fingertips. I didn't want Jenna in my house, in my kitchen, in my space. I didn't want to see the way she smiled, like this was the happiest moment of her life. It wasn't the happiest moment of mine.

'So,' I said slowly. 'You're . . . You've been dating Jenna this whole time, right?'

They exchanged a look before my brother focused his attention squarely on me. 'Yes,' he said. 'I have. I didn't want to tell you because – well, if things didn't work out, I didn't want it to be awkward for you at work.'

'I actually asked him to keep it a secret,' Jenna

interjected. 'I mean, you're distracted at work enough as it is. The library couldn't afford having you lose focus because of another personal issue.'

'I figured it out a while ago,' I said. 'I just hoped you'd break up soon.'

'Lissa,' Dad scolded. 'Stop that.'

'Sit down,' Logan said, his voice losing its cheery edge.

I didn't move, just looked back and forth between them for a minute. I had a sinking suspicion that dating wasn't the reason for this family meeting. Jenna was here, in my kitchen, no longer keeping it secret – no longer letting me live in the land of sweet denial. That meant something must have changed.

'Oh my God,' I gasped. 'You're pregnant, aren't you?'

'What?' Logan asked, his eyebrows shooting up into his hairline.

'No!' Jenna cried. I saw a hand fly to her stomach. 'Why, do I look . . . ?'

Logan shook his head and squeezed her hand on top of the table.

I thought I'd be sick.

'Then why are you telling us this now?' I asked. 'If you aren't pregnant, why not continue to keep the whole dating thing a secret?'

'Lissa, honey,' Dad said. 'Logan has some news for us. Go ahead, Logan.'

Logan glanced at Jenna again, and she gave him one forceful nod before he said, 'I'm moving out.'

I felt a rubber band begin to contract around my lungs. 'What?'

Jenna said, 'He's moving—'

'I heard him!' I snapped at her, unable to keep my cool. 'I . . . What? Where? When?'

'At the beginning of next month,' Logan said. 'Jenna and I are moving to an apartment in one of the suburbs outside of Chicago.'

'I'm going to Northwestern,' Jenna explained, looking at my father, not me. 'I'm going to finish my degree there, starting in January.'

'What about the classes you're taking right now at the community college?' Dad asked.

'My professors are letting me finish online,' she said. 'I want us to have time to settle in and learn the area before I jump right into school.'

'And I'm going to apply for grad school,' Logan said. 'Like I planned.'

'You can't leave,' I said, my voice coming out cracked and pathetic. I shook my head and tried again. 'You can't leave, Logan. You can't . . . you can't go that far

299

away. And you two barely know each other! You've been dating, like . . . like, a month. That's not enough time to move in together.'

'I know,' Logan said. He smiled at Jenna, and the sparkle in his eyes – that cliché glimmer you read about in romance novels – I saw it. 'We know it's soon, but this just feels right.'

And I could tell.

I didn't want to, but I could tell.

Logan was in love with her.

I felt a sense of panic boiling in my chest. I felt my lungs contracting with fear, frustration and worry. More than ever, I truly hated Jenna. Before, she'd just annoyed me, angered me, made me insane. But now? Now I hated her. Because of her, my family was being broken, again. And she was taking Logan away. I'd worked so hard to keep my family close, to keep them safe, and she was going to destroy that.

'Excuse me,' I said, turning away and running upstairs. I couldn't be in the room with her any more. Couldn't look at her or at Logan. Couldn't watch this happen.

Couldn't watch my family break apart again.

An hour later, I heard Dad calling me from downstairs. I thought about ignoring him, knowing what he wanted to say to me – that it would be all right, that this was bound to happen, things I didn't want to hear. I thought about putting the pillow over my head and pretending his voice hadn't carried up the stairs.

But I decided to be at least somewhat mature about this. I sighed and climbed off my bed, running my fingers through my hair before heading downstairs.

Logan and Jenna had gone already, but Dad was waiting for me by the bottom step, his hand resting on the banister. 'We should talk about this,' he said. 'Come on. I'll make you a sandwich.'

I followed him into the kitchen and sat down at the table while he rolled around the room, getting what he needed to make me a peanut butter and jelly sandwich, like he used to when I was little and upset.

'He can't do this,' I blurted out, knowing Dad was waiting for me to speak first. 'He can't leave us.'

Dad didn't respond. He pulled a knife from the silverware drawer and began spreading jelly across a piece of bread.

'And not with her,' I continued. 'She's . . . she's awful. So bossy and demanding and obnoxious.'

'I found her charming,' Dad said. 'Very smart, in control. A little obsessed with order, but that's the kind of girl Logan needs in his life. She reminds me of you and your mother, actually.'

'No,' I muttered, but I remembered Cash saying once that Jenna reminded him of me. As much as that made my stomach churn, I couldn't argue with the majority. Not successfully, at least. 'Besides,' I continued, picking up a napkin that had been left on the table and folding it into small, even sections. Fourths, eighths, sixteenths. 'He's so much older. It's creepy. She's, like, seven years younger than him. Can't he date someone his own age?'

Dad sighed and moved his chair back to the kitchen table, sliding the sandwich he'd just made across to me. 'Honey, I know this is hard on you,' he said. 'I know you've spent the last five years taking care of us – of Logan and me. But sweetheart, Logan is an adult now. He has to take care of himself eventually.'

'I'm scared that if he gets too far away, we'll lose him,' I whispered. 'I don't want to lose anyone else.'

'Don't look at it as losing him,' Dad said. 'Look at it as adding to the family. We have Jenna now, too. Someone to help you keep him safe – because you know she'll boss him around just as much as you do.'

He was trying to make me laugh, but it didn't work.

I put down the napkin, now folded into a compact little cube, and picked up my sandwich. 'Why her?' I asked. 'Of all people, why her?'

He shrugged. 'Sometimes it's hard to predict who will make a person happy. But in the end, that's what matters. Remember what I told you when you and Randy broke up? I told you that I'd accept any boy you brought home, no matter who he was, as long as he made you happy. Honey, we owe Logan the same.'

'I know.'

'You can't control everything,' Dad said. 'Sometimes you just need to relax and have faith that things will work out. Let go a little and let life happen. You don't want to miss out on the best parts of life just because you were afraid of getting hurt. Or, in this case, of Logan getting hurt.'

But it wasn't just about Logan.

Dad didn't know it, obviously, but he was also talking about Cash.

I'd been pushing him away, keeping him at a distance, running every time he got too close, because I was afraid of getting hurt. Afraid of how I felt about him. But in reality, I should have just talked to him. Like Ellen now wanted me to do. I could have solved all of this if I'd just asked him why. But instead, I tried to control everything about our relationship, tried to keep myself safe. And that hadn't worked at all.

But it wasn't too late.

'I have to go,' I said, standing up, my sandwich only half-eaten.

Dad looked startled. 'Are you OK?' he asked. 'I'm sorry. I didn't mean to upset you, honey. I just—'

'You didn't,' I told him. 'You're right. I can't control everything. Sometimes I need to let go and . . . not be afraid.' I took a breath. 'I'll work on it.'

Dad nodded. 'OK. Good. I know it won't be easy for you, but I think you'll be happier in the long run.'

'Maybe,' I said. 'Now, um . . . Can I use the car? There's someone I need to see.'

31

There was a soccer game going on down at the high school that afternoon. I showed up just in time to watch the last twenty minutes. The bleachers were pretty empty, probably because so many people had left for their fall break mini-vacations, but there were still several loyal fans sitting around cheering. I could see Ellen on the second bleacher, cheering for Adam with all her heart.

The way I used to cheer for Randy.

I sat down in an empty row, pulling my feet up on to the narrow bench and resting my chin on my knees while I watched. It was the first time I'd ever really watched a soccer game. Usually, I'd just pass the field and catch glimpses of the action during practice or on my way to the football field. Sometimes, due to horrible scheduling, the games would happen at the same time.

My family didn't watch soccer and I didn't know any of

the rules, but I spotted Cash running in the middle of the field, mostly along the edges. I remembered him telling me at the summer party that he was a midfielder or something like that. I wasn't sure what it meant, and I hadn't really followed his explanation then. Now, though, I wanted to know. I wanted to know what his job was on the team. What they trusted him with, relied on him to do.

One thing I knew for certain – I'd never seen anyone as graceful as Cash on the field. He moved swiftly, smoothly, past his opponents. He made it look like more than a game – like it was an art. I could suddenly see why he loved it. Why anyone might love sports. To me, it had always been just a game, but to people like Cash – like my dad and Randy, even – it was a life, an art, a passion.

The buzzer sounded just as Adam kicked the ball past the other team's goalie. Hamilton won, and everyone clapped and cheered. Slowly, the audience began to disperse, leaving the stands in packs, chattering and comparing their favourite moments of the game. Everyone seemed to be gushing about Adam or Kyle, the goalie. But I'd barely noticed either. Cash was the only one I saw on the field. The only one who mattered.

I stayed in the bleachers, nervously rapping my knuckles against the aluminium bench while the rest of the fans headed back to the parking lot and the teams shook hands on the field. Then the Hamilton players gathered at the bench, high-fiving and discussing the game with Coach Lukavics. When they'd finished, the boys all headed back towards the changing rooms.

All but one.

Cash's eyes met mine and, after a long pause, he started walking up the bleachers toward me. My heart pounded as he got closer. He looked amazing in his kit – more amazing than usual, I mean – but I tried not to think about that.

'Nice game,' I said.

'Thanks,' he replied as he reached my place in the middle of the stands. He sat down, leaving a few feet of space between us. 'I never expected to see you here.'

'Yeah,' I said, my knuckles tapping faster. 'Can we talk?'

'Sure – but, um, would you rather I shower and change first?'

I shook my head. 'No, let's just . . . I want to get this over with.'

He frowned but nodded. 'All right. What's going on?'

I took a deep breath and stared out at the empty green soccer field, keeping my eyes as far away from Cash as possible. I couldn't control how I felt about him. I couldn't fight it off or force it away. Every time he came near me, I melted, and hating myself for it wasn't going to do me any good. I knew I'd never move on if I didn't ask the one question that had been haunting me for months.

'How come you never called me? After that party over the summer, I mean. You kissed me, and I thought . . . We've avoided the subject ever since, I know, and it was probably for the best, but I have to know, Cash. Why didn't you call me?'

There was a long, heavy silence, and I wanted so badly to look at Cash, but I wouldn't let myself. I didn't want to see the shame on his face. The embarrassment he felt over kissing me multiple times. The awkwardness of telling me that I just wasn't special enough. I closed my eyes and bit my lip, waiting.

When he finally spoke, Cash sounded surprised. 'I didn't think you wanted me to.'

I turned my head to look at him then, not sure I believed what I was hearing. He was staring at me with the most intense expression in his green eyes, so genuine and sincere, there was no way I could doubt him.

'Lissa, I—' He paused, let out a breath, and laid a hand over mine to keep me from tapping my already aching fingers. 'Wow, I'm an idiot. That night – Lissa, it meant a lot to me. I really liked you. I, um, had for a while, actually.'

I blinked at him. 'What?'

'I'd seen you hanging out with Ellen back when she and Adam first got together.' He was the one avoiding my eyes now, his cheeks turning just a tinge red. 'I thought . . . I thought you were beautiful. I was going to ask her to help me out, maybe set us up or something, but then you two stopped talking, and I found out you were with Randy . . .'

My head was spinning. I couldn't actually be hearing this. Cash Sterling – Mr Unattainable, the boy every girl wanted but no one could have – thought I was beautiful. This had to be a dream – a good dream, but still, a dream.

Cash looked at me then, and I knew I wasn't imagining any of this. It was real. He was real. Everything he was saying was real.

And I was shaking.

'So that night this summer, at the party, I was so happy to be talking to you. Getting to know you the way I'd wanted to. I liked you even more, so when I kissed you . . . Lissa, I meant it. Then you kissed me back . . .'

'Then why—' My voice cracked, and I had to clear my throat. 'Why didn't you call me? Why didn't you try to see me again?'

'I guess I thought it was too much to hope for that you felt the same way,' Cash admitted. 'You kissed me back, but I thought— You'd just broken up with Randy, and the whole rivalry between the teams . . .'

He let the sentence trail off, and it took me a minute to understand what he was telling me. But when it hit me, I couldn't help but laugh. Despite everything.

'You thought I was using you?' I said. 'Like, to get back at Randy?'

He blushed. 'Yeah, I did. And then you two got back together a few weeks later, so I was sure that's what it had been about. But I didn't want to make you feel bad about it or weird around me, so I just didn't say anything. I did egg Randy's car, though.'

'Wait, back at the end of August? On Lyndway Hill?'

Cash nodded, looking ashamed. 'Yeah. That wasn't the only time, either. I know it was stupid, but I just . . . God, I hated the thought of you two together. Not just because you weren't with me but because Randy is such a jackass. I knew he didn't deserve you.'

'Cash, I – I thought you just didn't like me,' I told him. 'I thought . . . Well, you said at the lunch table that day that you'd only consider dating a girl if she was really special. You looked right at me when you said it, so I thought that was a hint. That I just wasn't enough or something.'

He shook his head. 'It was a hint, but in the, um, opposite direction. You'd broken up with Randy again,

310

and I was trying to tell you how I felt.' He blushed again. 'I'm an idiot. Lissa, I'm sorry.'

I was grinning from ear to ear, but I looked at my lap, still embarrassed. Cash liked me. He had all along. We'd just been too foolish to confront each other about it. If he'd spoken up – if I'd spoken up – things could have been so different. We could have been together. This whole drama never would have had to happen.

Except, maybe it would have. Because even if I hadn't gone back to Randy, the rivalry would have raged on, and even now, I was proud of myself for standing up against it. Against the stupid pranks and the insanity of fighting a war that has no purpose.

A war that has no purpose . . .

'Cash,' I said slowly, remembering the whole reason I needed to talk to him. 'Why did you take over the boys' side? Why'd you go up against me?'

He grinned. 'I was actually trying to help you out. When I offered to organize an attack against the strike, it kind of brought all the guys – from both teams – together. It was hard, but we started working together as a group. The strike was a great idea, Lissa. If there's one thing that'll bring a bunch of guys together, it's girls.'

I laughed.

'I had another reason, too,' he admitted, squeezing my

311

hand. I wrapped my fingers around his, listening intently. 'I also did it to get your attention.'

'What?'

He shrugged. 'You kept avoiding me. I gave you that copy of *Lysistrata* hoping it would give us something to talk about, but every time we'd start to connect, you'd pull away. You were still dating Randy then, so I didn't push it, but after Homecoming I couldn't fight it any more. I wanted to talk to you. To be around you. And you were so invested in this strike that I thought the only way I'd get you to stop avoiding me was to lead the boys' side.'

'So you were making me crazy on purpose? How is that any different to what I did to you – trying to . . .' I hesitated, embarrassed. 'To seduce you.'

'I wasn't trying to drive you crazy, just to get your attention,' he said. 'Lissa, I never tried to use you. Everything that happened between us – I meant it. Including that kiss in the library. I tried to tell you the other day at my house. That this' – he held up our entwined hands – 'is more than just a game to me. But . . .'

'But I wouldn't listen.'

'Yeah. Not that I blame you. This whole thing has been so complicated.' He shook his head. 'Obviously, I'm not good at this whole dating thing. I have very little experience.'

'It's OK,' I told him. 'I do have experience, and I've messed this up just as much as – if not more than – you have.' We smiled shyly at each other, our fingers still laced. 'At least now I know. And it isn't too late.'

'It's never too late.'

I leaned in then, ready to kiss him, to be with him, to start over from scratch and fix all the mistakes I'd made. But just before my lips met his, Cash put a hand on my shoulder and eased me away.

'Can we . . . Can we put this moment on pause?' he asked, though it looked like it was costing him an effort. 'Let me shower and change, and then we can get out of here. Will you wait for me?'

'Ye— No.' I stood up, shaking my head.

Cash's eyes went wide. 'No? Is something wrong?'

'Nothing's wrong,' I told him. 'No, everything's perfect. But I know that if we get out of here, the chances of me being able to control myself are slim.' The way Cash grinned when I said this made my cheeks burn. 'I'm still under oath,' I reminded him. 'And I won't let this strike be for nothing. The rivalry needs to come to an official end first.'

He nodded and got to his feet. 'OK,' he said. 'You're right. So how do we make that happen?'

32

Over fall break, an email was sent out to every football and soccer player at Hamilton High, as well as to their girlfriends. The message instructed them all to sneak on to school property on the Sunday evening before school started up again – the second Sunday in October. They were told to meet on the grass between the football and soccer fields just after sunset, and to park their cars on the gravel back roads that snaked along the edge of the woods about half a mile from the school.

Cash helped me write the email. He'd actually come up with the idea to meet between the fields. Sort of a safe ground for everyone.

Around five thirty on Sunday evening, I headed downstairs to wait for my ride. The living room was full of boxes that Logan had filled with his belongings. I kept pushing them off to the side, worried they'd get in Dad's way when he tried to navigate his chair through the living room. My brother – sometimes he just didn't think about these things.

'Hey, sis, wanna give me a hand?' Logan asked when I reached the bottom step. He was carrying a giant box labelled TROPHIES and nodding towards the front door.

'Why isn't your girlfriend here to help you move?' I asked, hurrying over to open the door for him.

'She's working her last shift at the library,' Logan said, carrying the box out to his truck. 'She'll be over in the morning so we can take this first load up to the new apartment.'

Cash and I had worked our final shift under Jenna's dictatorship on Thursday. She'd acted the same as usual, bossing us around, telling us how to do our painfully simple jobs like we were idiots, right up until we were locking up.

'You know,' she'd said to me as she shut down the computer at the front desk, "you're going to have to take on more shifts now that I'm leaving.'

'Why?' I'd asked.

'Because you're the only other person who loves this place enough,' she'd said, smiling at me. It was the first time Jenna had smiled at me like that. Like I was more than just a zit she couldn't get rid of. 'If you were able to put up with me, you must really love this place just as much as I do.' She looked over at the bookshelves, piled high with novels and memoirs and biographies. So many words and stories and facts. I looked too.

'I do love it,' I told her.

'Good.' She'd stepped away from the computer, hands moving to her hips, returning to normal Jenna mode. 'Because you're the only person I trust to take care of this place. Without me, it might fall apart . . . unless you can keep it in order.' She hesitated. 'I told Mrs Coles that she should give you more hours. She trusts my judgment, so if you need a few more bucks . . .'

'I'll think about it,' I said, stunned that she'd actually recommended me to the head librarian. Stunned, really, that she thought I was capable of doing as good a job as she did.

Because as much as Jenna drove me crazy, the truth was, she really had kept Hamilton Public Library running smoothly. The place would have been a wreck without her.

And now that she was leaving, she trusted me.

I still wasn't her biggest fan by any means. I wasn't happy that she was taking my brother away from me, that Logan was jumping into this relationship so soon. But she really did make him happy, so I'd decided to keep my mouth shut and accept it. Just the same way he and Dad would have to accept Cash, in spite of the rivalry between his soccer team and the football team they loved so much.

Though I hoped that rivalry was about to come to an official end. In about half an hour, actually.

'Are you and Dad going out tonight?' I asked Logan as he shoved the box of trophies into the back of his truck.

'I think so,' he said. 'He wants to go to a sports bar in Oak Hill. Watch a game together and have some fun before I leave. Why?'

'Just wondering,' I said. 'But . . . OK, he doesn't have to have a salad. He can eat fried food if he wants. But tell him just one beer. I mean it.'

'Yes, Mom.'

We looked at each other for a second, and then we both cracked up. I did sound just like her. My mother had been just as bossy as I was, just as protective. I told myself that she'd be proud of Logan, though. That she'd want him to go. And even though it was scary, letting him get so far away from me, where I couldn't always know he was safe, I knew I had to do it.

Just then, Chloe's convertible pulled into my driveway. 'Lissa!' she called. It was a little chilly, but she still had the top down. I could see Kelsey and Ellen sitting in the

317

backseat, bundled in sweatshirts. 'Come on. Let's do this.'

'Have fun,' Logan said, reaching over and ruffling my hair. He had no idea where I was going, that I was about to put an end to a rivalry he'd seen the beginning of. I thought about telling him, but honestly, I didn't think he'd care any more. That was his past. He loved the game, he'd been a part of the rivalry, but now he was an adult. He'd moved on, and the rest of the boys, this generation, were about to as well.

'Be careful tonight,' I said, exercising my last few hours of control over him. 'Don't get too drunk. You don't want to have a hangover when you're moving in tomorrow. Call me if you need anything, and take care of Dad.'

'Relax,' Logan told me. 'We're big boys. We'll be fine. Now go and hang out with your friends.' He shoved my shoulder. 'Don't keep them waiting.'

I nodded and waved to him before hurrying to Chloe's convertible, hopping over the edge and into the front passenger's seat.

'Ready to go?' Chloe asked, adjusting her sunglasses. We'd be driving right into the setting sun on our way to the high school.

'Yep.'

'Cool.'

'I'm freezing back here,' Kelsey whined.

'You'll live.'

'Why in God's name is your top still down?'

'Hey, you're the one who decided to carpool,' Chloe said, glancing over her shoulder as she backed out of my driveway. 'No complaining, or you can walk.'

Kelsey stuck out her tongue.

Chloe laughed and faced forward again, lighting a cigarette with one hand as she drove.

It was almost like they were becoming friends or something. While totally creepy, it was also pretty cute.

'Are you excited for all this to be over?' Ellen asked, leaning forward so that her head was between my and Chloe's seats. 'Are you proud of yourself?'

I smiled. 'A little.'

'You should be,' she said, leaning back again. 'And you should also be excited about your date with Cash tonight. Where are you two going?'

'I'm not sure,' I said. 'When he called me, he said he wanted it to be a surprise.'

Cash and I hadn't seen each other much over fall break. We'd called and texted almost every day, and of course there was work, but I wanted to hold off our real reunion until after tonight. After the rivalry was really and truly over and we could start fresh. That way I could relax and not worry so much about the rest of the world

319

– the oath, the battle we'd had going on. Nothing. It would just be Cash and me.

Just thinking about it made me smile. I couldn't wait to see him, to kiss him with no guilt or worry. I'd been daydreaming about it like crazy.

Chloe parked her car on the side of one of the gravel roads behind the school and the four of us walked up to the fields. A group was already waiting there, a mix of boys and girls, standing around talking until they saw us coming.

'Hi, Lissa!' Mary called, waving excitedly. She was standing by Finn, gripping his giant hand with her thin, delicate fingers. The smile she was wearing – that they were both wearing – made my heart sing.

Though I could never get the image of Finn singing 'Nsync out of my head. That was burned into my brain for life.

'Hi,' I said, waving back.

The crowd began growing then, as more and more people started walking up the hill towards us. I couldn't help grinning when I saw Cash approaching. He was walking with Adam and Shane.

Behind them, off in the distance, I also spotted Randy. It still hurt to see him, to remember the way he'd broken my trust, but not as much as it had a couple of weeks ago. And that hurt wasn't nearly enough to dim my excitement and pride tonight.

I turned to face Chloe. 'Do you think we're about ready?' I asked.

'I hope so,' Chloe said. 'The sooner we get this over with, the sooner I can get out of here and have my wicked way with Shane.' She glanced over my shoulder and winked at him.

'Chloe, do you like him?' I asked.

'Who? Shane?' she shrugged. 'As a friend. I'm not in love with him or anything, but . . . It's kind of like, we both know what we want. Neither of us wants a relationship, and we're both cool with that. I like that he doesn't make me feel like a tramp just because I don't want to have his babies one day.'

I laughed. 'Fair enough.'

Chloe didn't have all the answers, either. I knew that now. But she had known something all along that I hadn't: that being ashamed of what you want or how you feel is pointless, and letting anyone else make you feel ashamed is a waste. We all wanted different things, and that was OK. Chloe wanted sex without commitment. Mary wanted to wait until she was ready. And I wasn't sure what I wanted, but I didn't want to make any decisions until I knew. And I was proud of that.

'Everyone's here,' Cash said, coming over to stand next to me. 'Are you ready?'

'Very.'

I looked at Chloe, who nodded and whistled loudly, catching everyone's attention. 'Listen up!' she called. 'The less you talk, the sooner we can get this over with and you can all go home and do whatever it is you plan on doing – and I'm sure most of you have some interesting plans.' She grinned and a few of the boys cheered.

I could see several girls rolling their eyes, even in the steadily lowering light of the sun.

'All right,' I said, taking over from Chloe. 'So, as you know, the girls all took an oath when the strike started. We figured the only way to really finish this was if the boys did the same oath, ending the rivalry. Does, um, anyone have something you all can take the oath on?'

'I do,' Adam said. He was carrying a backpack, I noticed, and he swung it to the ground. 'Just a second.' He dug through the bag's contents for a minute before producing a magazine. He held it up, and once again the guys cheered while the girls groaned.

'*Sports Illustrated*?' I said to Adam. 'Really?'

'Hey,' he said. 'Ellen told me you guys took a vow on *Cosmo*, and that's about sex. So it's only right that we swear on *Sports Illustrated*, since this is a sports rivalry.'

'But was the swimsuit edition really necessary?' Ellen asked him.

'Yes,' he said firmly. 'Yes, it was.'

Chloe burst out laughing.

'Fine,' I said, walking over and taking the magazine from Adam. 'This will work, I guess. OK, everyone stand in a circle, please. This will just make it easier.'

They moved obediently, and I felt like the ringleader of a circus.

'All right. So here's how it's going to work. I'm going to say the oath and then pass the magazine to one of you guys. All you have to do is say, "I do," and then pass it on to the next person until it makes it all the way around the circle. Sound good?'

A few of the boys nodded. Others just shrugged. Cash gave me a reassuring smile.

'Adam,' I said, walking over to him. 'It's your magazine, so why don't you go first?'

'Gladly.'

'OK.' I cleared my throat, suddenly wishing I'd actually written down an oath for the boys to make instead of just winging it at the last moment. But I was trying to be more spontaneous, learning to let go a little. This was a baby step. 'Um . . . all right.

Do you hereby swear that the ten-year rivalry between

the football and soccer teams of Hamilton High will end here and now, that you will, uh, no longer participate in the pranks or fights associated with the rivalry, and that you will, at the very least, be civil to the members of the other team so that this rivalry dies once and for all?'

Adam took the magazine from me and laid his hand right over the model's chest. 'I do,' he said, grinning.

Then he passed the magazine on.

I watched as each boy agreed to the oath – many of them smiling at their girlfriends and not even glancing at the nearly naked swimsuit model on the cover of the magazine. I could feel Randy's eyes on me when his turn came, but I wouldn't look in his direction.

'I do,' he said.

And it continued.

'I do.'

'I do.'

'I, uh, do.'

Cash was the last person to get the magazine. He grinned at me as he agreed to the oath, and I grinned back. This wouldn't have happened without him, and I knew it. He'd done so much, been so helpful, even when I wasn't aware. Even when I kept trying to hate him.

'And I'll keep this,' Adam said, tucking the magazine back into his bag. He straightened up and turned to

Ellen. Then, without warning, he took her into his arms, lifted her off the ground and spun her around.

The sound of her laugh was like music.

One by one, the girls went back to their boyfriends. Some threw themselves into the boys' arms and started making out right away – kind of gross – while others walked over more slowly, clearly needing to say something that was on their minds.

Like maybe they'd thought about their relationships, about sex.

Like maybe this whole thing had changed them as much as it had changed me.

'Lissa.'

I glanced to my left and jumped when I realized that Randy was standing right next to me, a goofy grin plastered across his face. A few weeks ago I thought that grin was cute. Now, after all that had happened, it felt empty.

'What do you want?' I asked, folding my arms over my chest.

'I want to talk,' he said.

'I have nothing to say to you.'

I started to turn away, but he caught me by the arm. 'Lissa, wait. Please.'

'Dude,' I heard Shane say from a few yards away.

'Randy, leave her alone. You fucked this up already.'

'Shut up, Shane,' Randy barked over his shoulder. Then he looked at me again, his puppy face coming out. 'I miss you,' he said quietly. 'I'm sorry I acted the way I did. But it's over now. The rivalry and the strike. You got what you wanted, so . . . When can we go back to normal? To being us?'

I just stared at him, stunned, unable to believe he really thought his puppy eyes and a half apology were enough to make me want him back.

At the end of the summer, it had been enough.

But it wasn't any more.

'Never,' I told him. 'We're never going to go back to being normal, Randy. Because you are the same person you were two months ago. I'm not. I'm not the same girl who let you make me feel guilty for not doing the things you wanted me to do. I'm done with that, and I'm done with you.' I pulled my arm free of his and, feeling a little evil, smiled up at him. 'And I am so, so happy I never had sex with you.'

Randy flinched, looking wounded, but not wounded enough to satisfy me completely.

'Can't we go somewhere?' he whispered. 'Can't we talk about this? Lissa, I love you. You owe it to me to give us a shot.'

'I owe you absolutely nothing.'

'Lissa, please—'

'Hey.'

Randy turned to look over his shoulder as someone came near us. My heart began to race when I realized it was Cash. For a second, I was worried that he'd misinterpret the situation, that he'd see me and Randy talking and think I'd changed my mind, think we were getting back together again.

'Do you mind?' Randy asked. 'I'm trying to have a conversation here.'

'Yeah,' Cash said. 'I do mind.'

I felt a jolt of joy as Cash brushed past Randy and stopped by me. He reached out a hand, and I took it. Then, right there in front of Randy, Cash pulled me into his arms and kissed me.

Not a sloppy, groping, make-out kiss – the kind no one wants to see in public. It wasn't like that. But it was a warm, passionate, sweet kiss that, despite lasting only a few seconds, left me breathless.

'Ready to get out of here?' Cash asked, slowly pulling his mouth away from mine but still keeping me wrapped in his arms.

I just nodded, and he smiled.

'Excuse us,' Cash said, bumping past a shocked-looking Randy and holding my hand as he led me down the hill towards the back road where his car was located.

'You're smooth,' I told him as he opened the car door for me.

'I'm learning.'

A second later, when he climbed into the seat beside me and turned the key in the ignition, I asked, "So are you going to tell me where we're headed?'

'I was thinking of keeping it a surprise,' Cash said. 'Will that drive you crazy? I know you like to know the plan, usually so you can critique it. So I'll tell you if that'll make you more comfortable.'

I sighed and reached across the console to take his right hand as he used his left to steer. 'Don't tell me,' I said. 'Yes, it'll drive me crazy, but . . . I'm learning, too.'

Acknowledgements

Writing is a team sport, and the author only one player on the field.

I'd like to thank my MVPs, the people without whom none of this could happen. Kate Sullivan, who takes my best and pushes it to new heights – I could not have asked for a better editor. And Joanna Volpe, who not only knew what *Lysistrata* was but also supported this crazy, loose retelling from day one – thanks for believing in this, and in all my other wacky ideas; I always know I can rest easy when the ball is in your court.

Thanks also go to Cindy Eagan, Lisa Sabater, JoAnna Kremer, Stacy Cantor Abrams, Alison Impey and the rest of the crew at Little, Brown and Poppy. I'm so lucky to have you all on my team.

Much love to Shelby Bach, who was patient enough to explain soccer to me (I know what a midfielder is now!

Woo!) and Veronica Roth, who was always so willing to help. Special thanks also go to the girls of YA Highway, who have served as both my friends and my therapists over these past few years. And to Amy Lukavics – thanks for making me feel like the coolest girl in the world, even when I'm down.

I'd be nowhere without the support of my friends: Molly, Shana, Jamie, Ashlyn, Becca, Rachel, Gaelyn, Meredith, Alyssa, Hannah, Nicole, Cody, Kyle and so, so many others – I wish I could name you all. My friends, you have put up with quite a lot from me. For that, I am forever grateful.

Thanks also go to Nancy Coffey, Sara Kendall, Katharine Kittredge, Suzie Townsend, Diana Fox, Courtney Moulton, Lisa Desrochers, Kathleen Ortiz, Hannah Wylie and Michelle Hodkin – even if you don't know it, you have all inspired me. It's people like you who make me proud to play the game.

And finally, because I'm sure they are starting to wonder where their names are, I want to thank my family. Especially my mom, Elaine, and my dad, John. Thank you all for cheering me on, before I even stepped on to the field. Without your love and support, I couldn't have made it this far.

Turn the page for an extract from

1

This was getting old.

Once again, Casey and Jessica were making complete fools of themselves, shaking their asses like dancers in a rap video. But I guess guys eat that shit up, don't they? I could honestly *feel* my IQ dropping as I wondered, for the hundredth time that night, why I'd let them drag me here *again*.

Every time we came to the Nest, the same thing happened. Casey and Jessica danced, flirted, attracted the attention of every male in sight, and eventually were hauled out of the party by their protective best friend – me – before any of the horn dogs could take advantage of them. In the meantime, I sat at the bar all night talking to Joe, the thirty-year-old bartender, about 'the problems with kids these days.'

I figured Joe would get offended if I told him that

one of the biggest problems was this damn place. The Nest, which used to be a real bar, had been converted into a teen lounge three years ago. The rickety oak bar still stood, but Joe served only Coke products while the kids danced or listened to live music. I hated the place for the simple reason that it made my friends, who could be somewhat sensible most of the time, act like idiots. But in their defence, they weren't the only ones. Half of Hamilton High showed up on the weekends, and no one left the club with their dignity intact.

I mean seriously, where was the fun in all of this? Want to dance to the same heavy bass techno music week after week? Sure! Then maybe I'll hit on this sweaty, oversexed football player. Maybe we'll have meaningful discussions about politics and philosophy while we bump 'n grind. Ugh. Yeah, right.

Casey plopped down on the stool next to mine. 'You should come dance with us, B,' she said, breathless from her booty shaking. 'It's *so* much fun.'

'Sure it is,' I muttered.

'Oh my gosh!' Jessica sat down on my other side, her honey-blond ponytail bouncing against her shoulders. 'Did you see that? Did you *effing* see that? Harrison Carlyle totally just hit on me! Did you *see* that? Omigosh!'

Casey rolled her eyes. 'He asked you where you got your shoes, Jess. He's totally gay.'

'He's too cute to be gay.'

Casey ignored her, running her fingers behind her ear, as if tucking back invisible locks. It was a habit left over from before she'd chopped her hair into its current edgy blond pixie cut. 'B, you should dance with us. We brought you here so that *we* could hang out with you – not that Joe isn't entertaining.' She winked at the bartender, probably hoping to score some free sodas. 'But we're your friends. You should come dance. Shouldn't she, Jess?'

'Totally,' Jessica agreed, eyeing Harrison Carlyle, who sat in a booth on the other side of the room. She paused and turned back to us. 'Wait. What? I wasn't listening.'

'You just look so bored over here, B. I want you to have some fun, too.'

'I'm fine,' I lied. 'I'm having a great time. You know I can't dance. I'd be in your way. Go . . . live it up or whatever. I'll be OK over here.'

Casey narrowed her hazel eyes at me. 'You sure?' she asked.

'Positive.'

She frowned, but after a second she shrugged and

grabbed Jessica by the wrist, pulling her out onto the dance floor.

'Holy crap!' Jessica cried. 'Slow down, Case! You'll rip my arm off!' Then they made their merry way to the middle of the room, already syncing the sway of their hips with the pulsing techno music.

'Why didn't you tell them you're miserable?' Joe asked, pushing a glass of Cherry Coke towards me.

'I'm not miserable.'

'You're not a good liar either,' he replied before a group of freshmen started yelling for drinks at the other end of the bar.

I sipped my Cherry Coke, watching the clock above the bar. The second hand seemed to be frozen, and I prayed the damn thing was broken or something. I wouldn't ask Casey and Jessica to leave until eleven. Any earlier and I'd be the party pooper. But according to the clock it wasn't even nine yet, and I could already feel myself getting a techno-music migraine, only made worse by the pulsing strobe light. *Move, second hand! Move!*

'Hello there.'

I rolled my eyes and turned to glare at the unwelcome intruder. This happened once in a while. Some guy, usually stoned or rank with BO, would take a seat beside me and make a half-assed attempt at small talk. Clearly they hadn't inherited the observant gene, because the expression on my face made it pretty damn obvious that I wasn't in the mood to be swept off my feet.

Surprisingly, the guy who'd taken the seat next to me didn't stink like pot or armpits. In fact, that might have been cologne I smelled on the air. But my disgust only increased when I realized who the cologne belonged to. I would have preferred the fuzzy-headed stoner.

Wesley. Fucking. Rush.

'What do you want?' I demanded, not even bothering to be polite.

'Aren't *you* the friendly type?' Wesley said sarcastically. 'Actually, I came to talk to you.'

'Well, that sucks for you. I'm not talking to people tonight.' I slurped my drink loudly, hoping he'd take the not-so-subtle hint to leave. No such luck. I could feel his dark grey eyes crawling all over me. He couldn't even pretend to be looking me in the eyes, could he? Ugh!

'Come on,' Wesley teased. 'There's no need to be so cold.'

'*Leave me alone,*' I hissed through clenched teeth. 'Go try your charming act on some tramp with low self-esteem, because I'm not falling for it.'

'Oh, I'm not interested in tramps,' he said. 'That's not my thing.'

I snorted. 'Any girl who'd give you the time of day, Wesley, is most definitely a tramp. No one with taste or class or dignity would actually find you attractive.'

OK. That was a tiny lie.

Wesley Rush was the most disgusting womanizing playboy to ever darken the doorstep of Hamilton High . . . but he was kind of hot. Maybe if you could put him on mute . . . and cut off his hands . . . maybe – just maybe – he'd be tolerable then. Otherwise, he was a real piece of shit. Horn dog shit.

'And you *do* have taste and class and dignity, I assume?' he asked, grinning.

'Yes, I do.'

'That's a shame.'

'Is this your attempt at flirting?' I asked. 'If it is, you fail. Epically.'

He laughed. 'I never fail at flirting.' He ran his fingers through his dark, curly hair and adjusted his crooked, arrogant little grin. 'I'm just being friendly. Trying to have a nice conversation.'

'Sorry. Not interested.' I turned away and took another drink of my Cherry Coke. But he didn't move. Not even an inch. 'You can go now,' I said forcefully.

Wesley sighed. 'Fine. You're being really uncooperative, you know. So I guess I'll be honest with you. I've got to hand it to you: you're smarter and more stubborn than most girls I talk to. But I'm here for a little more than witty conversation.' He moved his attention to the dance floor. 'I actually need your help. You see, your friends are hot. And you, darling, are the Duff.'

'Is that even a word?'

'Designated. Ugly. Fat. Friend,' he clarified. 'No offence, but that would be you.'

'I am not the—'

'Hey, don't get defensive. It's not like you're an ogre or anything, but in comparison . . .' He shrugged his broad shoulders. 'Think about it. Why do they bring you here if you don't dance?' He had the nerve to reach over and pat my knee, like he was trying to comfort me. I jerked away from him, and his fingers moved smoothly to brush some curls out of his face instead. 'Look,' he said, 'you have hot friends . . . *really* hot friends.' He paused, watching the action on the dance floor for a moment, before facing me again. 'The point is, scientists have proven that every group of friends has a weak link, a Duff. And girls respond well to guys who associate with their Duffs.'

'Crackheads can call themselves scientists now? That's news to me.'

'Don't be bitter,' he said. 'What I'm saying is, girls – like your friends – find it sexy when guys show some sensitivity and socialize with the Duff. So by talking to you right now I am doubling my chances of getting laid tonight. Please assist me here, and just pretend to enjoy the conversation.'

I stared at him, flabbergasted, for a long moment. Beauty really was skin-deep. Wesley Rush may have had the body of a Greek god, but his soul was as black and empty as the inside of my closet. What a bastard!

With one swift motion I jumped to my feet and flung the contents of my glass in Wesley's direction. Cherry Coke flew all over him, splattering his expensive-looking white polo shirt. Drops of dark red liquid glistened on his cheeks and colored his brown hair. His face glowed with anger, and his chiseled jaw clinched fiercely.

'What was that for?' he snapped, wiping his face with the back of his hand.

'What do you *think* it was for?' I bellowed, fists balled at my sides.

'Honestly, Duffy, I have no earthly idea.'

Angry flames blazed in my cheeks. 'If you think I'm letting one of my friends leave this place with you, Wesley, you're very, very wrong,' I spat. 'You're a disgusting, shallow, womanizing jackass, and I hope that soda stains your preppy little shirt.' Just before I marched away, I looked over my shoulder and added, 'And my name isn't Duffy. It's Bianca. We've been in the same homeroom since middle school, you self-absorbed son of a bitch.'

I never thought I'd say this, but thank God the damn techno played so loud. No one but Joe overheard the little episode, and he probably found the whole thing hysterical. I had to push my way through the crowded dance floor to find my friends. When I tracked them down, I grabbed Casey and Jessica by their elbows and tugged them toward the exit.

'Hey!' Jessica protested.

'What's wrong?' Casey asked.

'We're getting the fuck out of here,' I said, yanking their unwilling bodies along behind me. 'I'll explain in the car. I just can't stand to be in this hellhole for one more second.'

'Can't I say bye to Harrison first?' Jessica whined, trying to loosen my grip on her arm.

'Jessica!' I cricked my neck painfully when I twisted around to face her. 'He's *gay!* You don't have a chance, so just give it up already. I *need* to get out of here. Please.'

I pulled them out into the parking lot, where the icy

January air tore at the bare flesh of our faces. Relenting, Casey and Jessica gathered close on either side of me. They must have found their outfits, which were intended to be sexy, ill equipped to handle the windchill. We moved to my car in a huddle, separating only when we reached the front bumper. I clicked the unlock button on my key chain so that we could climb into the slightly warmer cab of the Saturn without delay.

Casey curled up in the front seat and said, through chattering teeth, 'Why are we leaving so early? B, it's only like, nine-fifteen.'

Jessica sulked in the backseat with an ancient blanket wrapped around her like a cocoon. (My piece-of-shit heater rarely decided to work, so I kept a stash of blankets in the door.)

'I got into an argument with someone,' I explained, jabbing the key into the ignition with unnecessary force. 'I threw my Coke on him, and I didn't want to stick around for his response.'

'Who?' Casey asked.

I'd been dreading that question because I knew the reaction I'd get. 'Wesley Rush.'

Two swoony, girly sighs followed my answer.

'Oh, come on,' I fumed. 'The guy is a man-whore. I can't stand him. He sleeps with everything that moves, and his brain is located in his pants – which means it's microscopic.'

'I doubt that,' Casey said with another sigh. 'God, B, only you could find a flaw in Wesley Rush.'

I glared at her as I turned my head to back out of the parking lot. 'He's a jerk.'

'That's not true,' Jessica interjected. 'Jeanine said he talked to her at a party recently. She was with Vikki and Angela, and she said he just came up and sat down beside her. He was really friendly.'

That made sense. Jeanine was definitely the Duff if she was out with Angela and Vikki. I wondered which of them left with Wesley that night.

'He's charming,' Casey said. 'You're just being Little Miss Cynical, as usual.' She gave me a warm smile from across the cab. 'But what the hell did he do to get you to throw Coke at him?' *Now* she sounded concerned. Took her long enough. 'Did he say something to you, B?'

'No,' I lied. 'It's nothing. He just pisses me off.'

Duff.

The word bounced around in my mind as I sped down 5th Street. I couldn't bring myself to tell my friends about the wonderful new insult that had just been added to my vocab list, but when I glanced at myself in the rearview mirror, Wesley's assertion that I was the unattractive, undesirable tagalong (more like dragalong) seemed to be confirmed. Jessica's perfect hourglass figure and warm, welcoming brown eyes. Casey's flawless complexion and mile-long legs. I couldn't compare to either of them.

'Well, I say we hit another party, since it's so early,' Casey suggested. 'I heard about this one out in Oak Hill. Some college kid is home for Christmas break and decided to have a big blow-out. Angela told me about it this morning. Want to go?'

'Yeah!' Jessica straightened up beneath the blanket. 'We should totally go! College parties have college *boys*. Won't that be fun, Bianca?'

I sighed. 'No. Not really.'

'Oh, come on.' Casey reached over and squeezed my arm. 'No dancing this time, OK? And Jess and I promise to keep all hot guys away from you, since clearly you hate them.' She smirked, trying to nudge me back into a good mood.

'I don't hate hot guys,' I told her. 'Just the one.' After a moment, I sighed and turned onto the highway, heading for the county line. 'Fine, we'll go. But you two are buying me ice cream afterward. Two scoops.'

'Deal.'

 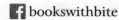

KODY
KEPLINGER
ONLINE

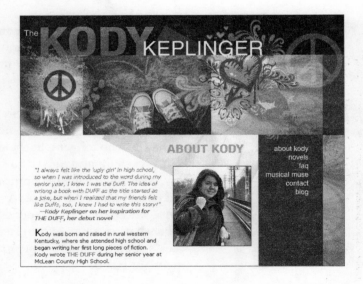